THE FINISHING
SCHOOL

THE FINISHING SCHOOL

Stephen Ferris

Nexus

This book is a work of fiction.
In real life, make sure you practise safe sex.

First published in 1996 by
Nexus
332 Ladbroke Grove
London W10 5AH

Copyright   Stephen Ferris 1996

The right of Stephen Ferris to be identified as the Author
of this Work has been asserted by him in accordance with
the Copyright Designs and Patents Act 1988.

Typeset by TW Typesetting, Plymouth, Devon
Printed and bound by
BPC Paperbacks Ltd, Aylesbury, Bucks

ISBN 0 352 33066 X

One

Lying at full length in her bath, Felicity Marchant
raised the sponge and squeezed it gently between her
hands. The warm water trickled down on to her breasts,
washing away the lather to reveal her perfect brown
nipples. She looked down at her own body, admiring
the way her nineteen-year-old breasts jutted, proud and
glistening, from the sea of foam that surrounded them.
Her head throbbed abominably, reminding her of last
night's party. Damn that party! Since the death of her
father, her last surviving parent, a few weeks ago, she
seemed to have gone overboard with wild parties. They
were supposed to assuage the pain of being orphaned
but they didn't. They just gave her these incredible
hangovers. Her only recollection of last night's excess
was of dim lights, loud music and a lot to drink. She
rather thought there must have been young men involved, because she dimly recalled being carried
somewhere and lying on the back seat of someone's car.
She did remember that it was with the greatest difficulty
that she had crawled inside the front door after having
been deposited outside it by persons who might as well
have been total strangers. She had slept there, her face
pressed against the hairy roughness of the mat, waking
with a disgustingly furry mouth and alcohol breath as
stale as her own body odours.

She would have to take better care of herself. After
all, she was now the sole owner of the estate. Mistress
of everything her father had accumulated during his

1

very successful business life. That was quite a considerable amount. Apart from the large house, extensive grounds, paddocks and stables, she knew that he had other financial interests which would ensure that she would never have to worry about earning a living.

It was today that his solicitor was due to come down to read the will. That was a formality, of course. Her father had always assured her that she, as his only child, would inherit from him. It would be interesting though, to see what small bequests he had made to servants and friends. With a twinge of sadness she remembered how he always called her 'Fliss'. It was a name she infinitely preferred and always used when thinking of herself. Who was there now to call her that?

She resumed her inspection of her own body. She ran her hands down over her stomach, brushing away the foam. Her skin was warm, healthy and pink. A small puddle of water remained in her navel and she tensed her stomach muscles and wriggled, just for the pleasure of seeing the little lake move over her skin. She flexed her knees and humped a little until the forest of her light brown pubic curls came into view. They were messy with lather and she brushed at that, too. She tried to tell herself that it was this accidental contact which made her think about masturbation but she knew that it was not true. She had known for some time that she needed an orgasm. Now she was about to give herself that gift. She deserved it after the traumas of last night.

She sat up and leaned forward to remove the plug from the bath. The shower head on its flexible hose was sitting in its little rack and she took it in her hand, turned it on and adjusted the temperature. It would be no fun to pleasure herself yet be unable to see the best bits because of suds. The last of the soapy bubbles gurgled away and she directed clean water down her back and under her arms. When they were washed clean, she lay back at full length again and showered the rest of her body, raising her knees to reach her lower extremities. She knew, from experience, that the shower head did not have enough pressure to bring about her orgasm unaided, but it was pleasant enough to lie for a while with it playing between her legs as a sort of starter for the main course.

She conjured up her favourite fantasy. She had been forcibly stripped and was tightly bound, hand and foot. Now 'they' (she never properly identified 'they') were playing with her body; touching and stroking. This bizarre imagery had been with her almost from the time when she first discovered the delights which her hands could cause to her own body. She could remember using her skipping rope to wind around her wrists in an attempt to make the dream reality. Such attempts were never satisfactory. What made her fantasy a turn-on was her inability to touch her body or to prevent it from being touched. If she fixed her own hands behind her she couldn't masturbate and there was no one to do it for her. It was a seemingly insoluble problem. Now she contemplated, briefly, using the belt of her towelling robe to enwrap her hands but discarded the notion. It would only result in the same frustration.

She rubbed her left forefinger in a slow circle around her left nipple. Dropping the shower head, she put her right forefinger on the bump of her clitoris and moved that in a similar fashion, circling slowly. Her nipples were erecting themselves now, under the influence of her finger and the cooling effect on her skin of the evaporation of the water. She felt her vagina beginning to lubricate. It was time for the next stage. She spread her knees as far as the sides of the bath would allow and thrust her right hand further between her legs, her fingers exploring to push aside the stray hairs which blocked the entrance to that lovely place. She felt the rubbery lips of her vulva give way to her and, with a small grimace, thrust two fingers into her warm, wet

3

tunnel of joy. Now she could see the involuntary contractions which rippled her stomach as she sought out the sensitive spot underneath her pubic bone and rubbed upwards, pressing the tissue against her skeleton. Her right thumb flicked at her clitoris and she jerked in time with it. Now it was not a matter of choice. She had to have that orgasm. Her fingers moved rapidly, plunging in and out with small sucking noises. Her left hand now pulled ceaselessly at her nipple, elongating it and pinching hard. Her knees rapped against the sides of the bath as her whole body went into spasm. It was coming! It was coming! Mmm! Ah! Yes! Glorious!

She relaxed, still twitching a little with the aftershocks, relief flooding over her with the end of tension. She flopped, allowing her spine to mould itself to the contours of the bath. Her head had begun to throb again. The solicitor must have arrived by now. She knew him well; a short, bald, fussy little man who was as much a friend of the family as its legal adviser. From the firm of Atkinson, Atkinson and Atkinson, his name was Mr Silsby; an anomaly which had always made her want to giggle and made her smile now.

After she was dressed, she took two more aspirins and went downstairs. Mr Silsby was already in the library, seated at a small table with papers spread out before him. The household's minimal staff were assembled there, too: Mrs Bedwell, cook-housekeeper; Mr Corley, the gardener; and Mr Lupton, the stableman. Until recently, he had been the stockman as well as the stableman, but her father had sold all the estate's cattle shortly before his death, partly for business reasons and partly out of consideration for Mr Lupton who was getting on in years, so that his work-load would be thus considerably reduced. At the back of the room were two austere looking ladies whom Fliss did not recognise.

Mr Silsby rose as she entered. 'Ah! Miss Marchant. We have been waiting for you. Such a sad occasion! Please sit down and we'll get on.'

4

Fliss draped herself on a convenient sofa. Her head still hurt abominably and she wished Silsby would get it over with. His preamble seemed to take for ever and she found her eyelids growing heavy. She waited as Silsby droned on, now only slightly interested in bequests to others. She jerked awake with a sudden realisation that what she had been hearing was not what she had been expecting.

'... that the said trustee, Selina Mary Doyle, shall hold my residuary estate upon trust until the said Felicity Lucinda Marchant shall attain the age of twenty-one years ...'

'What?'

Mr Silsby looked up from his reading, startled at Fliss's intervention. 'You have a query, Miss Marchant?'

'Yes. What's this about me not getting the estate until I'm twenty-one?'

He looked at her over his glasses. 'I'm sorry. I thought I made that clear in Clause Two. I'll read it again, shall I?' He shuffled his papers. 'Yes, here we are ... I appoint my partner, Selina Mary Doyle to be the executor and trustee of this my will ... etc., etc. What that means in simple terms, Miss Marchant, is that Miss Doyle is to look after your father's estate until you reach the age of twenty-one and will then hand it over to you.'

Something about the direction of his eyes made Fliss turn and look towards the back of the room. One of the ladies sitting there inclined her head in a curt nod and Fliss realised that this must be Selina, her father's partner. They had never met and Fliss knew her face only dimly, by photographs. As far as she remembered, Selina lived in Scotland and had been only nominally involved in her father's affairs. She had not thought that they were so close that he would make her a trustee.

'Oh! Can he do that?'

Mr Silsby smiled, drily. 'I assure you that he can. If I may assist you a little; I helped your father to draft his will and he told me at the time of his concern over your . . . forgive me, Miss Marchant . . . over your wild ways. He expressed the view that it would be safer for you not to receive all his estate until you had achieved a greater maturity, both physical and mental. I'm sorry. There was no politer way to put it.'

Fliss sat on through the rest of the reading, not bothering to pay attention to the small sums meted out to the domestic staff. As Silsby was taking his leave of her, the two ladies came forward and he shook their hands, too.

'So nice to have met you, dear ladies. I'm sure that Felicity will be in good, safe hands.' He gathered up his belongings and left, shown out by Mrs Bedwell. The other members of staff had already departed and Fliss was alone with these two women.

She studied them, covertly. Selina was tall and dark haired. Fliss guessed her to be around forty, even though she looked younger. Her clothes were grey and severe, her dark hair drawn back from her face. The other woman was a little shorter and plumper. She seemed a fraction less sure of herself and did not resemble Selina facially, but might have been her twin on account of the similarity of hair colouring and clothing.

Fliss decided to make the best of things. She held out her hand. 'Hello. You must be Selina.' She smiled. 'You must call me Fliss.'

The hand which took hers was cold and hard; almost as cold and hard as the voice that came with it. 'I am, indeed, your father's partner. This is my companion, Miss Crawford. Neither of us will have any truck with pet names, you'll find. Felicity you were christened and Felicity it shall be. I know your history. Don't expect me to be as soft as your father.'

Fliss recoiled. 'Here! Hang on a minute. It's only your job to run the estate, not to run me.'

She was rewarded with a long, cool stare. 'You will find, Felicity, that controlling the estate and the money supply is the same as controlling you. From the reports I have had, you are sorely in need of control.'

'Well,' said Fliss, defiantly. 'When you've gone back to Scotland, we'll see who runs things. You'll have to send me money for the upkeep.'

'But that's where you're wrong. We are not returning to Scotland. My companion and I intend to live in this house until you reach your majority. It was your father's wish that I keep a close eye on you and that's exactly what I intend to do.'

Within a very short space of time, Fliss learned to her cost exactly what that 'close eye' was to mean. The bank account into which her allowance had always been paid was closed. She was paid a much smaller amount in cash once a week. To receive it, she had to report to Selina in the library and produce accounts of her spending. Any item which Selina considered 'wasteful' was noted and that amount deducted from her pocket money for that week. Before she left the house she was obliged to seek permission; say where she was going and why, accepting an arbitrary time by which she must return.

She was even bereft of the solace of complaining to the staff, whom she had always regarded as friends and confidantes rather than as servants. Fliss experienced a genuine sense of sadness and loss when, only a few days after Selina and Alice Crawford moved in, all were sacked, being replaced with staff of Selina's choice. Instead of chubby, cheerful Mrs Bedwell, her aunt imported her own housekeeper from Scotland. Her name was Mrs Carstairs, but she was possessed of such a dour and sepulchral countenance that Fliss could never think of her by any other name than 'Mrs Danvers', so much did she resemble that character from *Rebecca*. As a further economy, Mr Lupson's replacement at the stables was Alex Ross, a gangling youth who doubled as gardener, thereby saving one set of wages.

Perhaps because she and Alice Crawford liked to ride, Selina did not carry her penny-pinching as far as getting rid of the horses altogether, for which Fliss was extremely thankful. About the only pleasure left to her was riding, which she did most days, after seeking Selina's permission. It was that innocent activity which led to the watershed of a severe change in her relationship with the new trustee.

Her black hunter, King, was the axis around which a great many pleasures revolved. First, there was a reason to wear jodhpurs and shiny, brown leather boots; garments which she found not only becoming on her trim figure, but inexplicably exciting. There was the pleasure of healthy exercise in galloping King around the paddocks and the bonus of sedate walks through beautiful countryside. She did not admit to anyone, least of all to herself, that the mild friction and bumping of the saddle, with the animal smell of leather, excited her sexually so that she was always ready for a masturbatory encounter with the shower head in her bath afterwards.

On this sunny morning, she cantered King back to the stable yard and slid gracefully to the ground. Alex Ross came out and took the reins from her to lead King into his stall. To Fliss, following him and for so long deprived of companions of her own age, his back view was suddenly very interesting. His face, neck and arms were burned a deep brown and she found herself wondering if that tan went all over. Her eyes went to his neat, tight buttocks in their covering of sprayed-on jeans and she found herself gulping.

She sat down on a bale of straw and watched him as he took off King's tack and hung it up then began to rub the horse down with a wisp of straw. Suddenly she felt very possessive and confident. She was mistress of this estate – well, near enough, anyway – and this was her man. He was there to do her bidding. She decided to put matters to the test.

'Alex!'

'Yes, Miss?'

She pointed. 'I don't like that bale of straw there. Put it over there against that wall, please.'

He stared at her, at the bale and the place she had indicated then shrugged, hefted it easily and carried it across.

Fliss was exultant. This was definitely exciting. 'In fact, I think I want you to put all the bales over there, please.'

'All of them?'

'Yes.'

'Why? What's the matter with where they are now?'

Fliss pretended anger to conceal her growing lust. 'Because I say so and because I'll have you discharged if you argue.'

This time, he stared at her for so long that Fliss almost caved in and backed down. She stared back as though she was totally confident until he shrugged again and began to move the bales. She watched him with deepest satisfaction, aware of the sudden dampness beneath her.

'You look hot,' she said. 'Why don't you take your shirt off?'

He paused in his labours, dusting his hands. 'That's all right, Miss. I'm not hot.'

'But it's not all right, Alex. I said take your shirt off, so take it off now. I'll hold it for you.'

This time her confidence was not feigned and she was able to retain her air of composure as she returned his stare, certain of his compliance. His removal of the shirt, revealing his upper body to her, was intensely thrilling. His tan did extend beyond his arms, she discovered. The feel of the coarse material of his woollen, plaid shirt was interesting, as was the faint smell of man emanating from it. When he continued his work and she thought he wasn't looking, she pressed the shirt to her face and rubbed her cheek with it. Overtaken by a sudden impulse, she unbuttoned her own white blouse, tugged it from the tight waistband of her jodhpurs and took it off. She unclipped her white brassière and slipped out of it, leaving her breasts bare. The hairy roughness of his shirt against her nipples was just as delightful as she had hoped it would be. She closed her eyes and savoured the sensation, her right hand dipping into her groin to massage the spot which was now so wet and inflamed.

A sudden cessation of the noise of movement made her open her eyes and look up. Alex was standing a few feet away, staring at her again, but in a totally different way and she read the lust in his eyes. He took a pace towards her, but she held up a warning hand.

'No! Stand there while I look at you!'

He stopped, obediently.

She massaged her naked breasts, pulling lightly at her erect brown nipples. 'Don't you think I'm beautiful, Alex?'

His voice was hoarse. 'Yes, Miss!'

'Would you like to see all of me – not just the top part?'

He cleared his throat with an effort. 'Yes, Miss!'

'If you're a good boy and do exactly what you're told, maybe you'll get lucky. Step up on that bale.'

'What?'

'You heard me!' She pointed. 'Step up on to that bale and stand there. Good! Now put your hands behind you! Go on, do it! That's right. Now I am going to come close to you. You are not to touch me or to move, is that clear?'

He nodded and she got up, dropping the shirt, and came across to stand close in front of him. Her face was level with his navel and the smooth, hairless expanse of his tanned chest towered over her. She reached up and ran her hands lightly over his torso. With interest, she noted that he jerked spasmodically as her finger-nails trailed across his nipples. For all the drunken parties she had attended, Fliss had never experienced more than the most clumsy and inexpert groping sessions and this man's body was completely fascinating to her. There was now a very distinct bulge in the front of his tight, blue jeans and she knew that what she wanted more than anything was to pull down his zip and release the maleness of him; to hold him; fondle him and maybe even to see what he tasted like. Her heart was pounding and she was having trouble swallowing.

In the stillness of the stable, the sound of the opening zip was deafening. He moaned softly and Fliss looked up sharply into his face.

'Stand still!'

She leaned closer, her face only inches from that intriguing lump in his white undershorts. Her fingers gently explored the excitingly hard outline of his penis under the soft material. In a moment, she was thinking, there would be flesh to flesh contact and that thought made her dizzy.

'Felicity!'

Fliss spun round as if she had been stung. Framed in the stable doorway were Selina and Alice. Fliss crouched, trying to cover her breasts with her arms. Selina came over to her and took her by the arm, shaking her roughly.

'So this is the sort of thing you get up to when I grant you the privilege of riding! Alex! You ought to know better. I shall speak to you later. Get dressed and get out!'

As Alex gathered up his shirt and left, Fliss tugged at the steely fingers which enwrapped her arm. 'I'm sorry. Let me get dressed, too, Selina.'

'No, I think not.' Selina gazed at Fliss appraisingly.

11

'I think it's time for the sort of lesson which will show you just what your situation is. So, you think it's fun to make someone stand half-naked on a bale, do you? Very well, Miss. Step up!'

Fliss could not believe her ears. 'What?' At least part of her confusion was caused by the realisation that Selina and Alice must have been listening for some time before they interrupted. 'You're surely not serious!'

'You'll find that I am extremely serious, Felicity. Now, are you going to get on to the bale or do we have to force you?'

The shock of her discovery and her semi-nude state deprived Fliss of all spirit. Meekly, she stepped up on to the bale and stood there, her face ablaze with shame, hiding her breasts with her arms. She was soon deprived even of this small protection. Selina grasped her wrists and pulled them out in front of her, crossing them. Alice came forward with a lunge-rein – a length of broad, strong webbing – and before Fliss could draw back or struggle her wrists had been most expertly bound. Selina held her about the waist so that she was unable to get down off the bale as Alice tossed the loose end of the rein over a beam above her head, then both women threw their weight on it, dragging Fliss' entrapped wrists far above her head and bringing her on to the tips of her toes. In this strained position, her rib-cage was thrown into prominence; her breasts stretched and flattened, only the nipples standing out from the taut, white flesh. She was acutely conscious of the humiliation of her exposure to the eyes of these two women who now stood in front of her. To avoid their eyes, she threw her head back and gazed up. That did not help. The sight of her imprisoned wrists and impotently twitching fingers reminded her all too strongly of her masturbation fantasies. Now those fantasies were becoming reality and she was aware of strong feelings of desire welling up in her, however hard she tried to suppress them.

When Selina came closer to her she drew in her stomach, fearing the touch which might exacerbate the embarrassment she felt at the knowledge that her vagina was liquefying.

'So tell me, Felicity. Is it fun?'

Felicity turned her head away, unwilling to give this woman the satisfaction of a reply. She jerked it to the front again as Selina raised one foot and thrust against the bale, moving it back a little so that Fliss was obliged to step forward to keep her feet under her.

'I asked you if it was fun,' Selina said, thrusting again and bringing Fliss' feet to the front edge of the bale. 'Is it fun to be half-naked and to be stared at?' Another kick at the bale meant that Fliss was now completely off balance. Only the extreme tips of her toes were on the edge of the bale and most of her weight was on her wrists.

'No, it's not fun,' Fliss groaned, completely subjugated. 'I'm sorry I did it. Please get me off this bale.'

'Of course, dear,' said Selina, maliciously and gave another thrust with her foot which set the bale skidding backwards and left Fliss dangling and kicking in mid-air.

She cried out as all her weight came on her bound wrists and her shoulder-joints took the strain. 'Please! Oh please! It hurts! Let me down!'

There was no mercy in Selina's eyes. 'It must be the weight of those heavy boots. We'll take them off for you, shall we?' She stood on Fliss' right and wrapped her arm around one upper thigh before pulling at her high leather boot. Alice did the same on the other side, then they stepped back again and watched Fliss, now in stockinged feet, struggle to free herself, kicking her legs.

'Those heavy breeches must be causing you some discomfort, too. We'll take those off for you.'

'No! No! Keep away!' Fliss kicked out at them as they came to her again, but they avoided her feeble efforts with ease. Alice stood behind her and clasped her arms about her waist, holding her still. Selina stooped and unzipped the legs of the jodhpurs. Fliss, looking down between her bare breasts and over her taut, white stomach, was horrified to see Selina's fingers at work on the buckle and zip of her lower garment. Then she saw and felt her breeches being tugged down over her thighs and calves, to be tossed aside with her socks and leave her wearing only flimsy white knickers.

Suspended by her wrists, her straining bare toes a good foot from the floor, Fliss saw the eyes of both women fixed on her only remaining covering and knew what they intended. 'No! Please! Not that! Don't strip me naked. I'll be good! I'll do anything you ask, only don't take my knickers off, please!'

'You have to learn, Felicity,' Selina said, surveying her helpless captive with glittering eyes. 'Being half-naked isn't fun, but being completely naked is twice as bad.'

Fliss crossed her legs in a futile attempt to thwart their intention but Selina just laughed; a short, cold laugh with no humour in it at all. She grasped Fliss' ankles and walked backwards with them, extending her at an angle while Alice took hold of the waistband of the knickers and ripped them down and off in one swift movement. Left to dangle again, Fliss crossed her legs once more and attempted to jerk herself around so that her back would be towards her tormentors in an effort to hide her pubes as much as she could. Behind her, Alice pushed her fingers as far as they would go between her clenched thighs and took a large pinch of tender flesh between finger and thumb, nipping and twisting viciously.

'Uncross your legs!'

'No! I won't! I . . . Ow! Oh God! That hurts! Ow! All right! All right!'

As Fliss parted her legs, Alice stepped between them

14

and tucked one of her knees under each arm. Marching backwards, she extended Fliss' nude body towards the horizontal until she was immovably fixed, face down and breasts dangling, secured at wrists and knees.

Fliss was sobbing now. 'Please, why are you doing this? What are you going to do to me?'

Her face, until now bright red with shame, drained of all colour as she heard Alice say, 'All ready for you to spank, Selina!'

Fliss craned her neck to see Selina, who stood in front of her, enjoying her humiliation. 'Oh God! You're just trying to frighten me, aren't you? You wouldn't really ... I mean, you can't be going to ...'

'Oh, but I am, Felicity. I'm going to give you what your father should have given you many times over; a sound spanking on your bare bottom. I think it's a language even you will understand.'

She moved to Fliss' right and out of her sight to stand alongside her target. With calculated cruelty, she waited for long seconds before beginning, savouring the helplessness of her victim and noting with interest that the bottom she was about to punish was actually twitching; the skin crawling in anticipation of what was to come. Raising her right hand high, she delivered a stinging slap on one cheek of the beautiful white buttocks so enticingly presented. The flesh jolted and wobbled under the impact and a red patch with finger-marks clearly delineated sprang up immediately. Fliss let out an agonised screech of pain, her body wriggling as much as the constriction of her bondage would allow. Even as a child she had never been spanked and the infliction of deliberate pain was quite alien to her. Fliss knew that she had never before experienced such discomfort. Each slap felt like the application of a block of ice, closely followed by a deluge of scalding hot water. She howled and bucked and yet, even in the midst of this shaming torture, she could not entirely rid herself of the inexplicable sensation of lascivious pleasure. Trapped there, bound, naked, helpless and tortured, she knew that she had two urgent priorities. One was the overwhelming desire for the relief of orgasm. The other was to urinate. The humiliation of allowing the latter to happen; of releasing a stream of pee on to the floor while these women were watching, was unthinkable and she clung on grimly, clenching her stomach muscles to restrain the impulse. She knew that she was close to involuntary orgasm and heaved a sigh of relief when the beating stopped and Alice released her legs. She hung there for several seconds, during which time she tried to prevent her thighs from massaging her clitoris while she absorbed the messages her bottom was sending her. True, the burning pain was dreadful but with it was something else; some imp which demanded the sexual stimulation which further punishment would bring; a voice within her which, against her will, was crying out to be beaten and shamed.

Then Selina grasped her legs as Alice had done and pulled her back into her spanking position. Fliss knew that her punishment was only half-completed and resigned herself to it, hating that part of her mind which became excited at the prospect. When Alice began to spank her, Fliss' gasps were not solely expressive of pain. Falling on to an already tenderised area, these slaps ought to have been excruciatingly unpleasant. They were not. Now the demon in her was working its perverse will. She found her hips thrusting upwards to receive each fresh sensation. Her howls were now suppressed as she kept her teeth clamped together, ashamed lest the women should hear her gasping, 'Yes! Yes! Do it to me!' She was tied as in her fantasies, being driven inexorably towards orgasm like some captive animal to slaughter. Ripples of her approaching climax were already coursing through her lower abdomen and she found herself hoping that the beating would not stop until that moment of release arrived. Here it was, now, and it was larger and more terrifying than anything her shower head had ever produced. She knew that the throes of orgasm would be taken for signs of torment. At last she could let herself go and scream, her head thrown back, heaving herself up by the arms as far as her constraints would allow so as to be able to feel her captivity more strongly. When it was over she sagged, limp and exhausted, half-fainting; scarcely noticing when they took her down and hurried her, still naked, into the house.

When Fliss woke she was lying face-down on her bed. No! Not her bed, she quickly realised. This was the old nursery, now kept as a guest-room. She rolled over, then winced as the coverlet came into contact with her sore and still-burning posterior. She got up gingerly and, standing in front of the dressing-table mirror, craned around to inspect herself. She drew in her breath sharply. Her bottom was a sea of fiery red from thighs to waist. She touched it gently, feeling the heat of it in her fingers. There was a bathroom attached to the nursery and she padded in there to avail herself of the cold water jet of the bidet which chilled and soothed her soreness. There was a pile of clean clothing on the dressing table but she did not feel able to wear anything on her lower half so contented herself with putting on a satin robe which was comfortingly cool to the touch.

Feeling somewhat better, she decided to go to her own room. When she tried to open the nursery door it was locked! Furiously she tugged on the handle, half-hoping that she was mistaken and that it was jammed by accident. It was not. Crouching down, she could clearly see the tongue of the mortise lock which secured it. Being a nursery, the windows were, of course, barred and always had been. There was no way out there. She was annoyed but not seriously alarmed. Selina could not possibly intend her any lasting harm so she decided to wait. Unwilling to sit, she resumed her face-down position on the bed. Presently she slept again.

She was woken by the rattle of the key in the lock. Remembering just in time not to sit up, she wriggled round to slide off the bed and stand up as Selina came into the room. Behind her, Alice was carrying a tray covered with a white cloth.

'I trust you're feeling better,' Selina said with mock solicitousness. 'We've brought you something to eat.'

Fliss was incredulous. 'You don't think you're really going to get away with beating me and locking me up, do you? As soon as I get out of here I'm going straight to Mr Silsby. I'm sure that after he hears how I've been treated he'll be able to revoke Daddy's will and you'll be slung out on your ear. You and your dike friend,' she added, bitterly.

Selina stepped forward and delivered a resounding slap across Fliss' face which made her ears ring. She staggered back and sat down on the bed, then hastily jumped up again, grimacing with discomfort.

'You stupid little bitch! What sort of a kid's game do you think we're playing? Your father was a fool. I gave him the best years of my life. Oh yes! You may well look surprised. You've heard of a sleeping partner? Well, I was his for years; in more senses than one. I gave him everything a man could need, but he wouldn't listen to me when he took it into his head to marry that slut who was your mother. After that, even when he was with me, I knew he was thinking about her. Fortunately, she died, but not before she had delivered herself of yet another slut to leech on him. Do you think I am going to allow you to waltz off with the inheritance which should have been mine and waste it? Think again! You will never see a penny of your father's money.'

Fliss stood rubbing her cheek, bewildered. 'But I have to. You can't stop me. By the time I'm twenty-one . . . .'

'By the time you're twenty-one, there'll be nothing left to inherit. I'll see to that.'

18

'But you can't . . . I mean . . . It's in the will.'

'Ah! The will! You really should read that will some-time, dear Felicity. You'll see that the sole executor and trustee – that's me – has complete discretion over invest-ments and the disposition of the whole estate. I propose to make those investments over the next couple of years. In your best interest, of course.' She smiled mockingly. 'It will be just too bad if those investments go wrong and you lose everything, won't it? And it will be pure coincidence if the companies in which I choose to invest should happen to be owned by me. Naturally, that fact will not be apparent even on the closest investigation. The process will be nice and slow so as to excite no comment. Just a gradual trickle of assets away from your estate and into mine until you are left in the gutter, as your father should have left your mother in the gutter where he found her. I pretended not to care when he married her instead of me and I forced myself to play the part of a contented mistress, biding my time. Now it's come and I'll have my revenge on his daughter, even if I can't have it on him, now.'

Felicity found her eyes prickling with tears at these unkind references to her mother but tried to pull herself together and fight back. 'And what do you think I shall be doing while this is going on? You can't keep me in this room for ever.'

Selina's smirk was hateful. 'No, I can't keep you in this room until you're twenty-one. That would be most inconvenient. However, I do know what you will be do-ing for the next two years or so. You will be at Finishing School.'

'What?'

'I have decided, out of the kindness of my heart, to pay an exorbitant amount of money so that you may complete your education. I have already discussed this with Mr Silsby and he thinks it is a splendid idea, if a little over-generous on my part.'

19

'What Finishing School? Where?' Fliss demanded, suspiciously.

'It is called Draco House. Where it is need not concern you. Suffice it to say that it is remote. It is run by a very dear friend of mine who will see to it that you receive the benefit of a secure, disciplined environment.'

'I won't go!' Fliss exclaimed, angrily.

Selina laughed. 'I rather think you will.'

'I'll run away!'

Selina laughed again. 'I rather think you won't!'

Still laughing, she left the room, followed by Alice, and Fliss heard the key turn in the lock. After a while, she took the cloth off the tray and began to eat the food they had left.

For the next couple of days, Fliss remained a prisoner in the old nursery. The marks of her spanking subsided quite quickly and she was able to dress and sit normally. It was clear to her that if Selina was to be stopped in her fraudulent enterprise, escape was a necessity, so she relieved the tedium by plotting and planning. It soon became apparent that it was impractical to consider using force while she was still in the house. Whenever she was visited with meals, Selina always had Alice with her. Fliss did not fancy her chances in a contest of strength with these women, each of whom was stronger and heavier than she. It seemed that the best chance would be when she was taken outside the house, which they would have to do in order to get her off to this Finishing School. Once in public, Fliss thought, there would be the opportunity to put up a fight; to scream and run; to create such a hullabaloo that she was bound to draw attention to her plight. To further improve her chances, she pretended complete submission and acquiescence so as to lull Selina and her henchwoman into a false sense of security. When she was ordered to pack her things for her forthcoming journey she did so meekly and without protest, content in the knowledge that this conspiracy against her would soon be exposed to public gaze.

Selina and Alice came to her as dusk was falling on the second day of her captivity. They were accompanied by two other women and Fliss eyed them with the first twinges of apprehension that maybe her plan was not as simple as it had appeared until now.

'These ladies are from Draco House. Allow me to introduce Miss Blair and Miss Colforth. They will see to it that you get there safely. Are you all packed?'

'Yes.' Fliss decided that there was nothing to be lost by continuing her deception of compliance. At the same time, she was eyeing the two newcomers with growing dismay. They were in their mid-twenties; tough-looking, hard and fit. In order to have any chance of breaking away from them she would have to take them completely by surprise.

Miss Blair came towards her holding a broad, black leather belt between her hands. 'Put this on, please.'

'Why? What's it for?' Fliss was growing seriously alarmed. 'I don't want to.'

Miss Blair nodded to Miss Colforth, who crossed the room and stood behind Fliss, who twisted her head nervously, trying to keep them both in sight at the same time.

'Look,' said Fliss, adopting a conciliatory tone while trying to keep the tremble from her voice. 'I've said I'll come with you. There's no need for anything else, is there?'

For answer, Miss Colforth reached around from behind her and grasped her wrists in steely fingers, raising them up and pressing them against her breasts, holding her securely, while Miss Blair came forward and buckled the belt around Fliss' waist. When it was secure, Miss Colforth forced her arms down over it. On either side of the central buckle, broad straps were attached to the belt at a near right angle and, while Miss Colforth held Fliss' arms in the appropriate position, Miss Blair buckled one of those straps about each wrist, so that

21

Fliss was secured with her hands over her stomach. She could flap her hands and elbows, but that was about all.

They released her then and Fliss stood still, tugging vainly at the straps, conscious of the fact that her means of attracting attention had been severely reduced. Screaming and running were the only resources left to her.

Selina was carrying a garment over her arm and she now unfolded it so that Fliss could see that it was a cloak. 'Have to keep you warm for the journey,' Selina said, smiling without warmth. She threw the cloak around Fliss' shoulders and buttoned it at the front from neck to hem, completely concealing the securing belt and cuffs.

Shivering with apprehension as it became more and more apparent that these women knew all about the transportation of recalcitrants, Fliss tried a desperate bid at reasonableness. 'Don't do this, Selina. Think about it. If you stop now, I won't tell anyone. I promise I won't. I'll do a deal with you to see that you get a fair share of the estate. I'll . . . What are you doing? No! Oh please, no! Not that!'

With a sadistic grin, Selina was ripping a length off a broad roll of flesh-coloured adhesive plaster. 'You talk too much, slut!' she said and pasted the strip across Fliss' mouth, sealing it tight shut. She took out a lipstick. 'Stand still!'

Desperately, Fliss shook her head and made such noises as she could.

'Either stand still or get another spanking. Your knickers can come off as easily with an audience as without, you know.'

Fliss knew that Selina was perfectly capable of carrying out her threat. Utterly cowed, she capitulated and stood still while Selina drew red lips on the plaster over her own.

Selina surveyed her critically. 'Nearly done, now,' she said.

22

Fliss saw that she now held a pair of sunglasses. They looked quite ordinary, except that the arms were joined together by elastic. There was nothing Fliss could do as Selina grasped her hair to hold her still while she slipped the glasses over her head and settled them on her nose. Fliss discovered that the centre part of each lens was completely opaque, allowing only very limited vision up, down and sideways. She could see nothing directly in front of her. She shook her head violently, but found that she was quite unable to dislodge these blinkers. She fought back tears of frustration as it dawned on her that now she was not only prevented from fighting or screaming, but that attempting to run would be useless if she could not see where she was going. Worse than that, to anyone seeing her at a distance without careful inspection she would not appear to be bound and gagged; just rather eccentrically dressed.

'All ready now.' Although Fliss could not see her, she could hear the triumphant sneer in Selina's voice. 'You won't mind if I don't come down to see you off, will you, dear?'

With Miss Blair on one side and Miss Colforth on the other, she had no alternative but to go where they led her. They led her out of the nursery and down the broad staircase to the front door. With her peripheral vision, Fliss was able to make out that their transport was not to be a car, as she had expected, but a large motor caravan. The women hustled her up the steps which led to the door at the back. Once inside, they seated her on a broad bed then Miss Blair pushed at her shoulders so that she fell on to it while Miss Colforth scooped up her legs. They arranged her on her back with a pillow under her head, then passed straps across her body at chest, waist and knees. She was completely immobilised. It was galling for her to recollect her hopeful, naive plans for escape. She was dealing with experts.

Miss Blair settled herself in the driving seat and

started the engine. Miss Colforth sat on the bunk opposite. 'I should try to sleep a little, if I were you. We have a long journey and you'll need your strength at the other end. I shall stay here and watch you. We will release you as soon as it is practicable. It's not our intention that you should be any more uncomfortable than is necessary to ensure that you don't escape or make a fuss. If you get hungry or thirsty or need the toilet, just snap your fingers and I'll attend to you. You can snap your fingers, I suppose?'

Fliss nodded, miserably. If this was a first taste of Draco House, she did not care for it at all. Her mind returned to that ominous phrase, 'You'll need your strength at the other end . . .' What did that portend? Deeply worried, she tried to take the advice offered and sleep.

Two

Fliss watched the coast disappearing into the distance as the big motor launch chugged on its steady course, occasionally pitching a little as it dug its bow into a larger than usual wavelet. It had not occurred to her that the school might not be on the mainland, a fact which substantially reduced the chances of escape. Miss Blair and Miss Colforth obviously thought that those chances had disappeared already. As soon as they had transferred her to this boat, they had released her. That must mean that the boatman was in their employ and a party to the conspiracy. Certainly he had given no sign that he found anything remarkable about a strapped, blindfolded and gagged young woman being brought aboard his craft. This seemed to be a well-planned and oft-repeated exercise. For her captors, the journey had been a matter of simple routine. For Fliss, it had been a trauma. She shuddered with distaste as she recalled her one attempt to break the stalemate. She had snapped her fingers and, when questioned, nodded to indicate that she needed to pee. When released for that purpose, she had thought, maybe there would be a momentary inattention on Miss Colforth's part which would allow some method of attracting attention to her plight.

All that had happened was that Miss Colforth had loosened the strap about her knees, pulled her knickers down and pushed a bed-pan under her body with a degree of expertise which indicated at least some nursing training. The humiliation of having that done was enough to deter her from snapping her fingers again, even though she was hungry and thirsty. However much she wanted a cup of tea, she was not willing to go through the humiliation of being fed from a cup like a baby to get it!

The boat lurched again, recalling her to the present. The motion might upset some people. Hopefully, she glanced at the women accompanying her. No, guarding her would be a better way of describing it. She certainly felt like some sort of convict on her way to prison. Miss Colforth had not let her out of her sight since they left the house. There was something scary about that.

Now an island was in sight in the distance ahead. She stared at it curiously. It was too soon to make out any detail, but it certainly did not seem to be very big. It was not until they were much closer that she was able to make out Draco House. It was huge, grey and rambling: the sort of nineteenth-century, crenellated, pseudo-castle which otherwise unimportant men, socially blighted by being 'in trade' but with lots of money and pretensions to grandeur were wont to have built for themselves. On a slight rise, it dominated the island. From it, a winding road ran down to a cluster of huts and a small pier. To its left there was flatter ground and a glimpse of woodland. Apart from those things the island seemed to be completely featureless.

It was already growing dark when the boatman brought the launch alongside the jetty. Her guards stepped ashore and Fliss followed them. Her suitcase was handed out to her and she waited as Miss Blair spoke to the boatman.

'Thank you, Mr Morgan. Put the stores in the warehouse as usual please, then return to your other duties.'

'Yes, Miss.'

'Come, Felicity. Pick up your suitcase. You will find no servants here. Follow me!'

Fliss trudged up the hill behind the two women, her

26

arms tiring rapidly, although she changed the suitcase from hand to hand frequently. Just as she was beginning to think that she would have to go through life looking like an orang-utan, they arrived at the main entrance to the school. The vast oak door was closed and Miss Blair pulled on an antique iron loop to ring the bell. There was a long delay before the door was opened by a young woman in an overall. Fliss later learned that she was one of the few domestic staff. Miss Blair went off in a different direction while Miss Colforth led her down a wide and echoing corridor. She opened the door of a side room and stood aside for Fliss to pass her. She went into the room and set her case down.

'Wait!' Miss Colforth said and went out, closing the door.

Fliss looked around the room. It was sparsely furnished but what there was looked to be of good quality. A cheerful fire burned in the grate. Perhaps this place would not be so bad, after all. That tentative opinion was reinforced when the door opened again and the woman in the overall brought in a tray of food and a pot of tea. At least she wouldn't starve. The woman offered no conversation. That seemed to be a habit in this place. Fliss was ravenous after her self-imposed fast and ate her supper and drank her tea with a young woman's healthy appetite. That need satisfied and being a little bored with her long wait, she decided to explore a little. She went to the door and tried the handle. It was locked. She was not really surprised. She sat down again and waited as patiently as she could.

When the door was opened again, it was Miss Colforth. She had changed her clothes and now wore a short, red, pleated skirt and a red, roll-neck sweater. Her legs were bare and she had on short white socks and white tennis shoes. She looked fitter and healthier than ever. 'Leave your cloak and suitcase here. Follow me!' she said.

Fliss trotted out into the corridor after her. The grey stone walls and flagged floor were dismal and forbidding. Miss Colforth's tennis shoes made practically no sound, but Fliss' high heels rang out a staccato beat which echoed eerily. Further along the corridor, Miss Colforth knocked at another door then opened it as before and stood aside for Fliss to enter. The panelled room was about twenty feet square. In the centre of it was a long, high table with a padded, black leather top. There was a long wooden bench at one side. That was the only furniture. There were five women already in the room. Miss Colforth, entering and closing the door behind her, made a sixth. Fliss stared from one to the other. All but one seemed to be in their mid-to-late twenties. Two women were standing near the table. One seemed older, maybe thirty-ish, and had an air of authority. She was fairly tall, slim, and wore her black hair drawn back in a bun. She was wearing a dark green dress with a white, starched apron over it. The other was shorter, just a trifle overweight and fair. Her uniform, for that was what Fliss now guessed it must be, was similar to Miss Colforth's and that of the other women except that her skirt and sweater were blue while theirs were red. The other three sat on the long wooden bench. They were identically dressed in the red outfits which, Fliss deduced, indicated a lower rank. Fliss recognised one as Miss Blair and it was beside her that Miss Colforth took her seat. Looking at the four of them in a row, shoulder to shoulder, Fliss was reminded of a brass ornament she had at home. One too many wise monkeys, she thought, irreverently.

She addressed herself to the woman in the white apron. 'Why have I been treated like this?' she demanded. 'When my solicitor finds out . . .'

The woman raised a finger. In spite of herself, Fliss' voice trailed off into silence. There was that about this woman with which one did not argue.

'I will tell you when you may speak,' the woman said. 'I am Miss Ames. I am the Principal.' She gestured to the woman in blue. 'This is my assistant, Miss Moncrieff.' She pointed individually to the women on the bench. 'Miss Blair and Miss Colforth you already know. This is Miss Snaith and Miss Kelly. This is your preliminary interview. It gives us the opportunity to find out something about you. Cleanliness is an absolute priority here. I have your medical history on file, of course, but it is necessary for the benefit of the other pupils that I should satisfy myself that you have no communicable skin or other diseases. Please undress!'

'What!' Fliss was staggered.

Miss Ames was dangerously patient. 'I'm sorry. What was there about the word, "undress", which you didn't understand? Remove your garments! Disrobe! Strip! Do any of those help you?'

Fliss temporised. 'Are you sure that's really necessary?'

'Completely necessary!'

'Well, do you have a screen, or something?'

'No!'

Fliss was running out of delaying sentences. 'But . . . In front of . . .' She gestured to the women all about her.

Miss Ames' patience became even more dangerous. 'Unless you are some sort of freak you will be showing them nothing they haven't seen a hundred times before. Give your clothes to Miss Colforth as you take them off. She will dispose of them. A uniform is supplied. You won't be needing them again.'

'But I don't need a uniform. I have lots of clothes in my suitcase,' said Fliss.

'There is nothing in your suitcase which you will need before you leave here.'

'But you don't know what's in it!'

'Whatever is in it, you won't need it. Now, are you going to undress? My tutors are perfectly capable of removing your clothing for you if you prefer it.'

29

'No, that won't be necessary,' said Fliss hastily, bowing to the inevitable. She unbuttoned her white blouse and handed it over, very conscious of the fact that her brassière was a filmy, lacy creation which did little to hide her breasts. She unzipped her light brown skirt and passed that over. This was worse! She had been particularly proud of the white knickers she was wearing. They were not tight or skimpy. In fact, they covered all her pubic area and even part of her thighs quite adequately. The problem was that they were so light and gauzy that they were practically transparent and they clung to every crease and hollow of her body in a way which, until now, she had thought wonderful. Now she wished she had chosen bloomers and tights that morning. The impression she was creating was not helped by the minimal white garter belt which, by means of long suspenders, held up her light stockings.

Almost gratefully, she removed the belt and stockings then paused. 'Won't this do?' she asked, piteously.

'No.'

Fliss unclipped the brassière and slid it off her shoulders, baring her breasts. Crouching, she wriggled out of the knickers and handed them over, too. She continued to stoop, shielding her body with her arms.

'Stand up straight! Put your hands behind you, please!' Miss Ames approached her, taking a small penlight from her apron pocket. Fliss felt the lobe of one ear being gripped between a cold finger and thumb and was aware of the glare of the torch. The other ear was similarly examined. That was, somehow, reassuring. It put the thing on a more clinical basis and made it more acceptable. She relaxed a little.

'Open your mouth, please! Wider! Say Ah!' The examination continued and was no longer particularly disturbing, even when she was asked to raise each arm so that her armpits could be inspected.

'Now turn round. Feet astride! Touch your toes!'

30

This was much more embarrassing. Face aflame, Fliss obeyed, very conscious of all she must be revealing by such a pose. She felt the brief touch of cold thumbs on her bottom cheeks, forcing them apart, and glimpsed the light of the torch again.

'Stand up!'

Gratefully, Fliss assumed an upright position. 'Can I get dressed again, now?'

'No, not yet. First it is necessary that I should remove your pubic hair.'

'Why on earth . . . ?'

'You are very new, so I will make allowances. I have already told you that cleanliness is extremely important. Shaving that area reduces the risk of any cross-infection from the outside world. It also marks you as a new pupil, so that staff and other girls can recognise the fact and also make allowances for behaviour which it may take you a while to change. As your hair grows, so will you become integrated into our system. Now do you understand?'

Fliss found herself appalled at the implication of this statement. Not only was she to be shaved, but there would be circumstances in the future in which others were going to be able to see that it had been done.

'I'm not going to let you shave my hair down there!'

'You will have it shaved. Will you stand quietly while I do it?'

'No, I bloody won't!' said Fliss, furious at the idea.

'Very well,' said Miss Ames, calmly. She nodded to the other women and they came towards Fliss.

She backed away. 'What are you doing? Keep away! Don't come . . .' She let out a screech of panic and surprise as they seized her, one taking each arm and leg. Sweeping her off her feet with ease, they carried her, naked, wriggling and still screaming, to the table. They dumped her on it without ceremony and she felt the coldness of the leather on her bare back and buttocks.

31

The two women who held her arms changed their grip. They grasped her wrists and pulled her arms out to the sides, so that they stuck straight out over the edges of the table. She felt them fumble with her hands and could not understand what they were doing until she felt the thumb and forefinger of each woman bite into the fleshy web between her own thumb and forefinger. They squeezed and the agony was incredible! Fliss had not known, until then, about the nerve centre at that location. Her whole body froze into immobility and the pressure relaxed to become just a pain.

She heard Miss Ames' voice. 'Keep still and you won't be hurt.'

Fliss' stomach churned as she heard the unmistakable buzz of electric clippers, then felt their coldness on her stomach. Careless of the pain in her hands, she lashed out with her feet, kicking wildly and struggling to get up. The women about her had obviously been prepared for that. The ease with which they overpowered her was astonishing. Two of them pulled her arms above her head and fixed them there with straps attached to the top corners of the table. Two more took her ankles and walked with them up each side of the table, pressing them down on either side of her head. In this doubled-up position, her hips came right off the leather surface. A long belt was slipped underneath her waist, pulled up inside her thighs, then out over them and down to the edge of the table. When the strap was pulled really tight on either side, holes in the strap ends located over hooked pegs set in the table side. Her thighs were spread so wide apart that Fliss felt her hips creak with the strain. The whole process seemed to take only seconds. When they stood back, her body was immovably fixed with her bottom turned up and her knees spread wider than they had ever been. Only her legs could wave in the air and even that movement was confined to the portions below the knees. With a sense of hopelessness, she set herself to endure what must come. This was absolutely dreadful! And yet . . . And yet . . . In the midst of the horror of what was being done to her, there was something else. She was ashamed to find that the very fact that she was being held down and so abused was giving her some sort of faint, sexual thrill. She tried to dismiss the feeling, but it would not go away.

Miss Ames took up the electric clippers and switched them on. In a most matter-of-fact way, she quickly clipped off most of the light brown pubic curls so conveniently presented. She even removed them far down in the cleft around her anal area. Fliss thought that she would detest the whole process but was dismayed to find that the humming tickle of the clippers was causing sex thoughts to fill her mind. Her masturbation fantasy was being fulfilled. She was strapped down; more strictly confined than she had ever been. These women were staring at her; could see her gaping sex and even her sphincter. Not only was she naked now; she was about to be made even more naked by the removal of her only remaining vestige of covering. The buzzing whirr of the clippers continued to be disconcerting. When they passed over the hood of her clitoris, the vibration was maddeningly arousing. In spite of herself, her vagina was lubricating and because it was stretched so wide open by her restraint, she was certain this was apparent to the watchers.

Miss Ames filled her palm from a can of foam and Fliss closed her eyes, holding her breath. When the first touch of it came on her body, her eyes flicked open in surprise. Miss Ames was spreading it in small circles on the stretched skin under her left armpit. She turned her head to that side and watched as the razor glided across the white surface. No one except she had ever shaved her there and the strangeness of it made her feel very odd but heightened her sexual tension. Miss Ames finished her shaving and wiped the armpit with a damp

33

cloth. Fliss turned the other way to inspect the other armpit. There was the faintest trace of stubble there; hardly noticeable but enough to provide an excuse, she supposed. She watched the same spreading of the lather and felt the razor on that side. There was definitely something very sensual about being shaved there. She realised that the armpit shave had been deliberate, to prepare her for what must happen to the remains of her pubic hair, and she felt her clitoris growing as her vagina twinged again. She looked down. Now that her curls had been clipped to an untidy stubble, she was certain she could see the tip of her clitoris in the gaping crevice between her thighs. She prayed that she was wrong or that, if she was right, none of the women would notice it. Now she could see Miss Ames between her legs and she was filling her palm with foam again. Fliss waited, both longing for and dreading that touch. When it came, the coldness of it there, in that place, was exciting, as was the way it was rubbed into her stubble with slow, deliberate circling. Miss Ames' fingers were passing across her clitoris and her exposed inner surfaces, moving her labia from side to side. Suddenly Fliss became intensely curious to know what the bite of the razor would be like and what her pubes would look like when it was hairless. In her turned-up position it was not difficult to see what was going on. She felt the scritch of the sharp blade on her and watched, fascinated, as a patch of pure white, hairless skin such as she had not seen in that place since puberty emerged in its wake. She shuddered, not from distaste. When Miss Ames reached the delicate area around her labia, she had to take hold of them with finger and thumb to stretch the skin for the razor. Fliss was humiliated to find that touch was sufficient to send her quivering into orgasm. It was tiny but she knew that the signs of it could not be missed by the onlookers and she flushed deepest red with the shame of it all. As Miss Ames wiped her clean with the damp cloth she was able to see herself properly for the first time. The whole area between her legs was completely hairless, bald and smooth, every wrinkle and crevice of her sex clear to see. She had felt the razor at work and knew that this total depilation extended everywhere, even beyond where she could see and that between the cheeks of her bottom and around her anus there was no longer even the lightest fuzz. She had never been so naked.

When Fliss was released from the table she sat up, rubbing her wrists and flexing her sore hips. Now that she was able to put her legs together, her newly shaven crotch and bottom felt decidedly strange. She wriggled experimentally, testing the sensation, but resisted the temptation to touch herself. Miss Moncrieff held out a towelling robe. She got down off the table and slipped her arms into it, wrapping it gratefully over her extreme nudity. When a pair of slippers were pointed out to her she pushed her feet into them and felt even better.

'That is the first stage of the cleansing process,' said Miss Ames, coiling the electric lead. 'Now go with Miss Colforth and Miss Blair to take a bath.'

Fliss was too numb with shock to argue. When the two women took her by the arms and led her out, she went without protest. The bathroom they took her to was large and white-tiled from floor to ceiling in the Victorian style. The very large bath was the old-fashioned, institutional sort; free-standing and set in the centre of the room. Miss Blair went over to it and started to fill it. By that time, Fliss had recovered some of her poise.

'Thank you,' she said. 'I can manage now.'

'Give me the robe!' said Miss Colforth.

Fliss shrugged. Obviously they intended to stay. Well, they wouldn't see any more than they had already. She handed over the robe, stepped into the bath and sat down. The two women took up positions kneeling on either side of her, each armed with soap and washcloth. Well, that was all right too, Fliss decided and allowed them to wash her. Actually, it was not an unpleasant experience. It was a long time since anyone had bathed her and she submitted to their ministrations with good grace. They washed her face, neck and ears and that brought back good memories of childhood. She was resigned to the loss of her pubic hair. There was nothing she could do about it now and it would grow again.

When requested, she raised her arms so that they could wash her newly shaven armpits. When they moved on to the front of her body she lay back and thoroughly enjoyed the movement of hands across her breasts and nipples and on her stomach. She was almost drifting off into a doze when she felt a hand insert itself between her thighs.

'No!' She jerked upright, splashing. 'I can do that bit, thanks.'

Miss Blair's hand intruded again and she knocked it away. 'I said, "No!" Don't touch me there!'

Both women got up and moved away. Satisfied that she had, at least, won that point, Fliss picked up soap and flannel to prepare for washing herself. She was taken completely by surprise when they suddenly bore down on her and seized her arms. They pulled them behind her back and she was shocked to see that Miss Colforth had the belt of her towelling robe in her hands.

'No! Oh God, no! Not that!' Fliss screamed, but she was too late. In a trice, the belt had been wound around her wrists, crossed, wound again and knotted. She tugged frantically, but this was the work of experts. The worst part was that even as she struggled her masturbation fantasy came strongly upon her again. She was tied; helpless; naked, and 'they' were going to touch her she was sure. Her stomach muscles contracted and she felt her vagina watering. This was a nightmare! To be bound was bad enough. To find that her mind and body were accepting this treatment and getting off on it was truly dreadful!

She watched apprehensively and clamped her thighs together as Miss Colforth picked up the soap and lathered her hands. She did not, however, return to the pubic area, but began to soap Fliss' breasts again, allowing her slippery hands to rove over the swelling surfaces. Fliss' nipples were now solidly erect and, after each pass, sprang to attention in a most embarrassing fashion. Before, having her breasts soaped had been merely pleasurable. Now the sexual stimulation was so intense that it was as if every nerve in her nipples had been fitted with an amplifier. She felt the shocks of the repeated caresses deep in her womb and began to be afraid that she would disgrace herself by coming.

Miss Blair pulled over a stool and set it beside the bath. Miss Colforth stopped her washing and rinsed her hands then they each grasped one of Fliss' arms and lifted her to her feet.

'What is it? What are you going to do?' Fliss' voice trembled with an emotion which even she was not entirely sure was fear.

They did not answer. Miss Blair sat down on the stool and Miss Colforth turned Fliss to face her.

Fliss felt hands on her shoulder-blades, pushing her gently forward. Her knees caught against the side of the bath and she overbalanced. Miss Blair caught her dextrously as she fell to her knees and Fliss found herself with her upper body laid along Miss Blair's lap, her face buried in the red skirt and her breasts pressing against those bare thighs. The other side of the bath prevented her from moving her feet backwards. The only movement she could make was to shuffle them apart sideways, which parted her already obscenely split thighs and bottom cheeks. Craning round, Fliss saw Miss Colforth soaping her hands again.

'What are you going to do? You can't . . .' Her voice

became muffled as Miss Blair pressed her head down into her lap and held it there. Fliss smelt the musky woman-scent of her and it excited her. Acutely conscious of the fact that her sex was now completely bald and that every detail of her most intimate parts would be visible to anyone behind her, she wriggled her soapy breasts against the flesh beneath them and waited. The first touch, when it came, was like an electric shock and she jumped. A soapy hand was running up and down the gaping cleft between her buttocks, causing the most exquisite thrills as it passed over her stretched anus. Now another soapy hand was between her parted thighs, rubbing back and forth over her shaven mons Veneris. She moaned and wriggled her bottom under the powerful influence of this sexual stimulation. She felt a soapy finger stop and centre itself on her sphincter. It pushed gently, then more insistently.

She twisted her face sideways, freeing her mouth. 'No! Oh no! You can't mean to . . . !'

'We have to wash everywhere,' said Miss Colforth.

Fliss felt the pressure become overwhelming. Not only the physical pressure but the sexual pressure. She had to fight hard against a tremendous urge to open herself; to surrender to that which she found herself lusting after. For the rest of her life, she would remember the jolt of the elastic muscles which collapsed, suddenly and completely, to admit that prying finger and the extraordinary way in which her body welcomed the first intrusion, ever, of any foreign object into that particular secret cave.

She cried out with joy as the soapy finger plunged in and out, massaging and cleansing her anus. Her naked bottom trembled and wobbled as she arched and thrust backwards to give the object maximum access, at the same time grinding her pubes against the rubbing hand underneath her. Now she had no time for such trivia as pretended pain or embarrassment. This was a dream come true. The words burned themselves into her brain again and again. Tied! Helpless! Naked! Masturbated by force! She knew that she was going to come and that her orgasm would be huge. She didn't care. The only thing that mattered was what was being done to her and how it made her feel. Now her sphincter was beyond her control, pouting and puckering to kiss the finger upon which it was impaled, sucking at it greedily as if to draw from it even greater pleasure.

'Yes! Do it to me! Make me come! Do it! Faster! Yes! Yes! Don't stop! For God's sake, don't stop!'

There was simply no way she could have concealed that climax, even had she tried. It was massive and seemed to affect every part of her which would move. Frantically, she eased her body back until her mouth was below the hem of the red skirt and she could kiss the bare thighs which supported her. 'Thank you! Oh God, thank you so much! Mm!' Still dizzy and panting, she hardly noticed herself being lifted, turned and seated again in the bath. She breathed hard, trying to regain her self-control, pressing her legs together and feeling the sting of the warm water on her stretched anus. She felt ashamed now, knowing that the two women had observed her at such a private moment. Her naturally philosophical temperament took over. There was nothing she could do to change what had happened. It was in the past. Let them make of it what they would. She relaxed and lay back, allowing the water to slosh over her stomach.

Miss Colforth was soaping her hands again and Fliss smiled inwardly. She didn't care. The humiliation of being watched in orgasm was over. Let them do their worst. The slippery hands sliding over her belly did not bother her and even when one of those hands dipped into the trough between her legs, she remained relaxed. Miss Colforth rubbed slowly and diligently up and down the full length of her sex and Fliss watched languidly. That rubbing was insistent, though, and she looked down at her own body as she felt a small qualm in the pit of her stomach. Then her breasts began to tingle and in fascinated horror she saw that her nipples were erect again. She tried to bring her hands forward to hide the fact, only to be forcibly reminded that she was still helplessly trussed. Her masturbation fantasy forced its way to the forefront of her consciousness again and she tried to dismiss it from her mind. Miss Blair was soaping her hands, now, and when she began yet another massage of those nipples, Fliss had to think the unthinkable.

The orgasm she had experienced when being shaved had been quite small and had been followed by a period of time, albeit short, so might be counted as a separate incident. She had never in her life had two orgasms in a row and believed it to be impossible. Girls who claimed to have done so must have been exaggerating, she thought. Now, however, there was no doubt that she was coming to the boil yet again. If only that constant teasing of her pubes and nipples would stop!

When Miss Colforth carefully soaped two fingers of her right hand, Fliss panicked. 'No, please! I know what you're going to do. You mustn't! Really, you mustn't!' She watched the lathered fingers come near her vagina and then a most extraordinary thing happened. Her brain told her legs to close and her thighs to clamp together. Instead of her limbs obeying her will, she saw her knees open until they pressed hard against the sides of the bath, while her crotch thrust itself up clear of the water. She heard her own voice, hoarse and almost unrecognisable saying, 'Yes! Oh yes! Please! Oh please, yes!'

The fingers thrust themselves into her vagina and her body arched, her breasts pushing up in search of greater nipple stimulation. She tugged hard at her bonds; not in an effort to get free, but for the thrill she got from satisfying herself that she was tightly tied and could not prevent what was happening to her. Now the fingers were probing; rubbing; washing; irritating that special place under her pubic bone. She felt her juices flood down on the fingers as if to wash them out, at the same time as her strong, young, vaginal muscles were sucking eagerly at them, trying to draw them further in. She bucked and twitched under their hands as she came in great waves; not as violently as before but somehow more deeply and satisfyingly. When it was over she lay drained for a while. Even after they untied her hands it took her some time to recover sufficiently to get out of the bath. She could not believe that she had orgasmed twice in such a short time with strangers watching her. The two women made absolutely no comment about anything they might have seen. She put on her robe and they took her back to the interview room.

Miss Ames and the other women were still in the same positions and might not have moved since she left. Miss Colforth made a whispered report to Miss Ames, causing her to glance sharply at Fliss, who simply stood where she had been put, staring dully ahead. She did not even demur when Miss Ames asked her to take off the robe and lie on the table. She just hitched herself on to it, swung her legs up and lay down on her back as ordered.

Miss Ames pulled on a pair of rubber gloves. 'Raise your legs and part your knees, please.'

Fliss did so. She did not even flinch when Miss Ames inserted a gloved finger into her vagina and examined her cursorily.

'So!' Miss Ames said, pulling off the gloves. 'You are not a virgin!'

Fliss was too drained to care. 'What? Oh! No!'

'You have had sex with a man?'

Fliss blushed, her attention caught at last. 'No.'

'Please explain your broken hymen, then.'

41

Fliss blushed even more. 'I can't!'

'Can't or won't?'

Fliss just shook her head. There was no way in the world she could ever explain to anyone just what had led her, at an early age, to experiment with a courgette. She was relieved that she was not pressed further on the point.

Miss Ames merely said, 'Put on your robe and slippers and come with me, Felicity.'

Fliss followed her out of the room, leaving the women tidying up. As they walked along the broad corridors, she noticed the vast number of doors, indistinguishable from each other, and wondered how anyone ever learned their way about such a rambling pile. When Miss Ames went into one of the doors she followed her and found herself in a room which seemed to be an office or study; maybe a little of each. It was wood-panelled and cosy. A bright fire burned in the grate. Although there were filing cabinets and a photocopier, there were also comfortable, chintz-covered chairs and occasional tables. The numerous bookcases held an assortment of volumes, many of them light reading matter; not formal office tomes. A broad, flat desk occupied the centre of the room. On it, an old-fashioned reading lamp cast a pleasing glow, epitomising the formal informality.

There was a small pile of clothing on the desk and Miss Ames gestured to it. 'That is the first part of your regulation uniform,' she said. 'It is your night attire. Please put it on now.'

Fliss sorted through the pile. It consisted of a heavier woollen dressing gown and a nightdress. She opened her robe to take it off but Miss Ames said, 'If you wish, you may change in there.' She pointed to a door. 'You will find that to be a small bathroom. You will find everything you need. Most particularly, there is talcum powder. I suggest that you apply it to those parts of you which have been recently shaved. You will be much more comfortable.'

Fliss gathered up the clothes and went into the bathroom. There was no bolt inside the door but she had expected no less and was unconcerned. If Miss Ames chose to walk in on her, she did not see how she could possibly see any more of her than had already been adequately displayed. She took off her robe, used the toilet then washed her shaved parts; not because she thought they were dirty but in an effort to remove her memory of Miss Ames' rubber-gloved inspection. She dried herself on one of the big, fluffy towels provided and picked up the talcum powder. Before she applied it she stared at her reflection in the big mirror on the tiled wall. Her new appearance was fascinating and she watched herself finger the bald skin of her pubic area, receiving physical and visual input which confirmed that the whole thing had not been some strange dream. She picked up a hand mirror and used it to obtain a better view of the unfamiliar genitals she had seemed suddenly to acquire. Her clitoral hood, the lips of her sex and even her anal area were now revealed as in some medical textbook. She found the contemplation of them very interesting and had a sudden urge to masturbate. She dismissed the notion angrily. Good God! She had come to climax three times, already! Was she becoming a nymphomaniac? She powdered herself and put on the nightdress. In plainest white, it was of a very old-fashioned design but not unattractive in a Victorian sort of way. The material was very warm but not one she could identify. The tiny collar buttoned high about her neck, the sleeves were wrist-length and the hem of it came down to her ankles. She pushed her feet into the new slippers which were decidedly unsexy but woolly and cosy. Similarly, the dressing gown was large, all-enveloping and made of the best quality woollen material. She went back into the study.

Miss Ames was at her desk, writing. She got up when Fliss came in and surveyed her. 'Better!' she said, and gestured towards one of the armchairs. 'Please sit down.'

Fliss sat, wondering what was coming next. She felt that there was little else this woman could do to her body. She was not so confident about what she might be able to do to her mind. She was still wondering when there was a soft knock at the door. On being bidden to do so, the overalled woman entered with a tray.

'Thank you, Dorothy,' Miss Ames said. 'Put it on the small table.' The woman did so and left, closing the door softly behind her.

Miss Ames seated herself in a matching chair with the low table between them. 'Cocoa and biscuits, Felicity. Help yourself.'

Fliss could not help thinking that she had strayed with Alice through the looking glass. One moment she was strapped down, being humiliated and shaved; the next, she was sitting in a comfortable chair being offered cocoa and bikkies. She picked up the mug. The cocoa was very hot and very good, indeed. She tried to remember the last time such a drink had been her nightcap instead of alcohol.

She sipped again. 'It's very good,' she said, grudgingly.

'Healthy fresh milk and healthy iron,' said Miss Ames. 'If you starve here, it will be by your own neglect. It is necessary that you be detained until Miss Doyle's plans for your estate are fully realised. That is for her financial benefit and mine. Whether or not you suffer during your detention will be in your hands and will depend on your behaviour.'

Fliss nodded. That was just a little reassuring, anyway. 'By the way,' she said, 'What's the nightdress made of? It's something I've never seen before.'

'Flannelette,' Miss Ames replied. 'Of the best quality, like everything we use. Warm, comfortable and healthy, yet condemned as old-fashioned by the young. Everyone

44

is dressed the same, here. That way, there is no discernible difference of status between the rich and the not-so-rich.'

'I see,' said Fliss. When put like that, the nightie seemed to be at least politically correct, even if not racy.

'Good,' Miss Ames said. 'We seem to have broken the ice. Your case is a little different from most of the girls we have here, though all of them are to a greater or lesser extent detained against their will; sometimes for their own good – sometimes for the good of others. The process of induction is strange for new girls and it is always a relief when it is out of the way and we can move on to other things.'

'Strange' was not an adequate adjective, Fliss thought, but kept her thoughts to herself.

'This little chat gives me the opportunity to tell you about the things we do here; what you may expect of us and what we, in turn, will expect of you. This is a Finishing School, and a good one. Here, you will learn about many things which will be useful to you in life. You will receive education in Menu Preparation and Supervision, Dress, Deportment, Conversation, Art, Literature, Entertaining, and some others. Your physical education will not be neglected. There will be regular sessions of healthy outdoor games and indoor gymnastics. *Mens sana in corpore sano* is one of our maxims, as well as cleanliness. And while we are on the subject of healthy minds, it was noticed that you came to orgasm while I was shaving you and you did it again, twice, while you were being bathed. Is masturbation a regular habit with you?'

Fliss felt her face turn beetroot red. 'I don't . . . I . . . Er . . .'

'I think we can take that as an affirmative, without going into detail,' said Miss Ames, briskly. 'It is to be expected. One of the infections from the outside world. You will find that our regimen, which feeds the mind

45

and exercises, as well as nourishes, the body, will help you to correct that. One of the things which all our young women need is self-discipline. They are all here because they have displayed a lack of it. In due time, they will learn it but until they do we supply the discipline for them. It is part of that learning process which causes all our subjects to be compulsory. It is only natural that there should be some you like and others you loathe. In your life outside you have been able to avoid doing things you dislike. Here, by a system of inducements, we teach you to stick at hateful tasks.'

'Inducements?'

'Yes, inducements. If you are observed to be doing less than your absolute best in anything you will be brought here. You will take your knickers down and bend over my desk. If you refuse to do that, Miss Moncrieff will assist me by holding you in that position while I take your knickers down myself. I will then spank your bare bottom in accordance with the scale your misdemeanour warrants.'

Fliss could not believe her ears. 'What? You can't be serious!'

'Try me if you doubt it!' Suddenly, Fliss didn't. 'For repeated or more serious offences, a slipper substitutes for my hand. If those fail to achieve the desired result you will be caned; never less than six strokes and always with your knickers down and on your bare bottom. If you continue to push matters beyond the caning stage there are other inducements which I won't bother to describe, now.'

'Good God!' Fliss was stunned.

Miss Ames smiled reassuringly. 'But I'm sure that nothing I have said need apply to you. I am certain that you will be a model of good behaviour and never find yourself across my desk all the time you are here. Now, drink up your cocoa. It is time for bed and I will take you to your room. Are you comfortable? This is your last opportunity to use the toilet.'

Fliss drained her mug. 'No, I'm all right, thank you.' She stood up.

Miss Ames went to her desk drawer and took out two curious objects which appeared to be green canvas bags stuffed full of something soft. 'Hold out your hands!' she said.

'Why?' asked Fliss, suspiciously.

'Because I just told you to hold out your hands, of course. Do you need some other reason?'

'What are you going to do?'

'If you continue to be intransigent I am going to send for Miss Moncrieff. She will hold you across the desk and you will find that having your dressing gown and nightdress pulled up around your waist has much the same effect of baring your bottom for a spanking as does pulling your knickers down. Now, this is the last time I shall say this. Hold out your hands!'

Sulkily, Fliss extended her hands in front of her. Miss Ames pulled open the neck of one of the bags and pushed it on to Fliss' right hand, like a glove. She buckled a strap around her wrist and fastened it with a tiny padlock. She did the same thing with the other bag on her left hand. Fliss found that the silk inner lining fitted her hands quite closely. The stuffing between it and the outer canvas meant that her arms now ended in green canvas balls, instead of in hands, fingers and thumbs.

'What's this for?' she said.

'It's for your own good. To help you through a trying time. When a girl has recently had her pubic hair shaved off, there is a great temptation, for a while, to touch and finger the area. If the girl also suffers from a tendency towards masturbation, as you do, it is almost inevitable that such a thing will occur, particularly when she is in bed alone and at night. Depriving you of the use of your fingers and thumbs for the first few nights will reduce the temptation and allow you to get used to your shaven state. Come along now and I will show you where you will sleep.'

Fliss followed her through the silent house to the dormitory level on the first floor, feeling totally humiliated by the ridiculous cabbages sticking out of her dressing gown sleeves. She thanked her stars that there was no one about to see them and guess at the reason for them. Her room proved to be small but adequate at about ten feet square. It was sparsely but well furnished and the paintwork was clean and light. Miss Ames had to help her with everything. The sleeves of her dressing gown were wide enough to take the strange mittens, enabling her to slip out of it with assistance. Miss Ames had to turn down the covers on the tubular metal bed so that she could climb in. Fliss expected her to pull them over her, but she did not immediately do so. Instead, she picked up Fliss' right hand and drew it to the side of the bed at hip level. From her apron pocket she took a metal object like half a pair of handcuffs, slipped it through the hasp of the padlock on the bag and clipped it shut around the metal frame of the bed. Even as Fliss tugged at it, she went around the bed and did the same on the other side. Only then did she pull up the covers and tuck the linen sheets under Fliss' chin.

'Goodnight!' she said, and went to the door. She switched off the light and went out, leaving Fliss in darkness with a great deal to think about. At first, she was consumed with self-pity and a large tear escaped the corner of her eye. However, practical as always, she tried to see the plus side of her situation. She had been maltreated, for sure, but she was warm and well fed and likely to remain so. The heavy linen sheets and pillowcase on which she lay were crisp and clean and the bed was comfortable. It would have been more comfortable if she had been able to turn on to her side. She tested the possibility of doing that but the attachment of her wrists to the sides of the bed made it impossible. Thinking about that made her stomach feel funny and sexy so she pushed it to the back of her mind. To do so, she

48

went over the extraordinary events of the day. That didn't help much. Being watched while she stripped! Having her hands tied behind her while she was washed in her most intimate places! Being shaved between the legs! It was no good. She could not avoid what was coming to the forefront of her consciousness. Miss Ames had been right. She needed yet another orgasm. In deepest frustration, she tugged at her wrist-bands but that simply moved those fat balls which were her hands and reminded her of them and her bondage. She rubbed her thighs together but knew that she had never been able to get off that way. Maybe if she could somehow move her pillow down between her legs she would be able to work herself against its sharply starched corner. She was about to attempt this when a noise caused her to freeze. Her door was opening!

In the inky blackness, she could see nothing so she called, 'Who's there?'

'Ssh!!' came an answering hiss. She heard the door close then a tiny glow appeared as someone switched on a miniature torch. The torch approached and shone in her eyes.

'Who is it?' Fliss asked.

'Madeleine Doran. Maddie to my friends. We've just come to say hallo!' The torch swept briefly around the room and Fliss saw that there were about half a dozen girls crowded into that small space.

'Felicity,' said Fliss. 'Felicity Marchant. Fliss to my friends. Sorry I can't shake hands.'

'Why not? Oh, wait a minute.' Maddie raised the bed-clothes and peeped underneath. 'Oh, look, girls! She got the mitts! We know why, don't we?'

'I don't know what you mean,' said Fliss, with dignity. 'I've no idea why she . . .'

'Aw, don't give us that. We've been there, don't forget. What did you do? Cream off all over Ames' fingers while she was shaving you?'

49

Fliss thought of maintaining her lofty ignorance, but could not restrain the impulse to giggle. 'Well, yes, actually.'

'I got the mitts first night because I came off in the bath,' said Maddie.

Fliss thought she could match that. Anyway, she was proud of her new-found orgasmic ability and was dying to tell someone. 'So did I. Twice, in fact.'

'In that case, you'll probably have them on every night for a week. Still, never mind. We'll be around to help you out.'

'Help me out?'

'Yes. You know. Do it for you.'

'Oh no!' said Fliss, blushing in the darkness. 'I couldn't possibly . . .'

Maddie addressed the other girls. 'Hey, Lady Muck, here, reckons her pussy's a bit special. Not for us common people. Peggy? Have you checked those curtains yet?'

'Yes, Maddie. No chinks.'

'All right then, dumbo. What are you waiting for? Put the light on.'

Fliss blinked at the sudden glare and stared back at the ring of faces about her. Now that Maddie was visible, she turned out to be tall and elegant, probably nineteen or twenty years old. To Fliss, her confident air implied that she had been here for some months, at least.

Fliss jumped as Maddie stretched out a hand and pulled back the bedclothes, uncovering her. 'What are you doing?'

'What we do to all the new girls. We're going to inspect your shave to make sure it's up to standard.'

'No! You mustn't!' Fliss was shocked at the thought, but there was that demon again, driving her up the scale of tension, her body telling her that this was exactly what it needed.

50

'Your hands are chained to the bed. Just how are you proposing to stop us?'

Fliss thought about this. 'I'll scream and wake everybody up.'

'Good job we always come prepared,' said Maddie, taking a bundle of handkerchiefs from her pocket. As Fliss opened her mouth to draw breath for a scream, Maddie stuffed the handkerchiefs into it and wound a dressing gown cord around her head so that she could not spit them out. 'Now let's have a look at you.'

Fliss squirmed impotently and shook her head violently, her protests cut off by the handkerchief gag, as Maddie took hold of the hem of her nightdress and pulled it up. Trapped by her body's weight, it wedged when she had been exposed only as far as mid-thigh. Fliss was annoyed to find that, without any command from her brain, her bottom eased up off the bed so that the nightdress could continue its journey but she managed to conceal the way her body had let her down by incorporating the shift of her hips into facsimiles of indignation. It came to rest on her stomach and she was naked from there, downwards. She felt all those eyes upon her and knew what the centre of their attention was. She blushed and clamped her thighs as far as she was able.

Maddie tapped her knees. 'Come on, open wide. We can always pull them apart, you know.'

Fliss' head-shaking became more furious. Maddie grinned and took hold of her right ankle. Looking into Fliss' face and enjoying her look of horror, she took her time over pulling the ankle to the side of the bed and tying it there with another cord. Fliss tried to kick out as Maddie grabbed the other ankle, but could only moan softly as that was attached to the opposite side of the bed.

Her groans increased as Maddie sat down on the bed alongside her hips and stroked the soft skin alongside her sex. 'Wow! Pretty smooth! Come and feel this, girls.'

Fliss thought her red face must be vying with the overhead bulb in lighting up the room as several strange fingers caressed her most sensitive places. She felt her juices build and flow; her clitoris bulging as her nipples erected themselves.

Maddie bent to peer closely. 'Whoops! Do you know you're leaking? God, you must need it badly. Never mind, we can fix that for you.' She got up and, stooping over Fliss' mid-section, she reached under her body to grasp the back of the nightdress and wriggle it further up. 'Come on, help a bit! We'll never get your tits out at this rate.'

Fliss shook her head vigorously, but at the same time contrived to ease her position so that the nightdress could be pulled right up. When Maddie threw the hem of it over her face, she was not only not able to move or speak, but could no longer see what was happening. Now her moans were not of protest, but of animal lust. Her nipple erection would be obvious, she knew, but she no longer cared. She was once more in the grip of her masturbation fantasy and she tugged at the fastenings on her wrists and ankles to reassure herself that it was not a dream. When the tutors and Miss Ames had brought her to orgasm, she did not think they had intended to do so. Her excitement was merely a by-product of their actions. This was hugely different. Not only were her hands tied but these girls had the clearly stated intention of bringing her off. There would be nothing accidental about it. They would masturbate her against her will until she came, she knew. Her breathing was short and heavy and her heart was pounding with excitement as she rejoiced in the vulgar exposure which, such a short time ago, had embarrassed her. She spread her legs wider and waited with tense expectation for the next move.

What came next was purest bliss for Fliss. To be touched and manipulated by many hands without being able to see and predict where the next sensation would occur was overwhelmingly sexy. No one had ever deliberately masturbated her before. A few boys had groped her rather inexpertly but she had never fooled around with other girls, so her experience of masturbation was as a solitary occupation; alone with her fantasies. This was something completely different! Eager mouths were on her nipples, sucking, tongue-tickling, and nibbling. When a mouth stopped, it was replaced by fingers which milked, pulled, rolled and stroked. These things alone would have been enough to drive her into a sexual frenzy but what was happening between her legs was stupendous. Down there, she was in the hands of experts who knew exactly what the effect of what they were doing would be. Someone was massaging her clitoris in precisely the right way – in slow, tantalising circles, while someone else had inserted two fingers right to the knuckle in her vagina and was pumping and rubbing in just the right places.

Time and again, Fliss thanked the Fate which had let her have three orgasms already that day. That prevented her from reaching instantaneous climax as soon as she was touched. It allowed her to remain in this paradise for quite a while and she revelled in it, squirming and twisting in response to the extreme stimulation she was receiving. Had she not been gagged she would have been unable to avoid screaming with the pleasure of it and she now resorted to snorting through her nose with the kind of panting rhythm which women in labour use during their contractions.

The climb up to the top of the mountain was slow, with many minor peaks along the way. When the pulsing which marked the onset of true orgasm came upon her she felt it as never before, deep inside her womb. It grew and grew until it seemed to be tearing her insides out. She was right at the summit now and she hung on there, poised for ages at that glorious point of maximum

53

tension before she launched herself, eagle-like into the throes of climax, jerking and writhing like an eel as the full weight of it hit her.

For a long while afterwards she lay in a swoon, her breathing shallow, her teeth chattering and her knees trembling while the last ripples of her stomach contractions coursed through her. She was hardly aware of her ankles being untied, her nightdress being pulled down to cover her nakedness and the bedclothes being replaced.

She was only dimly conscious of Maddie saying, 'Bet you sleep well, now!' She was asleep before they put out the light.

Three

Fliss was awakened by the sound of Miss Colforth drawing back her curtains as well as by the stream of sunlight thus admitted. Miss Colforth unlocked her hands from the bed frame and then unfastened the padlocks which kept the green mittens on her hands. Fliss sat up on the edge of the bed and stretched high and wide, wiggling her fingers in blissful freedom.

'Interview with Miss Ames this morning,' said Miss Colforth. 'Dressing gown and slippers. Bath first; interview second; breakfast third. This way.' She led Fliss along the landing to a bathroom which was not the same as the one she had used the previous evening. This one was smaller and less institutional.

Fliss waited for her to leave but instead of doing so, she sat down on a stool. Obviously, she was going to stay and Fliss could guess why. She had gone down in their books as the Beast from Hell; Champion Masturbator of the Universe! Whilst it was humiliating to be guarded in this way, there was enormous satisfaction to be gained from the fact that she had beaten the system by thoroughly enjoying the Orgasm to Beat All Orgasms last night. She resolved that if opportunity offered she would do the same again that night. She stripped self-consciously and bathed cautiously, being careful to devote only minimum attention to her erogenous zones whilst under the impassive stare of Miss Colforth. When she had finished her ablutions, dried herself and got back into her nightie and dressing gown, Miss Colforth took her to Miss Ames' study.

Miss Ames got up from her desk as Miss Colforth showed Fliss in, then left. Miss Ames invited her to take the same armchair as last night and seated herself opposite. There was already a tray on the low table.

'Tea?'

'Oh, yes please.'

Miss Ames poured two cups and handed one over. 'Did you sleep well?'

Fliss restrained the urge to giggle. 'Very well indeed, thank you. I'm only sorry I made such a fuss about the mittens. They turned out to be a tremendous help, just as you said.' And how, she thought. Without them, it would have been a dull old, run-of-the-mill, do-it-yourself job!

Miss Ames glowed with self-satisfaction. 'That's excellent! It is remarkable to find a girl who learns so quickly. I don't think they will be necessary again.'

That'll teach me to open my big mouth, thought Fliss, as her hopes of a return engagement that night were dashed. Back to pleasuring herself the old-fashioned way!

Miss Ames sipped her tea. 'Had your bath?'

'Yes, thank you.'

'You will start each day with a bath or a shower. That is one of our rules.'

'That's OK,' said Fliss. 'I usually do.'

'Hmm!' Miss Ames said. 'Here, it is part of our function to change your "usually" into an "always".'

Fliss changed the subject. 'Why haven't I seen any of the other girls about?'

'They were up and taking their morning exercise long ago. I let you sleep late because it was your first day.'

'Oh! I see. I don't have my watch. What time is it?'

Miss Ames looked at her wrist. 'It's past eight o'clock already.'

Fliss blinked. Good grief! She was going to be dragged out of bed at sparrow's fart every day!

56

Miss Ames fired another quote from her maxim machine gun. 'Early to bed and early to rise . . .'

Fliss could not prevent herself from displaying a grimace of distaste. Her own maxim had always been, 'Late to bed and late to rise, and bugger the big bags under your eyes!'

'And now,' said Miss Ames, rising. 'I would like you to try on your uniform.'

There was another pile of clothing on the desk and Fliss inspected it. 'I'll use the bathroom again, shall I?'

'No. That would be inconvenient. I have to see that everything is satisfactory.'

Jees! thought Fliss. Another striptease! Oh well, lady, whatever pedals your bike for you, I suppose. She took off her clothes and laid them on the desk. Even as she did so she wondered at her own aplomb. Perhaps she had become so used to being looked at while naked that the shock-value of the experience was wearing off. When she was nude she made no attempt to hide her body but stood and waited for Miss Ames to tell her what to do next.

'Try the socks and shoes first,' Miss Ames ordered.

Fliss sat down and pulled on the white ankle socks then pushed her feet into white canvas shoes.

'Stand up and put your weight on them. They are quite comfortable?'

'Yes.' Fliss now had difficulty in meeting Miss Ames' eyes. She was thinking how strange it was that just a moment or two ago she had been stark naked and quite comfortable about it but now, when she had shoes and socks on, she felt twice as exposed and embarrassed as before.

She was most relieved when Miss Ames said, 'Now the knickers.'

Fliss pulled them on, grateful for their covering. They were white cotton, of good quality but desperately sensible, with a broad gusset and all-embracing coverage.

'Good!' said Miss Ames. 'They'll do. We must hope that's the last time I see you pull your knickers up in this office. You use clean underwear and socks every day. You will have a sufficient supply and the laundry arrangements will be explained to you. Now put on the brassière.'

That was white cotton, too. Fliss picked it up, wrapped it round her middle and fastened it across her stomach. She rotated the fastener to the back, slipped her arms into the straps and pulled it up over her breasts. God, it was awful! Arguably the least sexy garment she had worn since her school navy blue bloomers! It fitted perfectly and comfortably, but, like the knickers, was earth-shatteringly sensible. It covered almost the whole of her chest area, revealed no cleavage whatsoever, and had straps as wide as the M1. She longed wildly for the gossamer scraps of transparency which had been in her suitcase.

Miss Ames tested the tension of the straps. 'Comfortable?'

Fliss could only nod. Words failed her.

'Now the skirt.'

Fliss stepped into it, pulled it up and zipped it, glad to have it to cover those yukky knickers. It was light grey and pleated. Of good quality material and cut, it hung well on her youthful body and, she was forced to admit, was not too bad at all. A bit short, perhaps. There seemed to be an awful lot of bare thigh and leg between it and her ankle socks.

The roll-neck sweater which followed was also light grey, exactly matching the skirt. Fliss heaved a sigh of relief as the gross bra disappeared beneath it. Like everything else in this place, the wool was of the best quality, soft and warm against her skin.

'Smart, but flexible and casual,' said Miss Ames. 'Your winter uniform is similar except that there are slacks instead of a skirt, and more underwear. Now come and sit down again. You will understand that there will be no telephoning while you are here. For you, such communications are against the rules.'

'You will write to Miss Doyle at least once a week, of course. You will do that, whether or not she writes to you. Your letters will always say that you are well and happy; that all is well and that you are enjoying your life here. Each letter must be given to me unsealed and I will advise you if there is anything in it you need to change. I find it irksome to have to keep correcting letters and I tend to do something which will modify impulsive writing.' She nodded meaningfully towards the desk.

Fliss shivered. She was trapped in this place! If she tried to tell anyone what was really happening here she would be bent over the desk, knickers down, and spanked; or worse!

At that moment, the woman in overalls arrived with a trolley. 'Ah, thank you, Dorothy. Breakfast, Felicity? As a matter of routine you will eat in the cafeteria with the others but this first morning is important and I share a light working breakfast with you, here.'

The trolley held fresh fruit and freshly squeezed orange juice, boiled eggs, toast and marmalade and a pot of excellent coffee. Fliss dug in eagerly and munched with unfeigned appetite.

Miss Ames was speaking again. 'I told you last night about some of the things you will learn. The reason for some of them is obvious. I would like to clear your mind about the others, so that you will not inhibit yourself from doing your best. We do not teach you about cooking and housework because we believe that it is a woman's inevitable destiny to spend her life doing these things. On the contrary. What you learn here, sensibly applied by you, can enable you to rise to such a position as would allow you to employ others to do these things for you. Whether that is by way of marriage or a career

59

is your choice. You will then be in the position of a supervisor. It is impossible properly to supervise a task which you cannot perform yourself.'

'We do not teach you art techniques in the hope that you will become a great painter but so that you may appreciate how a particular result was achieved and so talk intelligently about it. That is why it is important that you should persist with these studies whether you like them or not. The spankings I am forced to carry out are not for my gratification but for the good of the individual concerned.'

'But suppose I'm no good at something. Do I get spanked for that?'

'Perhaps, but generally, no. What you get spanked for is not trying hard enough. That, of course, has to be the subjective opinion of your tutor and they, like anyone else, can make mistakes. However, neither I nor my tutors have ever found one hundred per cent effort to be hard to spot, so concentrate your attention on achieving that and you will do well and keep out of trouble.'

The rest of their shared breakfast time was employed by Miss Ames to give further explanations of the myriad rules which would have to be obeyed, until Fliss felt her head spinning.

At last, Miss Ames got up and said, 'Now I will take you along to your first class. After that, you will be expected to study your timetable and find your own way about.'

To Fliss' relief, she quite enjoyed that class, which was Art Practical. It was quite fun to slosh acrylic paint about and she thought the still life of a vase she produced was not bad at all for a first go. One half was distinctly taller than the other and, to judge by its colour, it was constructed of Ganges mud but she was pleased with it. Even more significantly, so was Miss Blair. It was her praise, probably, that made Fliss overconfident and put her off guard.

60

The session which immediately followed was not a class; Fliss joined a different group of girls and moved on to laundry duty. Draco House had a large laundry room. It was partly automated but still required the attention of parties of pupils who took turns by rota. Fliss found that the work was not hard and not particularly unpleasant. It was just boring.

Miss Blair supervised for a while, until she was satisfied that Fliss was able to perform the simple labours required to service the washers and dryers, then said, 'I shall have to leave you alone for a while, girls. I have to run over the rosters with Miss Ames. Hilary! You will be in charge.'

A fat, pink, red-haired girl detached herself from a group around the steam press and came forward. 'Yes, Miss Blair.'

'Carry on with your work while I'm away,' Miss Blair said, 'And remember that Hilary is my deputy. She will report any indiscipline to me.'

As soon as Miss Blair left the laundry room Hilary hitched herself up on to a table and sat there, legs swinging. Presently, she was joined by two other girls and all three sat in a row watching everyone else work. Fliss thought that this was interesting behaviour. The three were obviously pals and accustomed to doing this. Incautiously, she allowed her eyes to remain too long in one place.

'What are you staring at, Marchant?' Hilary demanded, belligerently.

'Nothing,' said Fliss, dropping her eyes in confusion.

'Get your arse back to work then, before I kick it for you!'

Fliss bristled but the pale, slight girl who was helping her to fold sheets shook her head in warning so Fliss bit her tongue and turned obediently to her work.

'Olive!'

'Olive' was obviously the name of Fliss' work partner

61

because she went even paler and became suddenly very intent on what she was doing.

'Olive!' called Hilary, again. 'Get yourself over here. Don't make me come and fetch you!'

Olive looked at Fliss and Fliss read the sick fear in her eyes before she obeyed the order and went over to the group on the table.

'Stand there, Olive!' commanded Hilary, indicating a spot a few feet in front of her. 'Stand up straight and put your hands behind you. It's question and answer time.'

Trembling, Olive obeyed the instructions. 'What did I do, Hilary? What's wrong?'

'I ask the questions, not you. You know what you did, anyway. You got a parcel and didn't share it with us.'

'It was just clothes and things, Hilary.'

'No, it wasn't. It was a cake.'

'It wasn't, Hilary. Just clothes. I swear it.'

Hilary glanced at her cronies. 'We don't believe you, do we?'

'No!' they chorused.

'They found you guilty, Olive,' said Hilary. 'You know what that means, don't you?'

Olive folded her arms across her body, protectively. 'No, please, Hilary. Not again.'

'Oh yes! Again! Get your tits out, Olive!'

'Please, no, Hilary!'

'You want us to do it for you?'

'No.' Resignedly, Olive raised the hem of her sweater until it was just below her armpits, then pulled her regulation white brassière up, exposing her small breasts. She stood like that, flushed with embarrassment as they scrutinised her.

'Call those tits,' said Hilary, scornfully. 'More like bee-stings if you ask me. Take your sweater and bra off altogether and let's have a better look at you.'

62

Even more slowly, Olive removed the sweater, unclipped the brassière and took that off as well. Naked from the waist up, she resumed her upright position, hands behind her.

Hilary got down off the table and advanced towards her. She reached out and took Olive's nipples between fingers and thumbs. She manipulated and moulded them, watching Olive's face.

Olive looked down at what was being done to her. 'Don't hurt me again. Please, Hilary. They're still sore from last time.'

Hilary tightened her grip. 'You're forbidding me to hurt you?'

Olive gasped. 'No! I'm not, honestly. I'm just asking.'

'But I know you like it. You like having your nipples pinched.'

'No, I don't. I . . . Oh! Ouch! Yes! Yes! Whatever you say, Hilary.'

'I say, kneel down.'

'Why?'

'Don't argue!' Hilary pinched viciously, extracting a yelp of pain from Olive. 'Kneel down!'

Hilary retained her tight grip on the tortured nipples as Olive sank to her knees.

'Ask me nicely if you can kiss my pussy!'

Olive was aghast. 'No! I couldn't! Really, Hilary, I . . . Ow! Oh, that hurts! Agh! All right! Please may I kiss your pussy?'

'If you insist. Reach up under my skirt and take my knickers down for me.' Hilary pinched again. 'Quicker than that!'

Hastily, Olive did as she was told and, when Hilary's white knickers were about her thighs, Olive pushed her face under the grey skirt and nuzzled the proffered crotch.

'I don't feel that. Get your tongue in there!'

From the movement beneath the skirt, Fliss could see that Olive had redoubled her efforts.

'Want me to let you go?' enquired Hilary.

Olive's muffled, 'Yes,' was barely audible.

'If I do, I'll want you to fetch me something. Will you do that?'

This time, the acquiescence was louder and almost desperate.

For a while longer, Hilary enjoyed her victim's humiliation, then suddenly released her nipples and pushed her away. Olive lay in a curled heap on the floor, sobbing quietly.

'Get up!'

Olive dragged herself to her feet and resumed her position, hands behind her.

'I want you to get me something from that laundry basket.'

Hilary pointed and Olive turned to look behind her at the tall, narrow wicker basket used for carrying soiled clothes and bedding.

'What is it you want?' she asked.

'Go over there and look,' said Hilary. 'It's in among the clothes right at the bottom. You'll have to rummage about.'

Olive went over to the basket and looked in. 'Tell me what I'm looking for.'

'Just rummage about at the bottom. I'll tell you when you find it.'

Olive leaned over. The basket was so deep that it came to her waist and she had to put her head and shoulders right inside to reach the bottom.

At a nod from Hilary, her two friends came across and grasped Olive's ankles, lifting them straight up in the air so that she was forced to stand on her head in among the rumpled material. Her short grey skirt fell down, exposing so much of her white knickers that a strip of flesh was visible between them and the skirt. Hilary grasped the waistband of them and ripped them vertically upwards to her ankles, where her cronies took over and removed them completely. Each then pulled on the ankle she held so that Olive's legs were stretched straight and wide apart. She bucked and struggled as best she could, her naked bottom and thighs jumping with the effort. Of slight build compared with her tormentors and unable to use her hands because of the constriction of the basket, it was quite impossible for her to prevent them from spreading her wide, exposing the whole of her crotch area. From the very faint flush of dark growth on her lower belly and inner thighs, Fliss could tell that Olive's pubic shave had been recent and that she was, therefore, fairly new at Draco House.

With her cupped hand, Hilary smacked directly on that stretched and vulnerable vagina, each impact clearly audible. Olive kicked and screamed as much as she was able, but her legs were firmly held and the contents of the basket muffled her cries.

After six smacks Fliss could stand it no longer. She advanced on Hilary, eyes blazing. 'Hey! Pack it in, you big bully. Why don't you pick on someone your own size!'

Hilary swung round to face Fliss. At a sign from her, her cronies dropped the legs they were holding and the basket tipped over, allowing Olive to back out of it, crying.

Hilary addressed the crawling, sobbing figure over her shoulder. 'All right, sniveller. Get dressed now. We've got a new toy to play with.' Olive groped for her cast-off garments and gratefully began to scramble into them.

Fliss' heart was pounding furiously as she eyed the three girls now advancing on her. She tried to assess her chances of fighting them all at once and knew that she hadn't a prayer. They were all bigger and stronger than she.

'So, Marchant! You want to poke your nose in, do you? Want some of what she just had? Well, I hope you enjoy it because . . .'

Someone called from the far side of the room, 'Look out! Blair's coming back!'

Hilary came to a halt, her face working in disappointment. 'Some other time, Marchant,' she hissed. 'And if you dare to say one word about this you'll get worse than she did. That's a promise!' She turned away abruptly and busied herself with laundry work. Fliss had the presence of mind to do the same so that when Miss Blair re-entered the room she found the whole class apparently enthusiastically engaged about their proper business.

Fliss found herself hoping that the third and last class of the morning would find her separated from the objectionable Hilary but with a sick certainty she just knew that would not be the case. She was proved right. Hilary and her friends were part of the group which moved on with Fliss to Miss Moncrieff's Home Management class.

Miss Moncrieff worked on the principle that if her girls were to be competent to supervise staff, they had to know how the job ought to be done. On this day, her demonstration was intended to show how profiteroles should be made and presented. Fliss, as one who could not even boil an egg, found herself so interested that thoughts of her recent unpleasant encounter receded. She asked intelligent questions, trying to get the technique straight in her mind. Thus it was that when Miss Moncrieff was also called from the room, it was to Fliss that she handed the pot of chocolate sauce, with instructions on how to complete it.

Her mind was forced back to the earlier problem as soon as the door closed behind Miss Moncrieff. Hilary's cronies closed in on Fliss, grasped her by the arms and held her, while Hilary stood close in front of her, arms akimbo.

'Well, Marchant? I'm picking on someone my own size. What are you going to do about it?'

Fliss was still holding the chocolate pot and struggling to keep it upright. 'Look, just leave me alone, will you. I haven't done anything to you. If you don't let me go, I'll spill this.'

'Yes, you will, won't you? Then teacher's pet would be in trouble, wouldn't she?'

Hilary put her own hand over Fliss' on the saucepan handle and began to twist it inwards. Fliss struggled to prevent it, but the pot tipped and chocolate sauce splashed out of it, some of it going down the front of Hilary's grey skirt.

Hilary twisted the saucepan away from Fliss. 'Now look what you've done! I've got chocolate all over me! Well, now you'll get chocolate all over you! Hold her!' She dipped the palm of her hand into the cooling sauce clinging to the sides of the saucepan and dabbed with it at Fliss' face. Fliss threw herself about and tossed her head, but her arms were securely held and she could not prevent both cheeks being smeared with the sticky substance.

'Put her down!' Hilary ordered, and the two girls holding Fliss' arms twisted them behind her back, forcing her into a kneeling position. Hilary came closer and held out the hem of her stained skirt. 'Lick it off!' she commanded.

'Like Hell I will,' said Fliss.

Her captors increased the twisting pressure on her arms, forcing her chocolate-smeared face down onto the floor.

'I told you to lick it off.' Hilary said. 'Didn't you hear?'

Fliss grunted in pain and shook her head then, as her arms were twisted still further, groaned, 'All right! All right! Just let me up.'

Her arms were released and she got up on her knees, working her aching shoulder-joints.

'I'm waiting!' Hilary said.

Realising that she had no alternative, Fliss reluctantly

67

took the hem of the skirt from her and licked tentatively at the brown stain on it.

Hilary ran one finger down the side of Fliss' face, collecting chocolate. She reached past Fliss' hands and under the hem of her own skirt to wipe the sauce on her bare thigh.

'There's something else for you to lick off!'

'I can't do that.' Fliss protested.

'Do you want your arms twisted again?'

Dumbly, Fliss shook her head and with the greatest repugnance extended her tongue to lick the chocolate smear on the bare, pink flesh before her eyes. She tried to do it as efficiently as she could, to reduce the time she would have to spend on this degrading performance but as fast as she licked, Hilary transferred still more smears to her thigh, each one just a little higher than the one before.

Finally, she reached the edge of her white knickers. Fliss looked up into her face in mute entreaty but Hilary was gloatingly implacable. 'Go on! You know what you've got to do. You saw Olive do it.'

Thoroughly cowed, Fliss began to plead. 'Please, no. Don't make me. I don't want to.'

'Stop whimpering!' Hilary said, 'Or I'll have your arms twisted right off. Do you want that or would you rather take my knickers down and kiss my pussy?' She raised her skirt and waited.

With trembling hands, Fliss reached out and grasped the elastic waistband of the knickers. She pulled them down to mid-thigh, having to work to ease them over Hilary's plump bottom. The pubic hair which appeared only inches from her face was flaming red, like Hilary's head hair. It was long enough to show that Hilary had been at the school for some time, yet naturally sparse so that the scarlet of Hilary's outer labia showed through, contrasting with the pinkness of the rest of her skin. The faint scent of woman was unmistakable.

Fliss hesitated, horrified at what she was expected to do; trying to imagine what that redness would taste like. She licked her lips and closed her eyes . . .

A sudden violent push sent her sprawling backwards.

'Get off me!' Hilary yelled. 'How dare you, you lesbian bitch!'

Bewildered, Fliss sat up to see Miss Moncrieff approaching, a stern frown on her face.

'Miss Moncrieff,' said Hilary, pulling up her knickers. 'This girl attacked me. She spilt the sauce then, when I went to help her, she threw it all over me and tried to pull my knickers down.'

'Get up, Felicity,' said Miss Moncrieff. 'What have you to say for yourself?'

'It's a lie. She's the one who went for me.'

'I see.' Miss Moncrieff turned to the class. 'Did anyone see this?'

'We did, Miss,' said one of Hilary's pals. 'It was just as Hilary said. She wasn't doing anything. Marchant went mad and tried to get her knickers off.'

Miss Moncrieff turned to Fliss again. 'This is very bad, Felicity. I have to report this, you know.'

'But they're in it together,' Fliss protested, losing her temper. 'They're lying to save themselves. Can't you see that?'

Miss Moncrieff became angry herself. 'No, Felicity; as a matter of fact, I can't see that.'

Fliss' short fuse burned away completely. 'Then you must be blind, as well as stupid!'

It was the audible intake of breath from every girl in the room, simultaneously, which made it clear to Fliss that something had occurred which should not have done.

Miss Moncrieff took her by the arm and pulled her forward. 'Come with me! Hilary! Take over the class, please!'

With the tutor's steely grip on her arm, Fliss had to

69

trot to keep up with her brisk pace. With only a cursory knock on Miss Ames' door, Miss Moncrieff took her inside. 'Stand there!' she ordered, indicating a precise spot on the carpet. Fliss stood where she had been told. As she watched Miss Moncrieff make a whispered report to Miss Ames, she felt her knees trembling and her stomach turning over. What had she done? Worse still, what was Miss Ames now going to do to her? She soon found out.

'Oh dear, Felicity,' said Miss Ames. 'I am disappointed to see you here so soon after our little talk. Step up to the front of the desk, please.'

Fliss shuffled forward. 'Please, Miss Ames. It wasn't my fault. It was a mistake. I lost my temper. I'll apologise, shall I?' she added, hopefully.

'I'm afraid that won't do it, Felicity. Pull your knickers down to your knees, please!'

'No, really! Can't I . . .'

'Pull your knickers down! Now!'

White and trembling, Fliss fumbled under her skirt for the waistband of her knickers and lowered them.

'All the way to your knees, please!'

Stooping, and now red, rather than white, Fliss obeyed.

'Now raise your skirt to your waist, front and back! Higher! All the way round!'

Fliss did so and waited for the next order. She was well aware what that would be. There was a long pause and she realised that she was being kept like that deliberately. It was to be part of her punishment to be humiliated by having to stand there with her knickers down and her skirt held up so that her bald pubes and bare bottom were on display. Her inner tension communicated itself to her buttocks, which quivered so much that she could feel the soft flesh on them wobbling. She hoped that neither woman could see it.

It was almost a relief when the order finally came.

'Bend over and grasp the far edge of the desk with both hands! You are on no account to let go!'

Miss Ames got up and came around the desk to stand on Fliss' left, giving her right hand full play. Fliss craned around to watch her and saw her hand rise. There was a sharp, slapping sound as it connected with her left buttock cheek and the sting of it made Fliss cry out, her knees bobbing and her bottom performing a merry dance. Miss Ames waited until she was still, then delivered another, this time on her right cheek. After that, the spanking went on with a more regular rhythm, first on one cheek, then on the other.

'Ow! Ooch!! Jees!' Fliss gritted her teeth and hung on until all six had been delivered. Her bottom was warm and tingling. She eased herself back off the desk and stood up, rubbing her behind and allowing her skirt to fall about her. Hastily, she pulled up her knickers again. Actually, the spanking had not been nearly as dreadful as her imagination had told her it would be. In fact, it might even have been a bit of a turn-on. She could hardly believe that this could be the case but certainly her stomach had that funny feeling somewhere inside. She rubbed her bottom again through her skirt and knickers. She would have to have a look later and see how red it was.

'You understand that you have been spanked for causing a disturbance in class,' said Miss Ames.

'Yes,' Felicity answered.

'Now I must deal with the matter of insolence to staff.'

'What?'

'I'm sure you heard me quite distinctly. Your spanking dealt with only one offence, whereas you committed two. You were not only a disruptive influence. You were rude to Miss Moncrieff and that cannot be tolerated.'

'You're going to spank me again?' Felicity couldn't believe it.

71

'No. I'm afraid that insolence to staff goes way beyond being a spanking matter. It even surpasses the slipper. The only possible appropriate punishment is caning. Please pull your knickers down again and position yourself as before.'

'Cane me? You want to cane me?'

'I don't want to, Felicity. I have to. You have to learn to control your temper.'

'No!' Felicity exclaimed. 'You can't! I won't let you . . . Oh! Oh!'

She let out a piercing scream as the two women grasped her by the arms, led her to the desk and pushed her across it. Miss Ames held her there while Miss Moncrieff went round to the other side, grasped her wrists and pulled her arms straight out in front of her, pressing them down onto the desk. She felt Miss Ames' hands groping under her skirt, then her fingers were in the waistband of her knickers and she felt them drawn down over her hips to her knees. A draught of cool air on her told her that her skirt had been flipped up and that her bare bottom was now completely exposed and vulnerable to anything Miss Ames might care to do to it.

With wide eyes, she watched Miss Ames go to a cupboard and come back with a thin, whippy cane. 'No! Oh no! I beg you! Please don't cane my bottom. I'll be good! Really I will!' Yet, even as she pleaded, Fliss felt that 'thing' come over her like some evil curse. Miss Moncrieff was trapping her hands; her lower half was naked; Miss Ames was about to do terrible things to her bare bottom with that cane. Yet in spite of, or perhaps because of that, her juices were boiling, her nipples were erecting themselves and her clitoris was jumping about like a mouse trapped in a bag.

Now Miss Ames was standing on her left again. Fliss did not want to watch. She closed her eyes and gritted her teeth. She heard the swish of the cane in the air then

72

felt the first explosion against the bare skin of her buttocks. For a fraction of a second, it was as though someone had laid a long, cold icicle across her, then the burning fire began, spreading out on either side of the mark.

'Ouch! Dear God!' She wriggled her bottom, as though to shake off the agony. The second stripe was worse than the first. 'Ow! Oh!' Silently, Fliss cursed Miss Ames and Miss Moncrieff. She cursed herself for not holding her temper. She cursed her body for its sexual response which was making her vagina dribble and leak. The third and fourth strokes fell and now her lower half was a sea of fire. She could think of nothing except pain and masturbation. She knew she was going to come, soon. She prayed that the writhing of orgasm might be mistaken for that of pain. How could she! How could she! The fifth stroke came. If only there was something between her legs to rub against! She couldn't put her hands there. They were being held! 'They' were holding her down! Doing things to her! She thrust her bottom backwards and upwards, arching to welcome the cane as if to say. Here I am! Hurt me! Do it to me! Thrash my bare arse until I cry! Oh God! She was going to come. She was coming! Creaming off! Now!

The sixth stroke slashed across flesh already tender and she uttered a long, sobbing groan. Climaxing, she slumped, panting, her bottom quivering and her thighs rubbing together. She could feel a trickle of fluid escaping from her sex. As soon as Miss Moncrieff let her go, she stood up and covered herself with her knickers, dropping her skirt at once to conceal any damp patches.

'Very well, Felicity,' said Miss Ames. 'You may go to lunch, now. Before you do that, I would advise you to sit in a cold bath for a while. That will relieve you a little. Then take care how and where you sit down for a few days. Do you think I shall see you back here, soon?'

'No!' said Felicity. She was sure about that! 'Not for a very long time, I hope!'

Four

Although it was only a cafeteria system of feeding at lunchtimes, the food was plentiful, excellent and there were a variety of dishes to choose from. Fliss passed down the line, filling her tray. Her bottom still throbbed, but she had found Miss Ames' advice to be excellent. She had spent half an hour with her behind in cold water and that seemed to have taken all the burn out of it. She was looking round for somewhere to sit when someone called her.

'Fliss! Over here!'

Fliss recognised Maddie, about the only familiar face in the whole room. She made her way across to her table and set her tray down. She settled herself into the offered chair very gingerly, wincing as she did so.

Maddie knew the signs. 'Been in trouble already?'

Fliss nodded.

'Got spanked, eh?'

'Spanked and caned, actually.'

Maddie whistled, softly. 'Wow! Already! That must be a record. Got caught masturbating?'

'Certainly not!' said Fliss indignantly. 'I was rude to Miss Moncrieff.'

'Silly cow!' said Maddie, unsympathetically. 'What did you say to her?'

'I said she was stupid.'

Maddie was appalled. 'Oh no! You didn't!'

'I didn't think that was so bad,' said Fliss.

'Course it wasn't,' said Maddie. 'That's what's so

74

daft! If you're going to get caned, you might as well get your money's worth. Just think, you could have said, "Why don't you tie your tits in a knot and stuff 'em up your arse".'

Fliss giggled.

'Or how about, "Is it true, Miss, that if they wanted to operate on Miss Ames' piles, they'd have to surgically remove your head, first?".'

Fliss had just taken a mouthful of orange juice and choked, juice squirting down her nose as she tried to swallow and laugh at the same time.

Maddie clapped her on the back until she recovered. 'Next time, ask me first. I'll set you straight. How did you come to be rude to her, anyway.'

Delighted to have a confidante, Fliss poured out her tale of oppression and the injustice done her by Hilary. That seemed to strike a responsive chord. 'That puts you well up in my book,' said Maddie. 'For some reason, she gets away with murder. Wasn't even shaved when she came in. Anyone Hilary doesn't like can't be all bad.'

That was Fliss' first taste of the irrepressible chirpiness which, in days and weeks to come, she would always think of as Maddie's trade mark. Now that she had the chance to study her more closely she saw that her elegant look was helped along by very high cheekbones. There was a very slightly olive tint to her skin which was handsome but was, perhaps, not entirely due to sun-tan. It was most encouraging on such a dark day to come across someone who was so obviously not letting the system get her down. They ate their lunch and engaged in chatter about their backgrounds. Fliss found that Maddie was there because her parents considered her to be uncontrollable. She certainly had an assertive personality, thought Fliss. 'Uncontrollable' could well be an accurate description.

In her turn, Fliss explained the circumstances which

75

had led to her incarceration. 'I've just got to get out of here, Maddie. Can you help?'

'I will if I can,' said Maddie, thoughtfully, 'But it's not easy. If it were, I would have done it myself a long time ago. I'll give it some more thought, though.'

Even the knowledge that Maddie was thinking about her problem made it seem to Fliss that a solution was not far off, such was the confidence which the girl inspired by her breezy attitude.

'What have you got next?' asked Maddie.

Fliss consulted her timetable. 'Gym with Miss Snaith,' she said. 'I've got to get my kit and my towel from my room.'

'Me too,' said Maddie. 'Come on, let's do it now. You look as if you could do with a cheerer upper.'

They went to the dormitory landing and to Maddie's room. Once inside, Maddie stuck a chair under the door handle. On hands and knees, she took up her bedside rug and prised up a floorboard, scrambling to her feet with a packet of cigarettes and a bottle.

She opened the packet and offered it to Fliss. 'Fag?'

Fliss didn't smoke often but accepted one, more from a desire to break rules than from addiction to nicotine.

'Hang on a minute!' Maddie said. She went to the window and opened it wide. 'To let the smoke out!' She took a cigarette for herself, struck a match and lit both. She inhaled deeply. 'Ooh, Christ! That's better! Now then, vodka?' She poured a couple of generous measures into tooth glasses. 'I've got other stuff, but vodka's best for no smell on the breath. Sod it! I meant to pilfer some OJ at breakfast time. Can you take it with just water? Or neat?'

'Water, please,' said Fliss.

'It's in the tap,' said Maddie, handing over a glass.

Fliss added water at the little wash stand in the corner and took a sip. The fiery liquid warmed her and it was comfortingly familiar. 'Mm! Thanks! Where'd you get all this stuff?'

'If you don't know, you can't tell anyone,' said Maddie, puffing her cigarette. 'In this place, there's people you can trust and those you can't. A little bunch of us trusty ones sort of gang together to beat the system. Flick your ash in the basin and wash it down.'

'Oh!' A whole new picture of Draco House was forming in Fliss' mind. So far from Miss Ames and the tutors being omnipotent and having everything their own way, there was obviously a whole subculture of which they probably knew nothing which was working in the opposite direction. The notion was cheering.

'Come on!' Maddie got up and took a tin from under the floorboards. She pulled off the airtight lid and stubbed her cigarette out in the tin, then offered it to Fliss. 'Put your dog-end in there. No smell, see. Finish your drink or we'll be late. A smack on that sore bum of yours wouldn't be welcome, would it? Stick with me in gym if you can. I'll look after you.'

In the gymnasium's communal changing room, Fliss got into her exercise clothes rather diffidently, still unaccustomed to being voluntarily naked in the presence of others. There were ten girls in that session. Later she learned that this was about one quarter of the total number of girls at the school. The uniform for exercise consisted of grey shorts, hardly more revealing than the regulation knickers, and a properly fitted, athletic support bra which was, of course, white. The gymnasium contained all kinds of mechanical work-out apparatus, and Fliss was relieved to find that this session consisted of very routine bend, stretch and jump exercises which did not require her to sit down. Although she took little exercise by choice, her young body was still supple enough to cope easily with what she asked of it and she quite enjoyed the physical jerks. She bounced about enthusiastically.

Suddenly, Miss Snaith blew her whistle. 'Class, stand! Slacking, Madge!'

A chubby, fair-haired girl said, 'No, Miss . . .'

'Slacking! On the wall bars, Madge. Now! Line up, the rest of you!'

Fliss watched in astonishment as Madge trotted across to the wall bars. Facing them she hooked her fingers into the elastic waistband of her shorts and pushed them down to her knees, leaving her bottom bare. Standing close to her, Miss Snaith said, 'We'll have them right off, today, I think, then you can get your legs apart more easily.' For a moment, it looked as if Madge might argue, but she apparently thought better of it. She wriggled the shorts down her legs and stepped out of them. Miss Snaith held out her hand. 'Don't leave them on the floor. Give them to me and take up the position!'

As she looked at Madge, Fliss was reminded of her own experience in Miss Ames' office when she was trying on her uniform. Then, the fact that she had been wearing ankle socks made her feel more naked, rather than less. Madge, wearing only a white brassière and similar socks and shoes, gave off the same air of lewd exposure and must have known it. Her plump, pink thighs and even plumper pink bottom looked freshly-boiled with the embarrassment she felt. A moment later, that shame had to be increased enormously. As of long-established custom she bent forward and put her head between her parted knees until the back of her neck was pressed against the wall bars then forced her arms backwards, groping above her bent back with her hands until she could grip one of the bars. There was some doubt in Fliss' mind as to whether or not the length of her pubic hair was due to the fact that she had been at the school for only a short while. Perhaps that was the reason why her sex bore very sparse fair hair; perhaps it was a natural phenomenon. Fliss did not know. What was certain was that her vulva and anus, clearly visible between her parted legs and buttock cheeks, like

Hilary's, were of a fiery red colour, contrasting with the pinkness of her skin.

Fliss turned to Maddie. 'What's happening?' she hissed.

Out of the corner of her mouth, Maddie, behind her in the line, muttered. 'We all have to run past her and give her one smack on the bum.'

'Oh no! I can't do that!' said Fliss.

'Do it! And with all your strength!' Maddie gripped Fliss' arm in emphasis.

The front of the line started to move, the first girl running forward to deliver a resounding smack on that helpless backside.

'I can't do that, Maddie!' said Fliss. 'I couldn't smack her hard!'

'But you don't understand . . .' hissed Maddie, then, as the line in front of them dwindled, 'Oh Christ! You big daft cow! C'mere!' She grabbed both Fliss' arms and spun her around, placing herself in front of her in the queue.

There was no time for Fliss to ask questions before it was Maddie's turn to smack. She ran up to Madge, paused, then planted the most delicate of pats on her already red behind.

Miss Snaith blew her whistle at once. 'Not trying, Madeleine! On the wall bars!'

The queue re-formed in front of Fliss. Maddie turned and stared at Fliss with deepest meaning, then she turned to face the bars and did what Madge had done. She pulled down her shorts, gave them to Miss Snaith and positioned herself to be smacked, her head well down, her bottom sticking up and her arms strained unnaturally above her. Her black thatch was quite profuse between her straddled legs but even so it was clear that her vulva and anus, in contrast to the blonde's, were so dark as to be almost black.

Fliss turned to the girl next in line. 'What does it mean?'

'Now we've all got to run past again and smack them both. That's a pisser for Madge, because she gets nearly twice as many.'

Suddenly, Fliss realised what Maddie had done. She had known that Fliss would get smacked if she didn't slap hard enough and, to save Fliss' already tender bottom, she had sacrificed herself. Fliss found her eyes filling with tears. She thought that was the nicest thing anyone had ever done for her. Now she was presented with a terrible dilemma. Feeling as grateful and affectionate as she did, she was going to have to smack Maddie's bottom in a very few seconds and smack it hard if she was to avoid joining those two at the wall bars. For a moment she contemplated refusing to do it then realised that by doing so she would nullify the noble gesture; condemn herself and Maddie to another round of slaps. When her turn came she smacked with all her strength, fearful lest a failure on her part should mean further pain for Maddie. She had often heard the expression, 'This hurts me more than it hurts you,' and had not fully understood it. Now she did!

That episode concluded the gym session. As Maddie and Madge recovered their shorts and pulled them on, Miss Snaith blew her whistle. 'You two stay behind. I want a word with you. The rest of you. Shower!'

Fliss followed the others to the changing room and watched them as they stripped off for their shower. The therapeutic power of exercise was apparent. These girls gave no sign at all of being oppressed or despondent. The room was full of their happy chatter, at a volume almost equal to that heard inside an Italian bus. There was a lot of giggling and the occasional slapping sound followed by a joyful scream. Jostling and pushing, the naked crowd jiggled and wobbled its way into the shower which was, effectively, a large, tiled room with multiple shower heads protruding from one wall. Hot water was already hissing from the nozzles and the process of getting wet for the first time was the occasion for further laughter and screaming. Such behaviour was infectious and Fliss found her spirits rising to match theirs. She lathered and scrubbed, allowing the stinging water to wash the suds down her body. It was really rather pleasant.

The girl next to her, whom Fliss recognised as Peggy, one of the group of visitors that first night, called, 'Come on, everybody! Soapy circle!'

'What's that?' asked Fliss, brushing water out of her eyes.

'It's fun!' said Peggy. 'Look! You turn round and soap Olive's back. While you're doing that, I soap yours, see?'

Fliss did as she was told and saw that a circle of naked, soapy girls quickly formed, each having their back washed and performing the same service for another. Peggy had been right; it was fun. Fliss enjoyed the feel of Olive's slippery skin under her hands and to have her own back lathered was delightful.

Suddenly, she felt her arms gripped and she was pushed out of the circle until her back hit the tiled wall with a thud. It was Hilary; as naked as she was!

'At it again, are you? Can't leave their bodies alone. I hear you enjoyed having a soapy finger up your bum in the bath. They rubbed your pussy and made you come, too. We'll try that, shall we? But not until we've had a bit of a grope.'

To Fliss' horror, Hilary pressed her large breasts and stomach against her, pinning her to the wall, and attempted to kiss her, open-mouthed. She tried to struggle away but was trapped. The feel of that fat, wet body on hers was repulsive and she twisted her head from side to side to avoid being kissed on the mouth.

'Come on, you little bitch. You'll love it once you get used to it!' Hilary said. Her left hand slid between them to grope at Fliss' crotch. 'Come on, I said! I . . .'

81

She got no further. Before Fliss' startled eyes, a tanned hand appeared over Hilary's shoulder. It was Maddie! An equally tanned finger extended itself sideways underneath Hilary's nose, exactly at the point where it met her face. The finger pressed backwards and upwards with irresistible force, peeling Hilary off Fliss as easily as the skin is taken off a banana. Hilary screamed with the pain being caused by this maltreatment of a sensitive nerve centre. Her head was tilted far back against Maddie's other hand, which was at the back of her head. She staggered back until her feet caught Maddie's foot behind her, then she overbalanced and flopped on to her back in the puddly water of the shower. Maddie straddled her, her knees on her upper arms, pinning her, those big, pink breasts bulging up between Maddie's strong, brown thighs. Her legs thrashed wildly, her bright pink vulva and red pubic hair obscenely on show. Maddie's finger was still under her nose and her eyes were watering with the pain of it.

With her free hand, Maddie groped for a bar of soap on the floor. 'Open!' she said.

'No! Ouch! Get off me! Ow!' Hilary squirmed, her plump body wobbling with the effort.

Maddie increased the finger-pressure. 'I said, open!'

'Ow! Ouch! All right! All right! Aaah!'

'Wider!'

'Aagh!'

Maddie pushed the soap into the gaping mouth beneath her and pressed her hand over it, holding it there. Hilary's face was clear evidence of the ghastly taste of it, as was the way her heels beat a tattoo on the tiles.

'Glgrh! Mmffglrgh!' she screamed, bubbles escaping from under Maddie's hand.

'Had enough?' Maddie enquired, conversationally.

Hilary nodded emphatically. When Maddie took her hand off the soap, she spat it. She sighed with relief as the finger was removed from under her nose, only to tense again as Maddie transferred her attention to Hilary's small, pink nipples, taking a good pinch of nipple and flesh between her fingers and thumbs. She wriggled herself backwards down Hilary's body, pulling her by her nipples into a sitting position.

'You bitch!' Hilary screamed. 'I'll get you for this . . . Ow! Ouch!'

'You have a foul mouth, Hilary,' said Maddie, calmly. 'Just for that you can pick up the soap and put it back in. Go on! Do it!' She pinched harder, to make her demand clearer.

With a groan of pain and a grimace of disgust, Hilary groped for the bar of soap and put it back in her mouth.

Maddie hitched herself still further back, pulling Hilary with her.

'Come on, fat piggy,' she encouraged. 'Olive tells me you like a bit of nipple-pulling. Come forward, then. That's right. Right over on to your hands and knees.' Kneeling in front of her, Maddie's steely fingers under Hilary's plump body retained their tight grip on her nipples.

'You like the idea of fingers in bums, do you? Now you're going to beg Olive to stick her soapy finger right up yours. Come here, Olive. Listen to the way she asks. Don't do it until she gets it to your liking. Now, Hilary, you can take out the soap and ask!'

Hilary spat out the soap. It skidded across the wet, tiled floor as she gasped in pain. 'All right, you can do it.'

'Was that good enough, Olive?' asked Maddie.

Olive shook her head.

'Sorry, Hilary. Not quite humble enough,' said Maddie grimly, pinching harder. 'Try again!'

Hilary became frantic. 'Ouch! Oh God. All right. Please Olive, will you stick your finger up my bum?'

'Right up as far as it will go?' Maddie insisted, remorselessly.

'Agh! Yes! Oh, yes! Right up as far as it will go.'

'Good! Now get your big, fat arse up in the air and get your legs apart. All right Olive. You heard what she wants. Do it! The rest of you gather round and make sure you don't miss the moment.'

Totally humiliated, Hilary's eyes followed Olive's movements as she ostentatiously soaped her right forefinger. She shuddered and her bottom wobbled as Olive knelt beside her upthrust buttocks. Nearly everyone had suffered Hilary's tyranny and there were many willing hands to separate her buttock cheeks. Olive centred her soapy finger over the flaming red circle of her sphincter and thrust abruptly forward. Hilary's head shot back and she screamed and jerked, her plump thighs trembling with the effort of remaining still under this extreme irritation.

'Wiggle it, Olive. She'd like you to wiggle it, wouldn't you, Hilary?'

Hilary nodded despairingly her head now hanging in shame. 'Yes!' she muttered through gritted teeth. 'Just get it over with! Oh! Oh!' Her head shot up again as Olive carried out her wishes with great enthusiasm.

When Olive finally and with some regret removed her finger, Maddie released her grip and sprang up. Hilary remained where she was for some while, panting and retching a little from the taste of the soap before she crawled over and tilted her head back under one of the shower sprays to collect some water in her mouth, swilling and spitting.

Fliss felt Maddie's wiry brown arm around her shoulders and it was very comforting. Maddie addressed the awed onlookers. 'What you've just seen goes for all of you. Keep off!' She rubbed Fliss' wet head. 'This is my own personal toy! You mess with her; you mess with me! OK?' There were nods all round and Fliss got the very clear message that no one, but no one, wanted to mess with Maddie Doran!

During the next few weeks, Fliss learned a lot from Maddie. It was largely due to her guidance that Fliss didn't get spanked again. Not all the subjects on the syllabus were boring. She quite enjoyed several. Learning how to set out a table for a formal dinner was quite fascinating and she took pride in knowing which eating implement went where. Her interest in the culinary arts increased. She learned that cooking, so far from being tedious, could be a creative art. Her pubic hair ceased to be an irritating stubble and softened into a mist of darkness. Yet, through it all she never lost sight of her burning desire for justice; to see Selina thwarted and herself restored to her rightful estate.

Thanks to Maddie, she became 'street-wise' if, she thought to herself, one could use that expression about a group of people who never walked on a street! Maddie knew how to use the system against itself; how far she could push her luck and get away with it. She had, Fliss learned, extraordinary skills. She could open any locked door. She had several ways to do this, but her most common one was to use a small metal object like a dentist's pick, which she usually kept up the leg of her knickers.

She was an expert forger and could reproduce the signature of any of the staff with ease. She demonstrated that skill for Fliss one bright, sunny day. Maddie was lounging on her bed, cigarette dangling between her lips and Fliss was sitting on the floor, her knees drawn up so that her chin rested on them.

'You know, Maddie, if there's one thing I really hate about this place it's that we never get outside alone. At home I could go out any time I wanted and ride all over the place. Here, there's always someone supervising.'

'Well, just don't go to the next class, then,' said Maddie.

'But we've got to!'

'Not necessarily. We could go for a walk, instead.'

'Do you think they'd let us do that,' Fliss asked, doubtfully.

'Sure!' Maddie replied. 'Particularly if they don't know about it.'

'But how . . .'

'Watch and learn, O small one!' said Maddie. She swung her legs off the bed and took a sheet of paper from her writing case. She scribbled briefly then, 'Come on!' she said.

She led the way to their next assignment; Miss Colforth's drama class. Maddie approached her respectfully.

'Miss Blair says she's sorry, but she wants us for extra gym, Miss Colforth. She gave us this note.'

Miss Colforth glanced at it, then looked around. 'All right. I think we've got enough anyway. Off you go then.'

As Maddie led the way towards the laundry room, Fliss asked, 'Won't you get caught?'

'Never have done, yet,' Maddie replied, blithely. 'Anyway, hundred to one she never even bothers to check.'

From the empty laundry room, a small door gave access to a path, discreetly overhung with shrubbery, which led down the hill to the woods near the sea. Once they were certain of being unobserved they relaxed and walked casually in the warm sunshine. It was a lovely day, thought Fliss, and it was good to be free of the oppressive greyness of the school.

The woodland became more dense. Maddie led her off the path and they walked over soft mould in the dappled shade. Then the ground became rocky underfoot and Fliss could hear running water. The trees gave way to lower, more dense greenery which Maddie pushed through until they emerged on to a little patch of green grass, probably no more than twenty feet square. The concealing bushes were behind them and to their left. In front, a fast flowing stream formed a boundary, with dark trees beyond. To their right, there was a sheer granite outcrop, about twelve feet high, down the face of which was tumbling a white waterfall, feeding a large pool at the head of the stream. After the shadows of the woodland, the sun felt hot and good on the skin.

Fliss looked about her in amazement. 'Oh, Maddie! What a beautiful place!'

Maddie stood behind her with her hands on her shoulders. 'Mm! Bit special, isn't it?' They stood in silence for a moment then Maddie moved away to the base of the cliff. She knelt down by a low bush and groped at its base. She heaved and it became apparent that there was a small hollow in the rock there, because she pulled out a black, tin trunk. She opened it and came back with her arms full.

'What have you got there?' asked Fliss.

Maddie set them down one by one as if checking off an inventory. 'Booze to cheer us up; ciggies for peace of mind; chocolate for inner sustenance and a blanket to sit on. Who could ask for more?'

'Maddie! Wherever do you get all this stuff?'

'I can't tell you that.'

'Don't you trust me?'

'It takes time,' said Maddie, spreading the blanket. 'I'm pretty sure about you already, but I want to be absolutely sure. I showed you this place, didn't I? For the rest, you just have to be patient.' They sat down on the blanket. 'Have some chocolate.'

They munched a few squares of chocolate then had a drink and a cigarette. Maddie said, 'Well, I'm not going to waste the sun. I'm going to tan.' She stood up and pulled off her grey, roll-neck sweater.

As she stood for a second with her head and arms still in the sweater, Fliss looked up at the lean, brown, bare belly and navel on display. She felt something lurch inside her but could not explain to herself why that should have happened. A fraction of a second later, however, she sat up, resting with her hands behind her and exclaimed, 'Why, Maddie! Whatever have you got on?'

Maddie looked down at herself. Her large breasts were encased in a very sexy and skimpy bra. It was bright red; the straps were mere threads and the material of which it was made was lacy and almost transparent. Her dark nipples showed through quite clearly. 'Better than the standard armour plate, isn't it?'

'Oh, Maddie! You'll get shot at dawn if they catch you wearing that.'

'Better not let them catch me then, had I? See? It matches these!' She unzipped her skirt, dropped it and stepped out of it. Her panties were truly scandalous! As red as the bra and just as transparent, they were an abbreviated triangle of material which tapered to a mere string between her legs, allowing her pubic hair to emerge on either side.

'And how about the back, then?' she said. She turned round and Fliss saw that the only covering on her lower half was a red T shape, made from the string around her waist and the one which went from it and disappeared between the cheeks of her lovely, taut, brown bottom.

Fliss felt the same lurch as before, only more distinctly, now. Perhaps she had eaten too much chocolate?

Maddie sat down again then lay back, closed her eyes and stretched luxuriously. 'Ooh! Lovely sun!' she said.

Fliss remained sitting, looking down at her. Now that Maddie had closed her eyes, she was free to examine her without doing so from under lowered lids. That long, beautiful face with the high cheek-bones; the sharp angle of her jaw line; slender neck and strong, brown shoulders. Her breasts were receiving no support from that brassière but were so firm that her horizontal position hardly changed their shape at all. They stood up;

88

twin hillocks of perfection topped by the half-seen blackness of her aureolae. Her long, stretched stomach led Fliss' eyes downward to the scrap of material which constituted her panties. Lying down, her pubes were like a little mound sticking up out of the flatness of her belly and thighs. Those black curls protruding from either side of the tiny triangle were fascinating and, even as Fliss watched, Maddie flicked her hand at them, brushing as at some insect, as though Fliss' gaze was a tangible thing and could be felt.

Suddenly a little embarrassed by the intensity of her inspection, Fliss lay back herself with her hands under her head. Presently she sighed. 'You know, Maddie, it all seems so long ago that you saved me from Hilary.'

'Yeah! Pushy bitch! She could see you didn't like being kissed.'

'It wasn't so much that. I just don't like Hilary.' She paused for a long time. To her dying day, she would never know what inner compulsion made her say, 'I don't think I'd have minded if it had been you, Maddie.'

Maddie opened her eyes and rolled on to one elbow, her head resting on her hand as she studied Fliss' face. 'Have you fooled around with girls, then?'

Fliss blushed. 'No, of course not ... Well, I mean, there was that first night ... You know.'

'I don't mean that,' said Maddie. 'That was just a game. I mean serious, one-on-one stuff.'

'No.'

'Ever wanted to?'

Fliss blushed again. 'No! Well ... Maybe. Sometimes.' Fliss could see what this was leading to. She ought to stop it! It was so wrong! So wicked! So exciting! Her heart was banging against the inside of her chest, trying to get out.

'Would you like us to fool around now?'

Surely Maddie must be able to hear her heart now. She was choking! Her nipples were erecting and her vagina was twitching and wet. 'I don't know,' she said, in a voice she did not recognise. 'Will I like it?'

'You tell me,' said Maddie and leant over to kiss her gently on the lips.

Fliss had never been kissed by a girl. At least not with the thoughts she now had in her mind, which seemed to make a lot of difference. It was nice, she decided. Nice, and sexy and so very wrong! She was certain to go to Hell for what was in her mind! She must stop at once! Before this went any further!

'Mmm!' she said. 'That was nice. Please do it again.'

Maddie leant over again and placed her right arm about her. She kissed her once more, but this time the kiss was soft and clinging. Fliss felt Maddie's tongue flicking at her closed lips, demanding entrance. She opened her mouth wide and sucked it in as it plunged, delighting in this first exchange of bodily fluids. Her arms went around Maddie and she felt the smooth, strong back under her palms. It was warm and comforting. Her hands touched the material of the brassière and she went into a frenzy of sexual excitement, her clitoris throbbing and her pelvic muscles in spasm. Desperately, she scrabbled for the clasp but failed to find it. In an agony of frustration she rolled to her right throwing Maddie off balance so that she fell on to her back. She clawed at the flimsy garment, wanting to see breast flesh; needing to feel it squash in her hands; to bite and gnaw at it. She ripped and the centre strand broke. She ripped and ripped again, tearing the shreds from those desired objects. Suddenly, there they were in all their swelling perfection; naked and freely offered to her. She stared, eating them with her eyes. She had not known that there could be nipples like that! From glimpses at shower time, she had seen that Maddie's nipples were unusually large, as well as being almost black in colour. In erection, they were not like teats, but huge, glorious cones, a full two inches across at the base, and projec-

90

ting about an inch from the darkly engorged aureolae. There was only one way to pay homage to such objects. She bent her head and took one of the monsters into her mouth, suckling furiously. It filled her whole mouth with rubbery goodness and seemed to grow even larger. The sensation between her own legs was incredible. She could feel her thighs rubbing together, trying to capture her clitoris between them. She raised her head, keeping her treasure between gently clamping teeth until it was stretched and long, then she opened her jaw to let it spring back into place.

She moved her head across so that her mouth was directly over the other nipple. She worked her tongue and jaw to produce spittle, then opened her mouth and allowed it to fall on to that desirable thing, making it shine. She lowered her head and licked it clean, then sucked on it as fiercely as she had the first, swirling her tongue round and round that delicious mass. It was at that moment that her orgasm struck her and she wriggled and grunted, trying to prevent it. She groaned and moaned through it, chewing and nibbling, then flopped on to Maddie's breasts.

'Maddie, I'm so sorry! I've come off in my knickers. How terrible!'

Maddie heaved and rolled so that it was Fliss' turn to be on her back with Maddie's weight on top of her. 'You're just a little animal when you get going, aren't you?' She kissed the end of her nose. 'Well, if your knickers are wet, I'd better get them off you, hadn't I? Should have done it to start with.' She knelt up and flipped up Fliss' grey, pleated skirt. She pushed her hands down either side of Fliss' waist and reached underneath her to grip the back of the waistband of her white regulation knickers. 'Lift your bum up!' she ordered and, as Fliss obeyed, she yanked the knickers to her knees, then wiggled them down her legs and over her canvas shoes.

The feel of those knickers coming off, stroking her thighs and legs as they went, made Fliss' stomach lurch again, only this time she accurately identified the reason. Embarrassed at being naked below the waist, she flipped her skirt down. Maddie flipped it up again. Fliss tried to push it down and hold it there, but Maddie simply straddled her thighs, fumbling at the waistband of the skirt.

'No, Maddie! Don't! I'm shy!'

'You weren't shy when you ripped my bra off, were you?' said Maddie, tugging at the skirt and creating a wide strip of bare belly between it and the soft, grey sweater above. 'Come on! Let's have it off you!'

The sensation of her skirt dragging over her bare bottom and thighs as it was being tugged down and off to join her abandoned knickers did nothing to steady Fliss' lurching stomach and the knowledge that she was now stark naked from waist to ankles didn't help, either. She pressed her hands against her pubes but Maddie gripped her wrists and forced them to her sides.

'Lie still and let's have a look at you. I haven't had a close look since that first night.' Fliss lay still while Maddie brought her face to within about six inches of her groin area. 'Hmm! Your little hairs are getting quite long.' She blew on them, ruffling the fine, light down then tweaked one, making Fliss squeak. 'I'm not sure I didn't prefer you when you had no pussy hair at all. I could see more. Perhaps I ought to shave you off again.'

To Fliss, the prospect of being shaved by Maddie was extremely erotic. 'Have you got a razor in your box along with all the other things?' she asked, hopefully.

Maddie smiled indulgently at her enthusiasm. 'No. That's something else for you to be patient about.'

She concluded her inspection then changed position to straddle Fliss' hips. 'OK, it's show time!' she said and grabbed the bottom of Fliss' sweater, working it up to reveal her breasts encased in their solid, sensible covering.

Fliss willingly held up her arms so that the sweater could be pulled off over her head and as eagerly arched her body to permit Maddie to get her hands underneath her and release the brassière's hook. Maddie drew the garment up her extended arms and cast it aside. The sun was warm on her but Fliss shivered at the realisation that she was now naked; well, almost naked, she corrected herself.

'Are you going to let me, at least, keep my socks on?' she said, smiling.

'Thank you for reminding me,' Maddie said. 'No! You must have known when you ripped my bra that there would be a price to pay. Being stripped completely naked should teach you a lesson.' She reversed her position so that she faced Fliss' feet and leaned forward to unfasten her shoes. Fliss was presented with a wonderful view of her near-naked haunches. She felt her shoes and socks being pulled off and was astonished to find that having her feet made bare was every bit as erotic as having her knickers taken down. The crevice between the brown, muscled haunches in front of her was irresistible. She wanted to see what those frizzy, black hairs in the crack were half-concealing. She stroked the brown skin very gently. It felt like soft velvet and she shivered. Greatly daring, she took hold of the ridiculous string which was the back of the red panties. She pulled it up out of its resting place and substituted her finger, trailing it up and down.

'That's a silly thing to do while I've got your feet,' Maddie said. She placed her left arm around both Fliss' legs, crushing them securely to her breasts. With her right hand, she tickled the soles of Fliss' bare feet.

Fliss screamed and threw her upper body about, slapping at the brown buttocks. 'No! Oh no! Maddie! Mercy! I can't stand having my feet tickled!'

Maddie paused, still grasping Fliss' legs. 'Are you sorry?'

93

'Yes! Oh yes! Please don't tickle me any more.'

Maddie reversed herself again. She leaned over Fliss' face taking her wrists and pinning them to the grass beside her head. 'Any doubt about who's in charge?' she asked.

'No! You are, Maddie!'

'Right! So long as you understand.' Maddie bent and kissed her mouth, briefly, then let go of her wrists.

Fliss said, 'Anyway, you big bully, you've stripped me all naked and you're sitting on me but you've still got those on.' She dabbed at the red panties, thrilling at the feel of them under her fingers.

'All right! If you want them off, take them off!' said Maddie and shuffled forward until her knees were alongside Fliss' breasts. She raised her bottom and stuck her hips forward, daring Fliss to do something about it. 'Why don't you take them off like you did my bra? The set's ruined anyway.'

'May I?'

'Sure, go ahead!'

Fliss reached up and grasped the thin string which was the waistband of the panties, just to the right of the triangular centre section. She jerked her hands apart and the string snapped easily. The little jolt as it did so was echoed in her vagina and she gasped. She gripped the waistband on the left side and did the same thing. The centre section fell down and Fliss pulled it forward, sliding the material through Maddie's crotch until the whole garment came free and could be put aside.

Fliss stared up at the sex parts so close above her face. The shiny, black pubic hair was dense and frizzy. Even so, Fliss could see that the whole of her vulva was very dark brown, almost black. The crinkled, rubbery labial lips which poked through the hairs were almost dark blue. 'You're lovely, Maddie,' Fliss whispered.

'So are you, little sex-pot,' Maddie said. 'You know you turn me on, don't you?'

Fliss smiled, her happiness complete. 'I hoped I did. You turn me on, too.' She placed her palms against Maddie's hard thighs and stroked them. 'May I touch it, please?'

'If you'd like to.'

'Oh, I would!' Fliss was sure of that. Her contact with Maddie's nipples had been her first sexual handling of a woman's body and it had been wonderful. Even now she could see those fantastic nipples towering way above her, aggressive and threatening on the tips of those big brown breasts. However, what she was about to do made even the nipples pale into insignificance. She stroked that black pubic hair gently, savouring its texture while Maddie knelt, quiet and still, thighs wide apart, allowing her to do what she would. She trailed her finger to and fro, following the division of that dark vulva, her finger intruding slightly between the black lips. Maddie drew in a sharp breath.

Fliss looked up into Maddie's face. 'You're wet!' she said, accusingly.

'Wet from wanting you, Fliss.'

'That's nice!' Fliss took the wrinkled lips gently between the finger and thumb of each hand. She drew them apart and stared with intense curiosity at the gleaming inner surfaces thus revealed. She pulled them a little wider and Maddie's stark, white clitoris lanced into view from beneath it's fleshy hood. It was very long and pointed, almost like a miniature, uncircumcised penis. She felt her own juices flowing freely, trickling down between her bottom cheeks. She pulled the lips wider still and now she could see the red tunnel which was the entrance to Maddie's vagina. It was pulsing rhythmically; expanding and contracting.

She looked into Maddie's face again.

'Do you know, I can see right up inside you! It's so lovely. May I put my finger in there?'

'Yes please. I'd like you to.'

Fliss had to let go of the lips in order to free a hand but she used the finger and thumb of her left hand to spread them again, pressing against the frizzy hair for grip. Slowly and carefully she centred her right middle finger on the twitching vaginal channel and pushed it up, delighting in the way the hot, wet walls of that lovely place caressed her with their motion. Maddie groaned and her pelvis twitched in ecstatic reaction.

'Try to keep still,' Fliss said. 'I want to find your places.' She pushed her finger further in, turning her hand so that the pad of her finger could rub the soft tissue against the pubic bone. She felt a series of tiny bumps, like goose-pimples, and knew that she was in the right place. She rubbed in small circles. 'Is that good?'

'Incredible!' hissed Maddie, her thighs trembling with the strain of remaining still.

'I'd like to take you all the way and bring you off,' Fliss said. 'Is that all right?'

Maddie moaned with a sound that seemed to come from the area around Fliss' finger. 'Oh yes! Oh yes, please!'

'I'd like to do your nipples, too, but I don't have enough hands,' Fliss said. 'Will you do them for me? Do them the way you like best, then I can see what you do and learn how to please you.'

She watched as Maddie put the palms of her hands flat on her breasts and took a nipple in the cleft between the forefinger and thumb of each hand, noting that she did not use the tips of her fingers at all. She compressed them and pulled them away from her body until they were tremendously stretched and her breast flesh was also elongated. She rubbed her thumbs against her fingers so that each nipple was rolled back and forth, gradually sliding through until she lost her grip on it and it jumped back into its place, each breast resuming its correct shape.

Maddie's bottom was jerking uncontrollably now and

Fliss could see great undulating waves passing up and down her stomach. Maddie grimaced, drawing her lips back from her teeth in a wolfish grin. 'Christ! Oh Christ!' She gritted her teeth and pulled her nipples again in the same way.

Fliss maintained her rubbing but now gripped that long, pointed clitoris between the finger and thumb of her left hand, pulling and rubbing at it. Maddie's self-torture of her nipples became fierce and furious. Her head went far back and she began to shout, her voice rising up the scale and getting louder and louder.

'Ah! Aha! Do me! Do me! Yes! Yes!' She thrust her body towards Fliss' hands, grinding them down on to the breasts below. She wriggled there, covering Fliss' nipples with her sticky juices then collapsed, sliding her crutch down Fliss' body, leaving snail traces of its passage until it could rest on Fliss' thigh. She lay, panting into Fliss' ear and rubbing herself against her thigh while she calmed down. Fliss put her arms around her, hugging her nakedness close; unreasonably happy.

Finally, Maddie recovered and raised her head. Her face was beaded with perspiration and her short hair shone with wetness. She leaned across and kissed Fliss lightly on the lips. 'You're good,' she said. 'In fact, you're fantastic!'

Fliss giggled. 'That's very nice,' she said. 'I'm glad I'm good.'

Maddie knelt up suddenly then rose to her feet, taking Fliss' hand and pulling her up, too. 'I'm all sweaty and you're all sticky,' she said. 'Shower time!'

'Shower?'

'The waterfall, silly. I've got a towel in my box. We'll share it!' She grabbed Fliss' hand and dragged her at a run across the grass to the shallow pool.

At the edge, she did not slow down and Fliss screamed, 'No, Maddie! No! I like to get in slowly! Don't . . . Agh! Jees! It's so cold! Stop!'

97

Maddie ran on amid mighty splashes, still dragging Fliss and picking her feet high out of the shallow water to maintain speed. As the water got deeper she was forced to slow down, just as Fliss tripped and fell full length into about two feet of ice-cold water. She felt strong hands grab her as Maddie came back and pulled her to her feet, hugging her close so that Fliss' nipples, erected by the cold, bounced on her bare skin. Fliss hugged her back.

'Brrr! It's so cold! You're mad, you are! Absolutely crackers!' Fliss reached up and, taking Maddie's cheeks between her palms, she planted a cold, wet, trickly kiss on her lips.

Giggling, with their arms about one another's waists, enjoying the skin contact, they waded across to the waterfall and stood under it. It was exhilarating. The water thundered down on their heads and blinded them as they clung together, mouth to mouth and pubes to pubes. When the cold drove them out of their icy showerbath, they waded across the pool, holding hands, and scrambled back on to the grass. They dabbed each other perfunctorily with the towel then lay down again, their bare bodies amicably close, to allow the sun to toast them dry.

'We have to go soon,' Maddie said.

'Shame!' Fliss reached for the hand which was so conveniently close to her own. 'Can we come here again?'

'Better than classes, then?'

Fliss laughed, sitting up and looking around for her scattered clothing. 'Much better!' She paused in her search. 'Just think what Miss Ames would say if she could see us now.'

'Even better than that,' said Maddie. 'Just think what she would have said if she could have seen us a little while ago. You chewing my nipples off and then trying to tickle my belly button from the inside.'

They laughed together, then Maddie said, 'Shame to

98

laugh, though. Poor old, sex-starved spinster. Don't suppose she's had an orgasm in her life. She must have a pussy like a mouse's ear. If you wanted to stick your finger up her, you'd have to clear out the dust and cobwebs first.'

'I never thought about it that way,' Fliss said. 'It's sort of sad, really, isn't it?'

'Serves her right!' said Maddie succinctly, gathering the remnants of her underwear. 'Come on! Hurry up and get dressed. We'll be late for supper.'

Five

Agnes Ames sat at her desk in the glow of the reading lamp and worked at the reports stacked there. Although she was giving the appropriate amount of attention to her task she was still aware of other things going on in the room. Celia Moncrieff was behaving just a little oddly. That was the third time she had checked the photocopier's tray to make sure that it was full of paper. Now she was at the bookshelf, straightening a perfectly straight row of books. Agnes noted these things with an inner smile which she kept entirely to herself. She knew the signs. It pleased her enormously to torment poor Celia, so she gave no outward indication of having noticed anything out of the ordinary but continued with her reports. Presently, she knew, the thing would have to be brought out into the open.

Celia was standing in front of the desk now, her hands fluttering nervously. Agnes took no notice. Celia coughed quietly to attract her attention. Agnes looked up, appearing to see her for the first time. 'Yes? Oh, Celia. Thank you. That will be all.' She went back to her reports.

Celia coughed again. Agnes delayed a moment, taking the time to mark her place with her finger before she looked up again, frowning a little. 'Yes? Was there something else?'

Celia blushed. 'Have you a lot to do this evening, Agnes?'

Agnes considered. 'This evening? Let me see . . . I

have to finish these reports, then I thought I would wash my hair. I think there's rather a good programme on the television; then perhaps some Solitaire and an early night. Why do you ask?' She knew the reason perfectly well but wanted to force Celia to express it.

'Well, it's just that I . . . I mean we . . . It's been a long time, Agnes and I hoped . . .'

'Why, whatever are you trying to say?'

'Oh, Agnes. Don't be beastly to me. You know what I want. What I need . . . Please?'

'Celia! Are you trying to tell me that you have been a bad girl?'

Celia gasped, her teeth chattering with sexual tension as she whimpered, 'Yes! Oh God, yes! I've been such a bad girl.'

'You mean that you've done something so naughty that you think I ought to know about it?'

Celia nodded, speechless with the surge of excitement the carefully calculated words had aroused in her.

'You realise that any confession you make will have to be most severely dealt with?'

Celia's thighs were stirring restlessly, rubbing together under her skirt. 'Yes! Oh yes, Agnes!' she whispered.

'I see.' Agnes rested her elbows on the desk, pressed her fingertips together and regarded the squirming figure impassively. She looked at her watch, pretending to make a decision. 'It sounds as though this is the sort of confession which ought to be made in The Room. What do you think?'

'Oh yes! In The Room. I agree!'

'Very well. Eight o'clock, sharp. Don't be late.' Agnes resumed her writing.

'Thank you, Agnes! Oh thank you!' Celia almost stumbled in her haste to leave before the order could be rescinded.

Agnes resumed her report writing but more slowly and with less interest. She was distracted by the tingling

101

in her breasts and the fire in her belly which the prospect of a session with Celia always caused. It wasn't long before she pushed the papers away impatiently and rose. She switched off the reading lamp and left.

She took a leisurely bath in the private bathroom attached to her bedroom, pleased at the thought that Celia must at that very moment be doing the same thing. She dried and powdered carefully, applying perfume to her inner thighs and breasts as well as behind her ears. Disdaining underwear, she slipped a dress over her head, buttoned and belted it. Before her mirror she applied make-up with great care, using perhaps a shade too much lipstick. Slipping on some shoes she made a final check of her appearance in the full-length mirror then left her room, switching off the light.

Agnes made her way quickly along the corridors of the rambling old building to a door marked STAFF ONLY. Taking a key from her pocket, she unlocked it, passed through and locked it behind her. She went on through other, narrower corridors and up winding stairs which led to one of the wing turrets which few people ever visited. She used a different key to unlock a door there and entered what she thought of as her 'hobby' room.

The smell of leather excited her as it always did and she paused to look around with pleasure. The room was about thirty feet square and windowless, although a section of wall evidenced the fact that a narrow opening had been filled at some time. At the far end there was a vast fireplace. She crossed to it now and knelt to light the gas. The imitation log fire blazed in a most convincing way, warming the air. The only wall covering was a large, full-length mirror on one side, otherwise the walls were unplastered so that the natural stone of the old house's structure was a most perfect backdrop for the furniture and fittings. They consisted of bizarre apparatuses designed to restrain the human body in various positions. There was a padded bench, a leather vaulting horse and a plain wooden table, all fitted with leather cuffs and straps at different points. For standing confinement, there was a great X of thick oak and a pillory with holes for head and wrists. For sitting restraint a hard oak armchair was also equipped with similar cuffs and straps. For suspended bondage, two trapezes hung by steel cables over pulleys in the beamed ceiling. The cables led to modern winches attached to the wall, by which means any reasonable weight could be raised and lowered with ease. In addition to these, the walls were adorned with a collection of hand and ankle cuffs both of metal and of leather; whips, canes, paddles, belts and scourges. There were also devices for more delicate aspects of control, such as scolds' bridles, metal masks of intricate and ancient design, thumb or finger manacles, together with more modern gags, collars and blindfolds.

It was a vast collection and had taken a long time and a lot of money to acquire. Agnes loved it. To be in this room, even without a partner, was a thrill for her. She ended her survey and began her preparations for the evening's session. Going to one corner of the room, she climbed on to a chair and checked the setting of the wide-angle TV camera attached to the wall then cleaned the lens with a soft tissue. Getting down, she crossed to a cocktail cabinet against one wall and opened it. She poured herself a drink then stooped to a video recorder which occupied the lower part of the cabinet. She checked that a fresh tape was in place and wound back then closed the door on it.

Tossing back the rest of her drink at a gulp, she carried the soiled glass into the tiny bathroom adjoining and washed it before drying it and replacing it in the cabinet. She went to a long oak cupboard. Opening it, she pondered over the row of leather garments in order to make her selection for the evening. She decided at last, slipped out of her dress and put it on a hanger in the cupboard. Taking a tin of talcum from an upper shelf, she dusted her body carefully, paying particular attention to her arms and legs. She unzipped the back of the one-piece costume she had chosen and carried it with her to the wooden chair. Sitting, she forced first one leg, then the other, down the narrow tubes of fine, shiny leather, terminating in high-heeled boots which formed the lower half of the garment. She unzipped the cuffs to give a little extra room then forced her arms into the sleeves. She had to do a lot of wriggling to get the thing on to her shoulders and partly across her back. From the wardrobe, she took a piece of thin steel with a hook at one end and a handle at the other. Standing with her back to the full-length mirror and craning over her shoulder, she fished for the eye of the zipper against her bottom and drew it up slowly and carefully, closing the costume about her. It was skin tight and care was needed to avoid pinching herself with the zipper.

She zipped her cuffs and buckled the high collar at the back of her neck. Finally, she pulled on a pair of black, leather gloves made from such a fine skin that they might have been rubber, so elastic were they. From chin to toes, no bare skin showed. She was totally encased in tight, black, shiny leather. She admired herself in the mirror. The garment narrowed her already-narrow waist and threw her upper and lower halves into prominence. It had been tailored to accommodate her breasts which, although not huge, were distinctly adequate. The leather lifted and shaped them in a pleasing fashion and was thin enough to show her nipple erection. She turned to make sure that the costume was doing its job of containing her perfect bottom without a wrinkle and improving the shape of her already taut thighs. Satisfied, she slipped a leather cat-mask over her upper face and adjusted it. She took a thin riding whip from a wall bracket and tested it gently on her leather-covered palm. She was ready.

She had not long to wait. At exactly eight o'clock,

there was a soft knock at the door. Agnes rose and stood facing it, legs braced apart and whip in hand. 'Come!' The door opened and Celia slipped inside. When she saw Agnes' costume her mouth opened and she gasped with excitement. She closed the door behind her and stood with bent head, nervously entwining her fingers in front of her.

'Lock the door!'

Celia turned the key and resumed her former position. Her make-up was as careful as Agnes' had been. She wore a thin, white, lace-fronted blouse, charcoal grey skirt, black stockings and shiny, black, high-heeled shoes.

Agnes slapped her thigh with the whip. 'Well? Why have you come?'

'To confess and . . . to be punished.' Celia's low voice trembled, yet it was hard to tell if that was as a result of fear or passion.

Agnes held up an imperious hand. 'Wait! Before you say anything more, you know that I have to make a recording of what is about to take place?'

'Oh Agnes. Must you? You know how that embarrasses me.'

'What of that? I suspect you deserve to be embarrassed. Of course, if you wish to avoid that embarrassment you are free to leave. Close the door behind you.' Agnes turned away and walked to the other side of the room without a backward glance.

Celia hesitated, irresolute, making no move to leave and after a few seconds Agnes turned, feigning surprise. 'What? Not gone? Do I take it that you agree a recording should be made?'

Celia hung her head in shame. 'Yes,' she whispered.

'What? Speak up!'

'Yes.'

'Yes, what?'

'Yes, Agnes. Make a recording.'

'Very well, if you insist.' Agnes crossed to the cabinet, opened the door and switched on the recorder then came back to resume her wide-legged pose in front of her victim, again smacking the whip into her leather-gloved palm.

'Very well. Now that we are on the record, what have you to confess?'

'I've been . . . bad.' Celia glanced nervously at the camera's blinking red light as though it was some live Cyclops witnessing her shame.

'You mean you've been playing with your pussy again? Masturbating? Is that it?'

Fiery red, Celia nodded.

'Well, say so, woman! Let's hear it!'

The flush deepened. 'I . . . I've been . . . I've been playing with my . . . pussy again!'

'Come on! Say all of it!'

'I've been . . . masturbating.'

'Well, that certainly deserves punishment. Do you think so?'

Celia nodded again.

'Well then, say so!'

'I deserve to be punished. Punish me, Agnes, please!'

'You say that, in spite of what you see in this room. You realise how severe your punishment could be?'

'Yes.'

'Yet you still accept it?'

'Yes! Oh God, yes! I must have it! Do it to me, Agnes! Do it to me!' Celia fell on her knees, her hands clasped imploringly.

Agnes shook her head. 'Not yet! Get up! You haven't told me everything, have you? There's more.'

Celia nodded again.

'And I can see what it is. I can see through your blouse that you are wearing improper clothing; a black brassière. You know my orders. Black underwear is specifically forbidden. Yet you come to this room, knowing that I will discover your shame. What have you to say for yourself?'

'I've been very naughty, Agnes?'

'You have, Celia. Very naughty indeed and I shall have to deal with you accordingly. But first you must correct the wrong. Take off your blouse!'

Smiling, Celia unbuttoned the garment and let it slide off her shoulders to the floor. Her very large breasts were cradled in a flimsy black lace bra, over the top of which they bulged prodigiously.

'Now remove that obscene garment. Bare your breasts at once! That's right! No! Don't cover yourself with your hands. Fold your arms behind your back and let me look at you!'

Celia adopted the required pose. Unsupported, her breasts were not only large, but pendulous. Huge and white, they heaved with every panting breath she took as she thrilled at the open display she was making of herself.

Agnes increased the sexual tension. 'You know what I'm doing, Celia? I'm staring at your tits!' Celia gasped and bent forward slightly, rubbing her thighs together.

'Ah! I see that it excites you when I call them that, doesn't it? Well, Celia. I'm staring at your big, white, floppy tits and I'm planning what to do with them. Spank them perhaps? Whip them until they are red and sore?'

Celia bent further forward, yet kept her arms behind her. With her heavy breathing and shuddering, the twin melons swung and wobbled in a fascinating way.

'Bring your hands in front of you! Place the side of your thumbs very lightly and gently on the tip of each nipple. Gently, mind! A feather touch. I shall be able to see if you disobey. Good! Now rub in tiny circles. Slowly! Gently! Tiny circles!'

Celia's nipples were already fully erect, straining away from the engorged brown aureolae in the soft breast-flesh. What she was being made to do was torment of the worst sort to the waiting, wanting, rock-hard teats. Her upper body convulsed and her face contorted into a grimace. 'God! Oh God, Agnes! Don't make me do this! I can't stand it!'

'You can stand it and you will do it. It was your breasts which committed the offence and it is they which must feel the penalty.'

'How long must I do it?'

'Until I tell you to stop!'

'Agnes, I can't! I just can't! I shall come!'

'You most certainly will not! Control yourself! Stop rubbing your thighs together! I can see you!'

Moaning softly, Celia continued to torture herself for several long minutes more, until Agnes relented. 'All right, you can stop, now. Now take hold of each nipple between finger and thumb. Lift your tits right up! Come on! I said right up! Higher! Stretch them! Stay like that! That should cure your excitement!'

Agnes watched with deepest satisfaction as Celia almost stood on tiptoe to relieve the strain of what she was ordered to do to herself.

'Had enough?'

Celia nodded, her face screwed up in concentration.

'All right, you can drop them. What have you got on the bottom half? More black underwear?'

Celia hung her head.

'Right! Get that skirt off!'

Celia unhooked the skirt, slid down the zip and let the garment fall, stepping out of it. She wore a black lace garter belt with suspenders supporting her sheer black stockings and a very flimsy pair of black panties.

Agnes shook her head sorrowfully. 'You just won't learn, will you? You wore a black brassière and that had to come off, leaving your tits all naked. Now those knickers are going to have to come down, aren't they, and that's going to leave your pussy naked.'

Celia nodded again, quivering at the prospect.

'But before I pull them down I'm going to show you how useless they are. Why, they hardly cover your pussy at all.' She dropped her whip, went up to Celia and reached for the offending panties. She hooked the fingers of one hand into the sides of them at the front and compressed them in her fist until the material was just a thin cord. She pulled upwards and Celia groaned as the material bit into the division of her vulva, disappearing completely into her forest of brown, pubic hair.

Still gripping, Agnes yanked sideways. 'Turn round! Just as I thought. They're no more than a string at the back. Bend over! Spread your legs! Now reach back and stretch your cheeks apart! That's it! Both hands! Why, I can see everything! I can even see this!' She dabbed with her finger at the puckered, pink dimple which was Celia's sphincter. Celia jumped in surprise and her breath hissed through her teeth.

'All right, get up! Face me again! Arms folded behind you! Stay like that while I pull your knickers down!' Agnes knelt in front of Celia and allowed her grip on the panties to slide down until she held the gusset between the parted thighs. She yanked swiftly and Celia wriggled as she felt the waistband dragged over her hips and down her legs. She stepped out of the flimsy black panties and Agnes picked them up. She raised them to her face then removed her gloves and laid them down, the better to handle the black material.

'They're quite wet. I do believe you've been creaming in them. Let's see, shall we. No! Don't wriggle about! Stand still!'

It was very difficult for Celia to control her urge to dance about as Agnes placed the back of her hand against the thicket of hairs between her parted legs and rubbed it gently back and forth.

'I was right. You're simply soaking down there. Stand still while I mop you.' Agnes dabbed at the offending spot with the panties. 'Now hold yourself open while I clean you up. Come on! Both hands. Spread those lips wide and let me see you!'

Celia settled her legs a little further apart, knees slightly bent, and reached down under herself. Placing the tips of her fingers on either side of her sex, she pressed them against her body and pulled her hands apart to open the entrance to her vagina, revealing large expanses of moist, pink inner surface. She sighed deeply as Agnes rubbed the lacy material to and fro in the cleft thus exposed.

Agnes looked up into her face. 'I'll bet you're wet right up inside,' she said and wrapped a portion of the black material around one finger before inserting it gently into the wet orifice. Celia's sighing became a hissing pant.

'Looks to me,' said Agnes, 'as if you need something up there to mop up all that goo.' She began to push the panties into Celia's vagina, a little at a time. Celia continued to hold herself open but could no longer contain her wriggling.

Her bottom moved in vibrating circles under the influence of the intruding fingers and fabric. 'God! Oh! Oh! You'll make me come!'

'Don't you dare to come!' Agnes completed the task of inserting the panties and withdrew her fingers. 'All right. Get the rest off. Full strip! I want to see you naked! Now!'

Celia hurried to remove the garter belt, shoes and stockings, fumbling in her haste. When she had stripped herself bare she resumed her upright position before Agnes, hands to her sides. Agnes stared at her nudity, savouring the moment. Celia's figure was not one of classic beauty, being a little too thick and chunky for perfection. There was, however, a voluptuous quality about her; about the earth-mother width of her hips; the swell of her stomach and, above all, about the ample volume of her luscious breasts. For an instant, Agnes experienced a mad longing to possess a man's penis and semen so that she could impregnate that fertile body; cause those breasts to swell and fill; become ripe cornucopias of rich, thick milk. She would suckle on those long, strong, brown, maternal teats, drawing vitality from them. Suck and suck until they were dry, wrinkled and deflated. She gulped suddenly, tasting the delicious fluid in her mouth; smelling the womanliness of Celia. To increase that input she raised her fingers to her lips and tasted them. She shuddered with pleasure. Her fingers, still damp from their intrusion into that lovely, secret cavity were very slightly salty and as delicious to her tongue as they were to her nose.

Her voice trembled a little as she gave her next order. 'Take those panties out of yourself! And if I see you rubbing your clitoris while you're doing it, there'll be trouble!'

Agnes had pushed them in a long way and it was with no little difficulty that Celia managed to reach them. She had to part her legs very widely and bend her knees, stooping over herself to feel for them with finger and thumb. When the first scrap of material emerged, Agnes stopped her.

'Pull them out slowly! Slowly! And pull them upwards, close to your belly!' That was a cruel command. Such an extraction meant that the panties between the parted labia would be stretched across, and drag slowly over, Celia's throbbing clitoris; the very spot she had been forbidden to touch lest she should come to climax. It took every ounce of her self-control to prevent such a climax, her knees trembling and her bottom jigging as she gasped and grimaced at the sensation.

When they finally came free, Agnes said. 'Are they wet?'

'Yes, Agnes.'

'Soaking wet?'

'Yes.'

'Open your mouth!'

'What?'

'You heard! Open your mouth! Put the panties in. Right in! Now close your mouth. Chew on them and suck the juices out. Come on! Let me see those jaws moving!'

Celia obeyed, chewing and sucking. The smell and taste of her own body filled her mouth and nose, exciting her. Her hands strayed towards her groin.

'Get your hands away from your pussy! You're here to be punished for masturbating, remember! I think you will have to be tied if you're going to misbehave. Can you really taste yourself, now?'

Celia nodded.

'All right, let me see you swallow!' Celia gulped convulsively, sending her woman-taste all the way down inside her.

'You can spit them out, now.' Agnes held her cupped hand under Celia's mouth and she reluctantly parted with the sodden scrap of material.

Agnes tossed them aside. 'And now I think it's time we dealt with the offences of pussy-fingering and masturbation. That means that I'm going to have to spank you again.'

Celia trembled with delight. 'Yes! Oh yes! Please Agnes. I've been so naughty. I deserve to be spanked.'

'Indeed you do but, as this is a repeat offence, I'm afraid it won't do to have you simply bend over for it. I'm going to have to restrain you for this one. I rather fancy you'll have to have a taste of the pillory today.'

These words had a similar effect on Celia as a punch in the stomach. She crouched over, her thighs tight together and her hands pressed against her pubes. 'Yes! Oh yes!' she whispered. 'Do the words, Agnes. Please! You know what the words do to me!'

'Only if you pull yourself together and stop touching

yourself!' Agnes waited until Celia had resumed her position of attention, hands to sides, then she approached and stood close in front of her. 'So, it's the words you want, is it? Very well. You've been a bad girl, Celia. A very bad girl indeed! It's because of that you have had to strip stark, bare-arsed naked. You'll still be naked when I bend you over and lock you in the pillory. Fold your arms behind you again!' She reached out and took one of Celia's breasts in each hand, lifting and moulding. 'These big fat tits of yours will dangle down and I'll play with them. And when I spank your naughty bare bum very hard, they'll wobble and dance, won't they?'

Celia appeared to be on the point of collapse. She trembled violently. 'Do it! Do it now, Agnes, please!'

Agnes took a nipple between the finger and thumb of each hand and tugged gently. 'Come along then, Celia. Follow me to the pillory.' Celia followed as Agnes walked backwards. Every now and again, Agnes felt her pull back slightly so as to obtain the maximum impact from the fact that she was being led by her nipples. When Agnes raised the upper bar of the pillory, she willingly bent herself in half and placed her neck and wrists in the appropriate apertures. When the upper bar was lowered and locked she was trapped in her doubled-up position, her head and hands protruding from the front of the pillory and her rounded, naked buttocks thrust upwards in total vulnerability. Her long, full breasts hung down and Agnes toyed with them, slapping them lightly then lifting them up and letting them fall down of their own weight so that they bounced elastically.

She took up a position alongside the bare bottom, so willingly presented. 'Are you ready to be spanked?'

'Oh God! Yes! Spank me! I've been such a bad girl. Spank my bare bum really hard!'

Agnes had not the slightest intention of doing any such thing. She knew exactly how hard Celia liked to be

113

spanked to afford her the maximum pleasure and that is what she would do. Begging to be spanked harder s just part of the delight of hearing and using forbidden, wicked words. She began to slap the bare, white buttocks; first one cheek then the other in a regular rhythm. The slaps were hard enough to sting just a little and to cause the soft flesh to wobble and redden. After three or four slaps, she slid her left hand under Celia's belly and ran it along her body until her fingers could grope through the mat of pubic hair and separate her sex lips. Celia was lubricating furiously. Agnes rubbed her finger to and fro along the wetness then found and manipulated her bone-hard clitoris as she continued to slap.

Celia gave a great, hoarse cry. Her head shot back as far as the board of the pillory would allow and her whole pelvic area shook with violent tremors. 'Ooh! Oh! What are you doing to me? Oh my God! I love you, Agnes, darling. Do it to me! Just like that! Harder! Faster! I'm coming! Now! Don't stop! Yes! Yes!'

Agnes felt the lush juices of Celia's orgasm flow profusely over her hand. She slowed, but did not stop, her masturbatory movements. Her right hand continued its bottom-slapping but now only in the form of very gentle pats, hardly enough to move the flesh. She laid the side of her face against Celia's bare back, delighting in listening to the rapid thump of her heart, now slowing a little as she came slowly down from her peak of pleasure. Agnes felt a twinge of jealousy for a moment. She knew that this was only the first of many orgasms which Celia would have, each, apparently, more enjoyable than the first. Agnes had never been multi-orgasmic. However stimulated, one seemed to be her limit, so she had to use it wisely and not waste it on preliminaries.

When she judged that Celia had sufficiently recovered, she went around the front of the pillory and stood back a little, so that Celia could see her face without undue strain. 'Well, I hope that has been a lesson to you. That was for being a bad girl, wasn't it?'

'Yes, Agnes.'

'But it's not enough, is it? I have only dealt with your pussy-fingering. There is still the matter of the underwear to be dealt with, isn't there?'

Celia nodded. 'Yes, Agnes, I deserve to be punished for that. Will you spank me again?'

'Oh no, Celia. You've been much too naughty to be allowed to get off with a simple little spanking. It will be much worse than that.' She came close to the bent head, knowing that the woman-and-leather smell of her would be almost touching Celia's nose. She reached over the top of the panel which entrapped Celia's wrists and neck in order to slide her hands across her bare back and down the sides of her hanging breasts. Her fingers sought and found the nipples at the ends and she began to rub them, moulding, tweaking, pinching and milking. 'And now you will stand quietly for a while and imagine what that punishment is likely to be.'

Celia's body jerked in response to the tightening and relaxation of her gluteal muscles as she felt the full effects of her nipple torture. 'Not my nipples, Agnes. Please not my nipples! You know I can't stand it. You'll make me come again!'

'If you don't like it, why don't you stop me?'

'I can't! You know I can't!'

'No, you can't! I can do absolutely anything I like to you and there's nothing you can do about it. I own you. You are my naked slave and you belong to me, don't you?'

'Oh God! What are you doing to me? Yes! All right! Only no more on my nipples; I can't stand it!'

Agnes increased her teasing. 'Let me hear you say it, then.'

Celia's mouth hung open, now, her saliva dribbling down the board which held her. Her bottom never stopped leaping and gyrating as she strove to give herself the satisfaction of orgasm by rubbing her thighs together. She moaned and sobbed.

Agnes rubbed and tweaked faster still. 'Say it!'

'Aagh! Yes! Oh yes, Agnes. You own me! I am your naked slave and I belong to you! Oh! Ooh!'

Agnes released her nipples and stepped back. Celia slumped, panting hard. Her proximity to climax had been apparent and the treatment had stopped only just in time. Agnes went to the wall and fetched back a pair of double cuffs. These were made of soft leather lined with silk. Each one of the pair consisted of two cuffs, connected together by a metal swivel link. Working quickly, she buckled one cuff around Celia's left arm just above the elbow, leaving its connected partner dangling, then did the same with her right arm.

'What are you doing, Agnes? I can't see.'

'Never you mind. Would you like me to let you out?'

'Oh, yes please.'

Agnes unlocked the pillory and raised the top board a little. Celia removed her hands and Agnes slammed the board shut again before she could take her head out.

'Hey, Agnes! I'm not out,' Celia called.

'No, you're not, are you?' said Agnes. She took Celia's left wrist, pulled it up across her back and buckled it into the empty cuff at her right elbow. Going around the other side, she dealt similarly with Celia's right wrist so that she was cuffed, wrists to elbows, with her forearms resting in the middle of her back.

Agnes unlatched the pillory again and Celia stood upright at last, stretching her aching back. Agnes took her by the shoulders and propelled her across the room to face the long mirror.

'Look at yourself. That's what happens to naughty girls! They have their arms strapped behind them so that their tits stick out to be played with.' She reached around and lifted the large, white masses, making them bounce and wobble.

Celia wriggled with joy. 'Ooh! Is that what I look like! Oh, how dreadful!' Her thighs began their familiar movement under the impact of her reflection. 'Agnes?'

'Yes?'

'When you take me to do whatever it is that you are going to do to me, will you lead me by the nipples again?'

'I'll do better than that,' said Agnes. 'Stay there!'

She went to the cupboard again, returning with two lengths of thin, blue ribbon. Standing in front of Celia, she teased her nipples into erection then knotted the ribbon gently around each; tight enough so as not to slip off but not tight enough to interfere with the circulation. She passed each ribbon through the ring of a small sleigh-bell and secured it close to the nipple so that a length of ribbon was left hanging down. Gathering up the loose ends of the two ribbons in her hand, she tugged on them, softly. The nipples elongated, the milk-white breasts twitched in response and the bells tinkled. Celia went mad with excitement, her thighs now in constant motion as she sought the clitoral satisfaction she yearned for.

Agnes pulled more insistently on the ribbons. 'Time for your next punishment.'

Celia followed her as before; just slowly enough to cause tension in the ribbons, the little bells giving off their seductive sounds in response to her movements. Agnes led her into the middle of the room and, supporting her, helped her to sit down on the soft carpet. She went to the wall and released the ratchet on one of the winches there. Impelled by its own weight, one of the trapezes descended. There were leather cuffs at each end of the bar and Agnes spread Celia's legs very wide to fix her ankles into them.

Celia watched these preparations, her eyes shining. 'Oh God, Agnes! Not upside down? Are you really going to, or are you just teasing?'

'No, Celia. I'm not teasing. I've been telling you that this is what would happen if you went on being naughty, but you wouldn't listen. Now I'm going to

117

hang you up by your ankles, stark naked, with your legs wide apart and your big tits flopping down, and I'm going to spank your pussy.'

Deprived of the ability to rub her legs together and with her arms locked behind her, Celia bent forward, her face screwed up in frustration. 'Ooh! You're making me all wet. Touch me, Agnes. Do me, please!'

'You'll just have to wait,' said Agnes, calmly. She went back to the winch and re-engaged the ratchet. She began to turn the handle. Slowly the steel cable shortened, the trapeze was lifted and with it Celia's parted ankles. As it rose higher, Celia overbalanced and fell on her back with her legs in the air. Higher still and her bottom rose clear of the carpet, only her shoulders still taking her weight. Then she was completely upside down and clear of the carpet, her hair just brushing it. Her breasts, pendulous when she was upright, now stood out from her body in an amazingly youthful way and the ribbons on her nipples hung down past her face. Agnes continued to crank until her head was at least a foot from the floor then stopped and locked off the winch. She came over to the naked, suspended figure and pushed gently at her bare bottom. Celia swung and dangled, moaning softly with delight.

Agnes stooped and slapped gently underneath her breasts, so that the bells tinkled again. 'I rather think we're going to hear a lot of those bells in the next few minutes,' she said. She stood up and inspected the exposed pubic area at her face level. In its nest of brown pubic curls, Celia's vagina was gaping open under the tension induced by her bondage. Like the hairs around it, the open slit glistened with moisture. Agnes could smell wanting woman and it was all she could do to prevent herself from burying her face in that delightful thicket. Instead, she began to spank the unprotected pubes. She was very good at it and was quite aware of the fact. She knew just how hard and how fast to tap with

118

her hand and exactly where her fingers should fall so as to induce that glorious sensation she enjoyed so much herself. When Celia screamed with pleasure, she knew exactly what she was feeling. The delightful dilemma; the choice between wanting to throw her legs apart so that her clitoris might receive more of the delectable treatment and the desire to close her legs tightly because that pleasure was too intense to bear. Only, for Celia, one of those options was not open. Her legs were open, though, and would remain so until Agnes released her. It was enough to make anyone scream and cream.

As Celia bubbled into orgasm the lower half of her body wriggled and twisted like a snake, her beribboned breasts shaking furiously with a musical accompaniment from her bells. She continued to moan and pant, swinging gently to and fro and Agnes allowed her a little time to recover before uncuffing her arms. She went back to the winch and lowered the trapeze slowly until Celia could take some of her weight on her hands, then her shoulders, her back and, finally, lie at full length. Agnes unfastened her ankles and she sat up, rubbing them.

'Are you all right?' Agnes asked.

'Mmm? Oh, wonderful, thank you. That was so exciting! You are so good to me, Agnes. What can I do for you?'

'You can unzip me and help me get out of this costume.'

With Celia's assistance, it was easier to wriggle out of the leather costume than it had been to get in. Naked, she walked to the cupboard to put away her outfit. She knew that she looked good and she could feel Celia's eyes on her. She deliberately swung her hips so that the perfect inverted-heart shape of her bottom rolled enticingly. She hung the suit on its hanger but did not immediately go back to Celia, who was now kneeling on the hearthrug.

She parted her legs, put her hands on her hips and

thrust them forward, knowing how sexy that pose was. 'Want me?'

'You know I do, Agnes,' said Celia and there was no mistaking her sincerity. Lust mingled with adoration in her eyes.

'How much?'

'Very much indeed, Agnes!'

'Enough to lick me until I come?'

'Ooh, yes! I'd like that.' Celia could hardly wait.

'No fingers or hands. Just your tongue.'

'All right Agnes, if that's what you want.'

It was what Agnes wanted. Knowing that she would have just one orgasm, she wanted the pleasure of the things which would be necessary to bring it about to be as prolonged as possible. Being licked was, she knew, the best way of achieving that. She turned to the wardrobe again and took a small package from the top shelf. She went over to Celia and knelt beside her on the hearthrug. She opened the package. 'I bought you a special present,' she said.

Celia stared at the thing Agnes was holding in her hand. It was a long, pink, flexible dildo, but not like any she had seen before. The whole of its length was corrugated, like a vacuum cleaner hose. Around its circumference, just below the rounded tip, there was a ring of little rubber projections like short, pointed flower petals.

Agnes allowed her time to inspect it and absorb all its implications. 'Do you know what I'm going to do with this?' she asked.

'I think so.'

'What am I going to do with it, then. Go on, Celia. Say the naughty words. You know you're dying to.'

'You're going to . . . You're going to fuck me with it!' Uttering that word seemed to drive Celia into a sexual ferment. She fingered her sex, absent-mindedly.

Agnes decided to stir the pudding a little more. 'Yes!

120

While you're licking my hot, wet pussy and making me come, I shall be fucking yours with this lovely big prick. Just think how it's going to feel, rubbing and rubbing right up inside you, Celia. I'm going to fuck you until you scream for mercy and come, and then I'm going to keep right on fucking you.'

Celia grabbed at her breasts, rocking as though in terrible pain. 'Oh God! I can't stand it. Don't make me wait any more, Agnes.'

'All right. We'll start. First, you've got to kneel, facing me on all fours.' Celia adopted the required position with alacrity and Agnes copied her, so that their heads were very close together.

'Now we kiss. No hands! Just kiss!' They knelt, kissing each other like that, open-mouthed.

After several minutes Agnes said, 'Lick my face!'

Thoroughly steamed up, Celia licked feverishly at Agnes' cheeks, her eyes, her ears; everywhere her tongue would go.

Presently Agnes rotated herself, still on hands and knees, presenting her beautiful bottom to Celia. Lowering her head to the rug, she arched her back, opening her buttock cheeks as far as possible. 'Lick me there, Celia!' She shivered as she felt the busy, wet tongue work itself up and down her crevice, sending delightful frissons through her when it flicked on her anus. She rotated again, so that they were once more head to head. 'Now roll over sideways on to your back!' Celia did so and Agnes picked up the dildo. She crawled forward over Celia's upturned face, then further along her prone body until her knees were on either side of her waist. Celia pulled her arms through Agnes' parted thighs and put them over the backs of her calves. Agnes settled herself lower by spreading her legs wider, bringing her gaping sex lips down onto Celia's mouth. She thrilled as she felt the tongue begin its work again. She pushed Celia's bent knees far apart and kept them there by putting her forearms on her inner thighs and pressing down. Now the crisp, brown curls which so delectably adorned Celia's accessible crotch were close to her own face, glistening with love dew. Slowly and carefully she cleared away the hairs that blocked her view and stared into the opening of Celia's vagina, clearly visible as a dark tunnel inside the parted labial lips. The smell of her was heady; intoxicating. She placed the head of the dildo in position and pushed. She heard a great sigh from between her legs and pushed again. The thing was all the way in now and was so long that it must be near the neck of Celia's womb, even if it was not right inside it. She began to pump it in and out with slow, regular strokes. With the fingers of her left hand she spread Celia further open so that the light pink button of her clitoris came into view, fully erect. She continued to pump with the dildo but pulled the base of it up towards her a little so that now each corrugation was bumping over that unshielded clitoris at every stroke. She felt Celia go crazy, her stomach contractions being transmitted to Agnes' own belly by the closeness of their contact. She watched her orgasm with interest, observing the way her vagina twitched as it drew strongly on the source of its pleasure.

Now, what Celia was doing to her with her tongue became most pleasurable. She was concentrating on her clitoris, flicking at it, sucking and occasionally nibbling. Agnes increased the pace of her stroke and pressed with her finger so that Celia's clitoris was forced into almost painful contact with the corrugations. It was as much as she could do to hold down Celia's thighs, so violently did she react to this climax. She heard a voice from between her legs, slightly muffled. 'No more, Agnes! Please stop! I can't do another one!'

Agnes forced her own legs apart a fraction more so that her sex now pressed down tightly on that voice of protest, reducing it to muffled and incomprehensible noises. The tongue continued to lick through it all, sending the most delicious signals to her brain. She felt her own orgasm coming and redoubled her work with the dildo and her masturbating finger, in a frenzy to see another paroxysm from that vagina before she came herself. Now Celia was screaming as well as tonguing. The sound and the vibration sent Agnes over the top. She screamed with pleasure herself as she came, smearing her vaginal fluid over Celia's face. At the same time as it happened to her, she was rewarded by the sight of a really huge upheaval under her own face. Celia was in the throes of yet another orgasm, her legs and pelvis jerking helplessly.

Agnes slowed her movements then stopped, breathing heavily. She could feel Celia's breath between her legs, cooling her heated, wet sex. It was still twitching and pulsing in the aftermath of her orgasm. That climax had slaked her appetite, as she had known it would. She was satisfied with that and with what she had done for Celia. She had kept her word. She had fucked her until she screamed for mercy, then she had fucked her some more. Dear, sweet little Celia! It had been a wonderful session!

Six

Draco House was a miserable place, thought Fliss, but the island held other attractions. These woods, for instance, which had come to mean so much to her. The play of light and shade on the path was a delight, as was the earthy smell of the vegetation close about them. That beautiful scenery had played an important part in her relationship with Maddie, she knew. She ought to have been concerned about the sexuality of that camaraderie but she found herself unable to care. That part of their friendship was a source of great pleasure and she refused to worry about what others might think. She knew herself to be in grave danger of being in love, although she refused to accept that term inside her head. She watched the athletic form of Maddie just ahead of her on the path, noticing the length of her brown legs and the lithe swing of her hips. If she was too much committed to this fascinating young woman, what of it? Let it be so and let the pieces fall where they may.

Something had happened to intrude upon her reverie. She couldn't think what it was for a moment, then she knew. 'Hey!' she called. 'Hey! Isn't that the way to our clearing through there?'

Maddie didn't turn her head. 'Yes,' she said and kept walking.

'Aren't we going there today?'

'No.'

'Oh.'

Maddie stopped and turned to look at her. 'You sound disappointed.'

'No, of course not. Whatever you say is fine, Maddie. I just thought . . .'

'Wanted to get into my knickers again, did you?'

Fliss blushed furiously. 'No I didn't! Well . . . maybe just a bit.' Her blush turned to a shy smile.

Maddie smiled back. 'It's all right. I'm only teasing. I haven't gone off you. It's just that it's someone else's turn today.'

'Someone else? I don't understand. There's someone else?'

Maddie took her by the shoulders and kissed her lightly on the lips.

'Nothing for you to worry about, silly. This is business. Well, mostly business,' she added, reflectively. 'Today you find out where all the goodies come from; the drink and the cigarettes; the undies and the dildos.' She sniggered. 'And it isn't Father Christmas!'

She walked on down the path and Fliss, after a moment's hesitation, trotted along behind, a little concerned but intrigued at the same time. In another couple of hundred yards the path broke out of the woods and Fliss found that they were on the edge of a low cliff overlooking the green-blue sea. A little to their right, a steep path led down to a sandy beach of dazzling whiteness. Almost hidden by the overhang of the cliff, an ancient boathouse huddled defensively against the rock face, the weathered oak of its walls silvery-purple in the Spring sunshine.

'Why Maddie,' said Fliss, wonderingly, 'This is almost as perfect as our clearing.'

'Mm!' Maddie replied absent-mindedly. She was shading her eyes against the low sun and staring out across the white-flecked water. Apparently satisfied, she took Fliss' hand and led her towards the path. 'Come on,' she said. 'Not much time to get ready.'

125

She led the way down on to the beach then stooped to take off her shoes. 'Take yours off, too,' she said, 'Otherwise you'll get them full of sand.'

Delighting in the feel of the deep, soft sand between her toes, Fliss followed her to the boathouse and up the stone steps of the rock platform which supported it. The door was secured by a rusty chain and a huge padlock. Maddie fumbled under her skirt and produced a small device which looked like an elongated crochet hook. She inserted it into the padlock's keyhole and jiggled it expertly. The padlock opened and she removed it.

Fliss said, 'What are you? A burglar, too?'

Maddie held up the little tool and grinned as she swung the creaking old door back on its hinges. 'Comes in handy, sometimes. An uncle taught me to do that when I was seven. He should be coming out any day now,' she added, drily.

They went inside the boathouse and Fliss stared about her. It smelt faintly musty and seaweedy. There were many gaps between the planking of the walls through which the sunlight streamed, so that no window was necessary to enable her to see what it was like. It was hard to see why there should have been a padlock on the door. There didn't seem to be anything worth stealing in the place. A heap of old nets in one corner and a couple of rusty hurricane lamps on a shelf were about all the boathouse contained.

Maddie went to an inner door which was also padlocked and picked the lock with the same easy competence. This smaller room was completely empty, except for a stack of wooden shelves against one wall. She crossed to the wall on the seaward side. 'Look,' she said. 'You can see the beach through these chinks. And over this side . . .' she crossed the small room, ' . . . the cracks let you see into the main part where we just were. Now you stay in here and keep quiet until I come back for you.' She went out and closed the door behind her, leaving Fliss very puzzled indeed.

When she heard the rattle and click of the padlock, Fliss' puzzlement turned to alarm. She pulled at the door handle and banged on the stout oak of its panels. 'Maddie? Maddie! What's going on? Why have you locked me in?'

'Shut up, idiot,' Maddie said, her voice muffled by the thickness of the wood between them. 'You'll spoil everything. Do what I told you and keep quiet until I come for you.'

Squinting through the cracks and moving around the room to keep pace with her, Fliss watched Maddie leave the boathouse and go down on to the beach to stand at the water's edge. Presently, she heard the chug of a motor and a long, black, fishing boat nosed around a small headland and made for the beach. Maddie waved enthusiastically and the sturdy, red-haired man in faded denim shorts and heavy wool sweater at the tiller waved back. As it neared the beach, he cut the boat's motor and allowed the bow to nose gently up on to the sand then came forward and vaulted over the side into the shallow wavelets carrying a fisherman's anchor which he stamped into the sand. Fliss saw him go back to the boat and lean over the bow to retrieve a brown paper parcel. As he paddled back to the beach, Maddie went to meet him, greeting him with a hug and a kiss, then they came up the beach towards the boathouse with their arms about one another's waists. Fliss changed her position again so as to keep them in view as they entered the gloom of the outer room.

Maddie was chattering nineteen to the dozen. 'Come on, Fergus. Don't be a tease. What have you brought me this time? Give me my parcel.'

Grinning indulgently, he proffered it and she snatched it from him, tearing at the string and paper. 'Ooh! Vodka and whisky! You must have won the pools. Any chocolate? Oh yes. Here it is. And a whole carton of cigarettes. Well done! But what's this, you naughty man?' She produced a huge, pink dildo and masturbated it suggestively. 'What makes you think I need that with you around? Still, it does remind me that I have to give you your present.' She raised the pink, rubber head of the dildo to her lips and licked it, then slipped the extreme tip into her mouth, pumping it gently in and out and sucking on it. 'It's much too hot for clothes, Fergus. Why don't you slip out of that heavy sweater and those shorts?'

She fixed him with a stare and continued to manipulate the dildo as he struggled out of his clothes. Fliss, from her hidden vantage point, had an equally good view and found it very moving. She had never seen a man completely naked before. The revelation of his bare and well-muscled chest reminded her of her brief experience with Alex the stableman and she found her vagina watering with excitement. That excitement was greatly increased when he dropped his faded shorts to reveal the fact that he was already massively erect, his large penis jutting from a positive forest of dark red curls. That sight, with the knowledge of what was about to happen in the other room, made Fliss' stomach muscles contract and it took an effort to restrain the gasp of arousal which might have given away her presence. Almost without her own volition, her right hand stole down over the material of her short, grey skirt and rubbed gently at the division between her thighs. Now Maddie had put down the dildo and was stripping, too. She took her time over it, knowing the effect it was having on her willing audience. She pulled up her grey sweater and pretended to get caught up in it, so that her upper body was effectively revealed, her breasts encased in a filmy black brassière. When she dropped her skirt, her panties matched it perfectly, in their black, lacy scantiness.

Fergus took a pace towards her, but she held up a restraining hand. 'Down, boy! Wait for it. Why don't you go and lie down on our netting bed?'

Reluctantly, he made his way to the corner and arranged himself on the softness of the nets. Lying face up, naked, he caressed his rampant penis while he watched the remainder of the performance. With equal slowness, Maddie slipped the catch of her brassière and threw it aside. She hooked her thumbs into the elastic of her panties and drew them down over her swelling hips, gradually revealing to him more and more of her thick, black, pubic bush. To Fliss, the view from the rear was quite as fascinating and the sight of Maddie's exquisite brown bottom, now completely bare, was enough to evoke the most pleasant recollections. On an impulse, she fumbled with the catch of her skirt and allowed it to drop to the floor. Slipping her right hand inside her white, regulation knickers, she caressed her pubic hair then inserted a finger between her legs and rubbed it to and fro along her own wet slit, giving herself the most delightful sensations in the process.

Maddie crossed to the netting bed and dropped to her knees beside it. Leaning forward, she grasped Fergus' engorged organ in her right hand and bent her head to encircle the tip of it with her lips in imitation of her actions with the dildo. He gave a hoarse grunt and his whole body stiffened with pleasure. With his left hand he stroked the back of the dark head which was creating such intense sensations in his penis. Fliss had difficulty in believing what she was seeing. She had read about such things and heard coarse comments about 'a blow job' or 'giving head', but had not devoted much time to thinking about what that might imply. Now she was witnessing that very thing and it was vastly stimulating. Her vagina was overflowing and she could not resist the temptation to intrude a finger into its damp orifice in imitation of the flesh which now filled Maddie's mouth. She watched in fascination as more and more of that rigid lump disappeared from view and marvelled at the way in which Maddie appeared to be able to accept its whole length without choking. Fliss increased the rate of her own masturbation and shuddered into a small climax. Knowing that this was not the end of the matter for her, she continued to rub and thrust with her finger, confident that with the excitement of what she was witnessing, another orgasm would be bestowed upon her.

Maddie removed her mouth from Fergus' penis with a last, lingering, sucking motion, leaving it glistening with saliva, rock-hard and twitching. She knelt up and swung her leg over his prone body, staring into his face while she fumbled underneath herself to guide his organ to her vagina. Fliss' view was excellent and she masturbated more vigorously as she saw his pink length engulfed by that intriguing dark slit. Then Maddie was working herself up and down on it, flexing and relaxing her knees and Fliss could see the lips of her vagina distorting, being pushed first in, then out, with each stroke. She imagined how that must have felt for both of them. Suddenly, Fliss experienced an intense longing to be the possessor of a penis, so that she might be the one doing that thing to Maddie. That thought induced another orgasm which did nothing to assuage her lust, so that she continued to work just as hard at her masturbation.

Presently, Maddie raised herself off the intruding penis and Fliss thought for a moment that Fergus must have come. Then she saw that Maddie was simply reversing her position so that now her bottom was towards Fergus' face and the whole of the front of her naked, brown body was presented to Fliss' interested gaze. Once again, Maddie inserted the penis into her vagina and bounced enthusiastically. As she did so, she made it clear that this was not simply for Fergus' benefit. Unseen by him, she stared directly at Fliss then placed her right forefinger pointedly on her clitoris, masturbating in slow circles while, with her left finger and thumb, she pulled and worked at her incredible black nipples. Fliss needed little encouragement. She had worked her knickers down to mid-thigh and now she pulled up her sweater and eased her brassière up and over her breasts so that they fell free and she could manipulate her own nipples in imitation of Maddie's movements. She continued to stare intently through the crack in the boards and saw that Maddie was by no means indifferent to the effect Fergus' penis was having on her. She was no longer smiling but grimacing and frowning as though in pain. Occasionally, her left hand left its nipple massage and went down between her spread thighs, her fingers fluttering uncontrollably as she caressed the hairy thews and testicles so close beneath her, as if to reassure herself that they were really there. Almost the whole length of Fergus' penis was now revealed to Fliss as Maddie bounced more energetically. It was not only huge and hard, but almost purple with an excessive suffusion of blood. When Maddie threw back her head and shrieked in the throes of orgasm, Fliss came to climax with her, biting her lip to suppress her own groans; shuddering and clamping her hand between her damp thighs. Fergus was close to ejaculation, too. Fliss had still not recovered her breath when Maddie knelt up to allow the long penis to slip from her. Immediately, she grasped it with her right hand, working rapidly in an up and down motion. Fliss saw the lower part of Fergus' body where it protruded between Maddie's thighs, strain into a curve, his heels pressing against the netting as though he was attempting to unseat his rider. He gave a series of loud grunts and suddenly, from the purple tip of his organ there spurted a mighty fountain of creamy white semen which arced up and splashed across the front of Maddie's bare body, trickling down her breasts and stomach. Fliss had never seen such a thing before and found it so madly exciting that although she was no longer caressing herself and had already had three orgasms she came to climax again quite involuntarily. Trembling, she tore her gaze from the gap in the boards and went away to the other side of her small prison, crouching down against the wall while she attempted to regain her composure.

By the time she had recovered sufficiently to get up, rearrange her upper clothing and put on her knickers and skirt, Maddie and Fergus were already outside the boathouse and walking down the beach towards the fishing boat. Fergus had dressed in his sweater and shorts, but Maddie was still naked and apparently quite unconcerned about her nudity. The tide had come in a little and the boat was now bobbing gently in the light swell, almost afloat and grounding only lightly and occasionally. Fergus broke the anchor out of the sand and put it on board. He gave Maddie a long kiss which she returned with enthusiasm then climbed over the bow and went to the stern, where he started the motor. He chugged off in reverse for a short distance then put the tiller over and swing the bows of the boat out to sea. Maddie continued to stand, naked, at the water's edge, waving until he passed out of sight around the headland then she turned and made her way back to the boathouse.

The padlock rattled and Maddie's cheery face appeared round the edge of the opening door. 'See everything?' she asked.

Fliss was a little embarrassed and blushed. 'I wasn't really taking any notice,' she replied.

Maddie snorted. 'Not much, you weren't! I could see enough through the cracks to know what was going on in here.'

'Oh!' Fliss' blush deepened then, in the manner of all who have been disconcerted, she sought to hit back. 'Anyway,' she said, 'I don't know how you could allow him to use you like that – a common fisherman, too!'

Maddie had been about to lead the way out of the room, but stopped dead and turned back, her hand still on the door's latch. 'Now just a minute, Miss. In the

132

first place, he wasn't using me; I was using him. I got a very nice seeing-to, thank you very much, and a parcel of goodies into the bargain. And not so much of the hoity-toity "common fisherman", please. Fergus would be many women's notion of the ideal man. He's got the prick of a donkey, the brains of a pilchard and a pre-disposition to give nice presents. Who could ask for more?' Maddie grinned engagingly and, in spite of herself, Fliss could not resist a giggle at this description.

Maddie grinned again and reached out to ruffle her companion's hair. 'Not just a bit jealous, then?'

This was so close to the truth that Fliss became defensive again. 'Certainly not!'

'It's all right, you know,' said Maddie. 'You're allowed to be jealous. I rather like it, in fact.' She thought for a moment then decided. 'Yes, I definitely like the idea that you're jealous. Gives me something to make up to you and I'll do that just as soon as we get to our clearing.'

'Oh,' Fliss said, brightening. 'Are we going there after all, then?'

'Course we are. Several reasons. First, I have to stow these goodies in my trunk.' Maddie stooped and picked up the brown paper parcel, re-wrapping it loosely. 'Here,' she said. 'You carry that.' She picked up her own clothes and bundled them under her arm. 'Secondly,' she continued, 'I need to shower under our waterfall and get all this gunk off me. And thirdly . . .' she paused with a sly glance, ' . . . Well, thirdly, I'll let you guess about, shall I.'

Fliss had thought that after her recent orgasms, nothing could arouse sexual expectancy in her but those words and that mischievous look from her beloved were enough to send the mercury in her passion thermometer soaring and threatening to burst out of the top. She felt her throat drying and she gulped.

Maddie pretended not to notice and sauntered out of

the boathouse. Fliss gathered her reeling senses and followed her naked form. 'Aren't you going to dress?'

'What for?' asked Maddie, nonchalantly. 'I'll only have to strip off again. Who's to see, except you, and I thought you'd enjoy the view. I'll walk in front all the way and let you watch me and wonder if I'm going to let you smack my naughty bare bottom.' With an exaggerated, mincing walk which caused her elegant haunches to swing from side to side, she led the way off the beach and back up the cliff path.

The hand that was shaking Fliss' shoulder was insistent. She tried to snuggle and wished it would go away. It couldn't possibly be time to get up, yet. When she finally opened her eyes, she was alarmed to find that it was pitch dark. She shot up in bed. 'What . . . ? Who . . . ?'

'Sshh! You'll wake everybody!'

'Maddie? Oh, Maddie! It's the middle of the night. What do you want?'

'Come on, get up. I want to show you something.'

'What?'

'Something I found. Oh, do come on!'

Fliss climbed out of bed, shivering and sleepy. She put on her dressing gown and slippers. 'This had better be good, Maddie.'

'Oh, it is. Believe me!'

Fliss followed her along the corridors. She could hear her own heart beating. If they were caught out of bed together, there would be red bottoms to show for it, at least. Now Maddie was kneeling at a door marked STAFF ONLY. In the glow of the tiny torch she was shining on the lock, Fliss could see that curiously shaped piece of metal and once again marvelled at Maddie's uncanny ability to make it open anything. Within seconds, the door was unlocked. They passed through and Maddie knelt again to lock it behind them. She led the way onward, up winding flights of stairs, higher and higher.

Maddie knelt at another door. She opened it and went
into the pitch blackness beyond. Fliss followed her and
Maddie closed and locked the door behind them. Fliss
was very glad of the glow of the tiny torch. She blinked
as Maddie switched on the light, then gasped as she
looked around her, taking in the strange furniture and
implements. 'Maddie! Whatever is it?'

'It's Miss Ames' own private torture chamber, that's
what it is! Isn't that something?'

'My God!' said Fliss. 'You were right. This was worth
getting up for.'

'There's a cocktail cabinet here,' said Maddie. 'And
it's loaded. There's even a little refrigerator with ice.
Want a drink?'

'Oh, Maddie. Do you think we should?'

'Course we should. The old bag'll never miss it. Gin
and It?'

'All right.'

Maddie poured two generous measures, added the
vermouth and handed one to Fliss. As she stretched out
her hand to take it, she paused. 'Oh look, Maddie! There's
a video recorder. Why do you suppose she needs
one of those up here?'

'Bet I know,' said Maddie and squatted on her heels
to inspect the machine. 'There's a tape in it and a TV
over by the fireplace. I'll just wind it back, then we'll see
what's what.'

While the tape was rewinding, they went over to the
big fireplace, taking the bottles with them and Maddie
switched on the TV then lit the gas. Fliss squatted on
the hearthrug while Maddie went back to start the tape
running then they sipped their drinks while they
watched in complete amazement the recording of the
so-respectable Miss Ames in session with Miss Moncrieff. Not until the picture flickered and died did either
speak, then Maddie said, 'Imagine that! The po-faced
old hypocrite, spouting all that shit about cleanliness

135

and medical inspections when all the time she's getting her jollies out of strapping us down and shaving our pussies!'

They allowed the growing heat of the imitation blaze to warm them for a while then, setting their empty glasses down in the hearth, they continued their inspection.

'Come and look at this,' said Maddie, crossing to the big, oak cupboard. She opened it to reveal the row of bizarre costumes. Fliss fingered them, amazed.

Maddie was holding a garment to her face, smelling it and rubbing it between her hands. 'Look at this. It's real leather.'

Fliss took it from her and gave it the same treatment. 'Certainly looks like it.' She held it up. 'But whatever is it? I can't work it out, can you?'

Maddie took it back from her. 'Well, the bottom bit is long boots with high heels. It must be for Miss Ames. None of the others would fit in. It's too long for ordinary boots, though, and look at the top bit. It's like a pair of slacks, except that there's no front and back, just these wide bits at the side and a belt. They wouldn't hide much, would they? Need to keep your vest and knickers on!'

They giggled and passed on. The next item was even more mysterious. Also made of leather, it seemed to be a glove, although it was much longer than a normal evening glove and about twice the diameter. From top to bottom ran a double row of laceholes and there was a strap and buckle stitched on where the wrist might come.

'Whatever can that be for?' asked Fliss, wonderingly.

The next item was easier. An arrangement of straps formed into a sort of bridle with a bright red ball gag attached.

'Oh, I've got it now.' Fliss picked up the second object again. 'Look, you put somebody's arms in here, then lace it up. It pulls their arms together and keeps them straight, then you buckle up the wrists.' Even to give that description gave her tremors between the legs. 'They're bondage things. Look at the trouser bits again. See, they have rings at the knees and ankles, so they can be clipped together.'

They took the articles with them to the fireplace, sat down and refilled their glasses. The strange leather apparatus lay on the hearthrug between them and Fliss could not take her eyes off it. She knew what she wanted. She had known ever since she first identified its purpose. She had a couple more gins. Maddie was equally liberal with herself.

At last, Fliss broke a long silence. 'You know Maddie, I'd really like to try those on.'

'You would? Why?'

'Oh, I don't know. I suppose its the feel and the smell of the leather. Don't you think it's sexy?'

Maddie considered the question. 'I suppose they are. I know you get off on that stuff.'

'Thing is, I couldn't manage by myself. I could do the bottom bit, but someone else has to do the laces on the arms. I'd just like to see myself in the mirror.'

'OK, if that's what you want.'

Fliss got up and took off her dressing gown, slippers and nightgown, putting them in a neat pile on the table. She stepped, quite nude, to the fireplace and picked up the leggings. They were an extremely tight fit and it took their combined strength to force her feet to the bottom of them. She stood up, teetering on the six-inch heels while Maddie buckled the belt about her waist and pulled it tight. She tottered over to the mirror and inspected her image. The sight which greeted her was every bit as sexy as she had hoped it would be. The shiny black garment covered her thighs almost to the crotch, but left her pubic area completely open and available. Against her white stomach, the securing belt was starkly black. The side pieces joining belt to legs formed a perfect frame for the light fluff of her pubes. She turned and looked over her shoulder. That mirror image was just as seductive. Her bare bottom, also framed in black, bulged out above the constraining leggings, almost demanding to be spanked. She shivered with pleasure.

'Now help me with the arms thingy.' She interlaced her fingers behind her back and, as Maddie held the neck of the apparatus for her, she plunged her hands into it. As with the leggings, it was quite a struggle to get her hands to the end of the long pouch but she managed it and Maddie pulled the top up until it was as far as it would go, which was just above her biceps.

'Now tighten the laces for me. Pull on them. Really pull! Ah! Yes! That's it!' The complete restriction of her arms and the way the device pulled her shoulders back, throwing her breasts into prominence, was a most exciting sensation. When Maddie pulled the wrist strap tight and secured it, she felt completely trapped.

'I wonder how you're supposed to fix the knees and ankles,' Fliss said.

'I don't know. Wait a minute!' Maddie went to the cupboard and rummaged. 'There are some padlocks here. That'll be it.'

Fliss pressed her legs together and Maddie linked the rings at ankles and knees. The sound of the padlocks clicking shut was a real turn-on for Fliss and she found her vagina wet and her thigh muscles tensing to squeeze her clitoris. She met Maddie's eye and saw a new light there. She felt a sudden surge of power as she realised that, although she was the one in restraint, what the sight of her nearly naked, confined body was doing to her companion meant that Maddie's enslavement, although mental, was just as complete.

Partly to tease and partly to increase her own stimulation, Fliss said, 'Just think, Maddie. Now you've got me like this you could do anything you liked to me and I couldn't stop you.'

Maddie gazed at her and Fliss exulted in the lust she read in her eyes. 'You talk too much,' Maddie said and picked up the head-piece with its bright red gag.

'Oh no, thank you, Maddie. I don't need that.'

'I think you do. Stop you being so saucy. Open your mouth.'

'No, really! I don't want it.'

'Please yourself.' Maddie sat down on the hearthrug and picked up her drink.

There was a long silence. In the mirror, Fliss could see Maddie sitting behind her, making no attempt to release her.

'What are you doing? You're not getting me out!'

'No, I'm waiting.'

'Waiting for what?'

Maddie poured herself another drink. 'For your mouth to open. You'll be pretty tired by morning, I imagine.'

Fliss was beginning to regret her teasing, but could see no alternative. 'All right then, but just for a little while, eh, Maddie?' Her tone was conciliatory. It was ominous that Maddie did not appear to respond to that but just picked up the head-piece again and came in front of her with it, eyebrows raised questioningly.

Resigned now, Fliss opened her mouth. Maddie slipped the leather cage over her head and pushed the red ball into her mouth. It was rather large and her jaws ached as they strained to encompass it. Maddie fastened the buckles under her chin and behind her head. Now there was no way Fliss could eject the ball with her tongue. She looked at herself in the mirror. Despite the discomfort there was no doubt that the sight was tititlating in the extreme. From the forehead band, a wide strap divided on either side of her nose and was stitched to the strap which held the ball. This arrangement made it seem to Fliss as though not only her mouth, but her eyes as well, were captured by the device.

139

'There's a ring right at the top. I wonder what that's for?' Maddie looked up. 'Oh! I know!' She disappeared from Fliss's view. When she came back, she was carrying a length of cord. Standing behind Fliss, she put her strong arms around her and half lifted, half dragged her to a position directly beneath one of the trapezes. By releasing the winch lock, she lowered the bar until it almost touched the top of Fliss' head. Putting the cord through the ring on top of the helmet, she passed it around the bar, pulled it tight and knotted the ends together. She went back to the winch, took up what little slack there was and locked it off. Fliss realised that whereas, before, she could have bent in the middle at least, now she would be quite unable to move at all.

Maddie surveyed her, hands on hips. 'Well, Missy. Not so cheeky now, are you?' Maddie stood in front of her and each read the other's eyes, then she moved to one side and began to slap the underside of each breast in turn, one after the other. They were gentle slaps, just sufficient to lift the weight of the breast and allow it to fall back into place, bouncing and jiggling. Fliss could see this happening in the mirror and the effect pleased her. It was like a vigorous massage and it seemed to go on for a long time. Fliss's skin began to glow. It felt wonderful. Then Maddie was standing directly in front of her again. 'Great nipples you've got,' she said and Fliss knew what she was going to do, even before her hands moved. The grip of finger and thumb on each straining protrusion sent an intense thrill through her. When Maddie started a milking action, pulling, stroking and rolling, Fliss groaned behind her gag with pure joy. Added to the normal pleasure such manipulation would cause was the certainty that there was nothing she could do to prevent it. She could not move or speak. Maddie would go on doing what she was doing for as long as it amused her. Fliss was awed by the depths of the sensations she was feeling. Her breath whistled through her nostrils as the stimulation reached deep into her vagina which began to pulse in time with the hand movements. She was going to come, she knew. She did not believe that could be possible without her vagina or clitoris being touched, but that was what was going to happen to her if Maddie didn't stop that tantalising stroking and pulling. Maddie did not stop. She stared, steadfastly into Fliss's face and Fliss knew that she was aware of the precise effect she was having. The pace of her milking increased until Fliss could stand it no longer. Her orgasm rushed upon her with full force. Unable to cry out or touch herself in any way, she was forced to undergo it stoically erect, with only the desperate quivering of her body to show the turmoil inside.

Maddie continued to stroke and pull until she was certain that the climax was over before she began to release her captive. As soon as her head and legs were free, Fliss staggered on her high heels to the table and bent herself over it, pressing her burning nipples against its cool surface. Maddie worked to free her arms; not accomplished without a lot of tugging. The leggings were even more difficult but it was done at last and Fliss sank on to the hearthrug with a groan.

'My God! Do I need a drink! It's strong stuff, that leather!'

She had a stiff gin. So did Maddie. They had a couple more then, slightly tipsy, they resumed their examination of the cupboard, tittering together over the strangeness of the things it contained.

From a shelf near the bottom of it, Maddie dredged up another leather item. She held it up for inspection, 'Now *that's* more like it!'

Fliss took it from her. It was like a pair of leather knickers, except that from the crotch area there protruded a very large rubber penis. 'I guess that's for a man who hasn't got a big one,' she said. 'No! Wait a minute. Oh look! It's got another one inside, sticking up. It must be for a woman to wear. That one goes inside her and the outside one goes . . .' She stopped. There was a glint in Maddie's eye which was unmistakable. 'Maddie! Are you thinking what I think you're thinking?'

'Could be. Seems a shame to waste it and we ought to know how these things work, oughtn't we?' Probably neither would have been so forward had the drink not worked upon their inhibitions. For Fliss, another factor was that the image of Maddie being serviced by Fergus and the envy she had felt was still vivid in her mind. The fact that Fliss had not bothered to dress again after the previous episode may have had something to do with Maddie's acquiescence. Whatever the reason, they laughed together and went hand in hand to the hearthrug, taking the fascinating article with them.

'Take your things off quickly, Maddie. I can't wait to see that gorgeous body of yours again.' Maddie grinned and removed her dressing gown and nightgown. She cupped a hand beneath each breast and exhibited them to Fliss. 'I thought you fancied them. Want a feel, do you?'

She arched her back in pleasure as Fliss reached out and stroked the objects of her fascination. When Fliss buried her head in their deep cleft, and pressed them against her face, nuzzling and feeling for the nipples with her thumbs, Maddie groaned and stroked the back of the head pressed against her chest. They sank on to the hearthrug together and Maddie lay down on her back with her knees raised.

Fliss pushed at them. 'Open your legs. I want to see all of you!'

Maddie spread her legs and Fliss stroked and fingered her exposed vulva. 'I guess you'd like me to be the one who wears this, wouldn't you?'

'That would be nice, I think.' Maddie watched with interest as Fliss stood up and inserted her legs into the leather pants. She pulled them up about her thighs then paused as the internal penis prevented further upward movement. Instinctively, she turned away to do what had to be done but Maddie stopped her.

'Don't hide yourself. I want to watch.' Fliss turned back obediently, her embarrassment at what she was about to do mingling with a certain sexy thrill. Maddie was lying on her back, her youthful breasts so firm that they were hardly diminished at all by her position; those huge, dark nipples pointing at the ceiling. Her legs were still splayed so that Fliss could have a good view of her crotch. She played with herself, gently parting her sex lips and rubbing her finger up and down between them, knowing full well what effect that would have on Fliss. With her eyes riveted on that delicious prize, Fliss grasped the tip of the inside penis and inserted it into her vagina. She was certainly wet enough to need no artificial lubrication. She grunted as she felt the full thickness of the thing, hardly smaller than the external one. She pulled the pants right up and grunted again as this forced the whole length into her. She tightened the belt and came forward, walking slightly awkwardly, becoming aware of the small rubber projection at the base of the dildo inside her. It was doing marvellous things to her clitoris as she moved. She looked down between her breasts at the erect penis which now erupted from between her legs. Was this what it felt like for a man when he approached the woman he was going to have?

She sank to her knees and crawled forward until she was between the parted thighs, lowering herself as Maddie reached out and took the rubber penis in both hands to guide it to her waiting vagina. Her nipples, still very tender from their earlier torture, brushed lightly against Maddie's breasts and the touch was magic.

Pushing and probing with her hips, Fliss sought to gain entrance for her artificial appendage. 'Am I doing it right?'

'Gently, Fliss. Not so eager!' Maddie adjusted her position slightly. 'Now go on. Slowly! A bit more! There! I've got it all, now.' She sighed deeply, a beatific expression on her face. 'Now move to push it in and out. Yes, that's right. Ooh! Oh! Aah! That's good. That's *so* good!'

Fliss straightened her elbows, pushing herself away from Maddie's bosom. Free to move again, those breasts were joggling in a constant state of agitation which Fliss found quite captivating. She bumped her pubes against Maddie's at every forward stroke, simply for the delight of seeing the quivering jar with which those tanned globes responded. Looking down her own body, Fliss could see the length of the penis disappearing into Maddie's hairy crevice, distorting the dark lips which gripped at it with every stroke. For the second time in her life, she regretted not being a man. The vagina which was impaled upon her was wet, she knew. Its walls were sucking greedily at the intruder which was ravishing it so deliciously, yet she had no way of sharing that. She could not feel the wetness or the contractions and that was deeply frustrating. She felt she would have given anything to feel what a man would feel, but had to make do with the sensation of the penis inside her own vagina and the rubber button which was now beginning to make its presence well and truly felt, massaging her clitoris with every forward thrust.

Maddie was pushing her away.

'What is it. You haven't finished?'

'No. I was getting too close and I don't want to finish this way. Let me turn over.' Maddie rolled over and got up on all fours, parting her legs. The golden expanse of her behind was overwhelming, the hirsute bulge of her sex prominent between the equally golden thighs. 'Kneel up and put it in from the back. Ah! Yes! That's it! All the way!' Now reach around and do my clitoris for me. Ooh! Yes!' The taut bottom twitched and wriggled against Fliss' bare belly. 'Now feel my tits. Do my nipples! Harder! Pull them longer! Pinch and roll! Make them ache! Oh God! Do it to me. Fuck me hard, Fliss! Now! Harder! Faster! Here I come! Here I come! Oh! Ooh!' Her head shot back and every muscle in Maddie's body tightened. Her left hand slapped lightly at her own breasts, beating rapidly and making them jump and wobble. She bucked and humped until it was all Fliss could do to keep the penis inside her. Maddie's climax seemed to last for ever. When it ended, she collapsed on her face, taking Fliss down with her.

Fliss made to withdraw, but Maddie prevented her. 'Don't take it out, Fliss. It feels so good.'

Fliss was most content that this should be so, and they lay curled up together on the hearthrug, holding one another close. Presently, they slept.

Seven

Since the episode in the shower room, fear of reprisals by Maddie seemed to have prevented Hilary from making further physical attacks on Fliss. However, she continued a campaign of emotional abuse, as though she was trying to make Fliss' stay at Draco House as intolerable as possible. Unless Fliss locked everything away, she would find that her possessions had been hidden, damaged or interfered with in some way. It was hard to say for certain that Hilary and her cronies were the culprits but their sneering laughter at any discomfiture on Fliss' part made it fairly evident that they had a hand in the mischief.

Hilary had an annoying habit of referring to Fliss as 'The Duchess' and exaggerating her father's wealth. Whenever Fliss entered a room Hilary would call the class to order with comments like, 'Attention, staff! The Duchess has come to inspect her estate.'

At first, Fliss had found this hateful and wounding but under Maddie's guidance and tuition she learned to let such thing slide off her and, occasionally, to retaliate with some pithy insult. On this particular day, Fliss had emerged from the communal shower to find her towel, sopping wet, lying in a puddle on the floor of the changing room. As she picked it up and wrung it out, Hilary sneered, 'Oh dear, Your Highness. Is your towel wet? Shall I send for the upstairs maid to dry it for you?'

Fliss turned to face her. 'When you have your breast reduction, Hilary,' she said, 'why don't you have a bit taken off your fat arse as well? We could keep a Chinese takeaway in pork balls for a year.'

Most of the other girls in the changing room had no great love for Hilary and guffawed loudly. Even her toadiest friends could not refrain from smirking.

Hilary reddened with anger and lost her cool. 'You high and mighty little bitch!' she screamed. 'Let's see how grand you are when you get out of here. You'll have nothing. No big house; no land; no staff; no stables. The only way you'll see anything more of your precious King is if you happen to buy the right tin of dog food!'

The picture this conjured up in Fliss' mind was dreadful. She loved her horse and the thought that he might even at this moment be loaded and on the way for slaughter made her feel sick. She tried not to show that she had been affected, but could manage only a routine insult. She raised her right middle finger in an American gesture of derision. 'Rotate on this, Hilary!' she said but her heart wasn't in it.

So it was that Maddie found her in her room later, face down on the bed and sobbing. 'Why, whatever's up, Fliss?' she said, sitting on the edge of the bed and patting the heaving shoulders.

Fliss raised a tear-stained face. 'I've got to get out of here, Maddie. I've just got to get out of here now! Today!'

'OK! OK! What brought this on?'

'Hilary said . . .'

'Oh Lord! Didn't I tell you not to take any notice of her?'

'I know, but this time I'm sure what she says is true. They're going to have King put down.'

'Have you slipped your trolley? The King of where? And who's going to depose him?'

Impatience dried Fliss' tears. 'No, you don't understand. Not *the* king. King, my horse. Selina will have him sent for slaughter.'

'All right, calm down,' said Maddie, soothingly. 'Tell me exactly what Hilary said.'

'She said the only way I'd see anything more of King is if I bought the right tin of dog food.'

'She actually said that?'

'I just told you, didn't I?' said Fliss, exasperated.

'OK. Don't get snitty. I meant that she actually used the name "King"?'

'Yes.'

Maddie pulled at her chin. 'Interesting!'

'No it's not, it's disastrous.'

Maddie was patience personified. 'No, it's interesting because if I didn't know your horse's name was King how did Hilary? You're not best mates, are you?'

'No,' said Fliss, suddenly interested herself. 'I've never told anyone here that, I'm sure. And remember the way she knew about what had happened to me in my first bath here?'

'She been opening your letters, do you think?'

'No, of course not. You know I never get any.'

'Dead fishy!' Maddie thought for a moment. 'It's got to be Miss Ames, then. She knows all about you and Selina, doesn't she? Hilary's enough of a sniveller to be in her pocket.'

'Oh yes,' said Fliss. 'That must be it.'

'All the same,' Maddie said, stroking her chin again, 'It won't do any harm to check.'

In pursuance of the plan they had formulated, Fliss made sure that she was well scrubbed and that her uniform was impeccable when she tapped timidly on the door of Miss Ames' study. On being bidden to enter, she did so and closed the door behind her.

Agnes Ames looked up from her paperwork. 'Yes, Felicity?'

'Please, Miss Ames, I was wondering if I would be allowed to write an extra letter?'

'To whom?'

'Oh, no one different. Just Selina Doyle again.'

'Why do you want to write an extra letter?'

'I just wanted to make sure that King was being looked after.'

'King?'

'My dog.'

Miss Ames peered at her over the top of her steel-rimmed spectacles and Fliss' heart stopped beating under that piercing gaze, then Miss Ames said, 'Very well. I'm sure King is being well treated, but you may write if it will set your mind at rest. Close the door behind you.'

Fliss could hardly prevent herself from running back to her room, where Maddie was waiting for her. 'It's not her!' she gasped. 'I told her King was a dog, like you said, and she didn't bat an eye.'

'Curiouser and curiouser,' Maddie mused. 'Could Hilary be in direct contact with Selina, do you think?'

'I don't know. What do you think?'

'I think we'll never know unless we take a chance. Are you game for a daring plan?'

'Yes, if it's one of yours.' Fliss was quite sure about that.

'Come huddle with me then, child,' said Maddie, 'and listen . . .'

Hilary in the throes of deep sleep was an even less appetising sight than Hilary awake, if that were possible. In the dim light of Maddie's pencil torch, she lay on her back with her mouth open, snoring gently.

'Sleeping beauty waiting for the Prince's kiss,' breathed Maddie to Fliss at her side. 'She'd wait a long time, don't you think? You got all the stuff?'

Fliss nodded, not trusting herself to pitch her own voice as softly as Maddie's.

'Right! I'll nod three times, remember, and on the third nod, we do it, OK?'

149

Fliss nodded again.

The effect on Hilary of being roused from peaceful slumber by the coordinated attack which followed must have been terrifying and completely disorienting. As Maddie vaulted on to her recumbent body, trapping her arms at her sides beneath the bedclothes, Fliss thrust the red ball gag which she had so recently worn into Hilary's still open mouth, quickly buckling the leather bridle over and behind her head. Working together, they rolled Hilary over on to her face. Maddie pulled her arms back behind her and Fliss secured her wrists together with handcuffs. The rest was easy and could be taken at a more leisurely pace. They rolled the fat body over again and sat Hilary up on the edge of the bed. They pulled a duvet cover over her head and down to her waist, where they secured it with a cord then they sat on either side of her to get their breath back.

Hilary writhed and twisted her body about, shaking her head in a fruitless endeavour to be rid of the blinding duvet cover until Maddie hissed in her ear. 'Listen, you. I've got a big hat pin in my hand and if you don't stop jigging about I'm going to jab it into your fat bum. Understand?'

Fliss knew that Maddie had no such implement but Hilary didn't and froze into immobility at once.

'Now we're going for a little walk,' Maddie went on. 'You're not going to give me any trouble at all because you don't want me to use you as a pincushion, do you?'

The shrouded head shook vigorously.

'Get up, then, and come with us.'

With Fliss and Maddie on either side of her gripping her upper arms, Hilary went with them obediently enough. They led her through the broad corridors, instructing her when they came to steps or other obstacles. They paused for a moment while Maddie picked the lock on the door which led to the turret room then they were in the passageway and could breathe again as

150

Maddie locked the door behind them. Hilary stumbled a little on the steep stairs but at last they had her in Agnes Ames' pleasure room and locked that door behind them, too.

By prior arrangement they left her standing while they went to the cocktail cabinet and poured drinks for themselves. As Maddie had known it would be, this treatment was most effective. Hilary had been expecting dreadful things. What she had not been expecting was that nothing would happen and her unease was made plain by her shifting about and head-shaking. They watched the hooded figure as they took their time over finishing their drinks then they approached noiselessly. The shock of being touched so unexpectedly made Hilary leap nervously and she trembled as they unwound the cord and removed the duvet cover. Her eyes above the gag widened in surprise and horror as she took in her surroundings.

'Ah!' said Maddie. 'I see even you didn't know about this place. I've brought you here because I feel in the mood to torture someone tonight and I've chosen you. No special reason for that. It's just that when the moon is full, I get these urges and I just have to satisfy them. You do understand, don't you?' Maddie's sinister, lunatic chuckle sounded entirely authentic and would have curdled the blood of a heroine. Hilary was no heroine.

'But first,' Maddie went on. 'We have to get you nice and naked, so that I can get at your juiciest bits.' She turned away to cross the room and when she came back she was holding a large pair of dressmaking scissors which she snipped menacingly in the air. Stooping, she took the hem of Hilary's regulation nightdress in her left hand and snipped at it with the scissors in her right. Grasping both sides of the snip she ripped suddenly upwards so that the material parted with a loud, rasping noise and Hilary's plump pink knees, thighs and stomach came into view in the flapping rent. The seam beneath her bust held until Maddie snipped again, sliding the scissors up between her breasts then ripping again. This time, the tear connected with the neck of the nightdress and it fell apart, exposing the whole of the front of Hilary's body.

Passing behind her, she inserted one tip of the scissors into the cuff of her long sleeve and snipped upwards, following Hilary's outer arm until she arrived at the shoulder then cutting across to the neck. When she did the same thing with the other sleeve the nightdress fell away, leaving her victim completely naked. Maddie stalked around Hilary in a slow circle, staring at her, to her acute embarrassment then stopped in front of her.

'Hmm!' she said. 'I think you're ready. Do you know,' she added, conversationally, 'I've never been able to use absolutely everything in this room on one person. It's so disappointing. They always faint before I've finished.' The goose-pimples as Hilary's flesh crawled were clear evidence of the fact that she believed that.

Maddie's frown turned to an insane beam. 'But you're made of sterner stuff. You'll give me good sport, I'm sure. Come over here and take a look at all these goodies.' She led Hilary by the arm around the room. 'See here. We have a pillory for your neck and wrists; and here's a big oak "X" with straps to fix you on it. Then there's the trapezes to hang you upside down or however I fancy and this padded bench to strap you down on, face down or face up.'

Maddie's voice became livelier with crazy enthusiasm as she led Hilary to the large table. 'Look at all these,' she said, picking up the implements one by one, then laying them down again. 'There's a cane and a leather whip; a strap and a birch. Want to try these springy clamps on your nipples now? No? Well, how about these screw clamps? Oh well, later perhaps. We'll start off gently. I'll just redden up your bum a bit with this table-tennis bat. Bend over!' Hilary shook her head violently and made grunting sounds through her nose.

'Don't want to?' Maddie was obliging. 'All right, no need. It's just that, if you bend over, I'll give you twelve, and if you don't I'll give you thirty-six. It's up to you, of course, but I shall be very upset if you spin out the lesser beatings then go and faint on me before I can give you all the sterner ones.'

With only a moment's hesitation, Hilary bent far forward, her plump breasts hanging and sagging, pear-shaped, towards the carpet, her handcuffed wrists in the small of her back, leaving the target of her plump bottom completely clear. Maddie administered the promised twelve strokes with a firm hand, each one delivered with a stinging, slicing action which quickly reddened the bare, pink buttocks and made them wobble and dance with every blow.

Grasping Hilary by the hair, Maddie pulled her upright. She stood, breathing hard through her nose, her eyes bright with tears. 'Now Fliss is going to take your gag out,' Maddie said. 'Don't worry about screaming. I like to hear it. No one else will, though. This room is quite soundproof.' She turned away and went across to the other side of the room to rummage among the equipment there.

Fliss removed the red ball gag and its securing bridle and Hilary worked her stretched mouth. She stared anxiously at Fliss. 'What's this all about? What's got into her?' She nodded towards Maddie's unseeing, unheeding back.

Fliss lowered her voice to a conspiratorial whisper. 'I thought everybody knew about her. She goes with the moon, you know. One day she's perfectly normal, then comes the full moon and she goes off into one of her insane rages. Just humour her and I'm sure it will be all right. At least,' she added, pensively, 'I'm fairly sure it will be all right.'

'Oh God!' Hilary moaned, then stared in horror. 'What's she doing now?'

153

Fliss turned to look at Maddie who was striding up and down, muttering to herself and brandishing a huge knife. 'Oh dear!'

'Oh dear?' quavered Hilary. 'What does "Oh dear!" mean?'

'I hoped she'd forgotten about that. She's been reading about the Death of a Thousand Cuts,' Fliss said. 'You remember? Red Indians used to do it.'

'Do what?'

'Snip bits off people.'

Hilary turned a delicate shade of green. 'Snip . . .' she stammered. 'Snip . . . bits! What bits?'

'No special bits. Just bits.' Fliss scissored her fingers in the air. 'Sort of here and there all over. Don't worry, though. I'm sure I can talk her out of it. Trust me and do what she says.'

Maddie came back to them. So great was Hilary's relief at seeing that she had put down the knife that she almost welcomed the sight of the leather cuffs Maddie was carrying. Hilary did not even demur when the two girls went behind her and buckled one cuff about each wrist above the handcuffs, then led her across the room to the great oaken 'X' on the wall beside the fireplace. A wide, low stool stood at its foot and, mindful of Fliss' injunction to humour the insane Maddie, Hilary stepped up on to it when bidden and turned her back to the 'X'. Mounting the stool with her, Maddie and Fliss unfastened the handcuffs then raised her arms wide and high to the top corners of the 'X', clipping the leather cuffs to rings there. Working quickly and using straps already attached to the structure in the appropriate places, they buckled them around her upper arms and waist. They made her straddle her legs, then fastened more straps around her thighs, knees and ankles so that she was held in a wide-stretched and completely defenceless pose; only the tips of her toes on the stool. When Maddie pulled the stool away, even that support was denied her and she hung in the straps, her pink flesh bulging over them.

Hilary's voice was even more shaky, now. 'What are you going to do to me?'

Maddie's sinister laugh chilled her to the marrow. 'You'll see! Or, rather, you won't see. Blindfold her, Fliss!'

Fliss pulled the stool a little closer and climbed on it to pass an elasticated, padded blindfold over Hilary's head. She paused when the blindfold rested on Hilary's forehead and, with her mouth close to Hilary's ear, she hissed, 'Don't worry. I won't let her do anything, you know.'

'Thank you! Oh, thank you!'

With Hilary's view temporarily blocked by Fliss' head, Maddie took the opportunity to squeeze a little toothpaste onto her finger and work it around her teeth with her tongue until it foamed up, so that the last thing Hilary saw before Fliss pulled down the blindfold was the menacing figure of Maddie advancing towards her, huge knife in hand. She was muttering to herself, her face was twitching uncontrollably and the corners of her mouth were flecked with foam.

As soon as Maddie was sure that the blindfold was in place, she whirled around, went back to the side table and put down the knife. From the refrigerator in the cocktail cabinet, she took an ice cube, then came across to stand with Fliss in front of their unsuspecting victim.

At a nod from Maddie, Fliss said, 'Now Maddie, be sensible. You know you can't do that. Be good and put down the knife.' Her voice rose to a shriek. 'No, Maddie! No! You mustn't!'

Maddie leaned forward and swiped the ice cube three times across the naked pink belly in front of her face. Hilary let out a great howl of terror and her whole body jumped and twitched as far as her bondage would allow.

Fliss and Maddie clung together, grunting and straining

as though there was a struggle taking place. 'No, Maddie! I won't let you! That's enough!'

'Why are you trying to protect her?' shouted Maddie. 'You know she hates you.'

'No, she doesn't! Not really. You don't hate me, do you Hilary? Tell her you don't hate me.'

'I don't hate her! I don't!' Hilary screamed. Melted ice-water trickling down her plump stomach added to her frenzy.

'She must do,' Maddie sounded unconvinced. 'Why would she do and say all those nasty things to you if she doesn't?'

Fliss wavered. 'I suppose you're right. I can't think of any other reason.'

'There is a reason! There is!' Hilary's words tumbled over themselves to get out.

'What reason?' said Maddie, suspiciously.

'Someone told me to. Someone paid me to.'

'Pah!' Maddie snorted. 'I don't believe that for a moment. Let go of my arm, Fliss!'

'No, Maddie! Wait just a minute. Give her a chance. Who paid you, Hilary?'

'Selina Doyle. She wanted me to watch you all the time and to make trouble for you.'

There was a pause while the two conspirators eyed one another in triumph and relief before they returned to the job in hand.

'No,' Maddie said, then more decisively, 'No! She's just saying that. She can't prove it.'

'I can! I can! I've got letters she sent me. They're under my mattress.'

'No,' Maddie said. 'She's lying to save her skin. That can't be true. Miss Ames sees all the mail. She couldn't get letters direct.'

Hilary's voice rose to an imploring squeak. 'I did. I swear it. Miss Ames got some, too.'

'Huh! If that's true, where are they.'

'In the grey filing cabinet in her office. Second drawer down. A red folder right at the back.'

'I'll check this, you know,' Maddie growled. 'If you're lying to me ...'

'I'm not! I swear it!'

'We'll see.' Leaving Hilary where she was, Maddie and Fliss left the turret room and made their way back down into the main part of the school. The lock on Miss Ames' office door was no match for Maddie's burglary kit and neither was the lock on the filing cabinet. There was a red folder, just where Hilary had said it would be. Maddie laid it down on the big desk, opened it and examined the contents by the light of her pencil torch.

'Is it any good?' asked Fliss, craning over her shoulder.

'Any good! It's pure dynamite and it's going to blow you right out of this Hell-hole. And me with you, I hope. Come on. Let's collect Hilary's letters as well.'

Later, in the comparative security of Maddie's bedroom, they laid their trophies out on the bed and examined them more closely. 'Well, it's all here,' said Maddie. 'Conspiracy; theft; embezzlement. Selina's letters to Miss Ames. And look, Aggie's even signed her own copies of her letters to Selina. How obliging!'

'But what good are they if we're trapped on the island?' said Fliss, puzzled.

'We're trapped, but these letters needn't be. It's Fergus' day today. He won't take me off the island. I've tried that before. But I'm sure he'll take a parcel with these papers in it to a bank on the mainland with instructions to send them to the Police if we don't come in person to collect them in, say, two weeks.'

'Of course,' said Fliss, admiringly. 'But what about Hilary? She'll spill the beans.'

'Not if they can't find her, she won't. They'll never think of looking in the turret room. Not until it's too late, anyway. We only need a few hours, then we're safe and they can talk to Hilary all they like. Come on, let's raid the kitchen for some food then we can lock her in. She'll have food, water and a bathroom. She'll be quite safe there for a while.'

When they returned to the turret room, Hilary was still hanging in her straps on the great wooden 'X' where they had left her. Fliss climbed on to the stool and removed the blindfold then both girls stood back and watched with keen interest as she craned her head to stare down at her entirely unmarked stomach. The expressions which flitted across her face were worthy of their attention. Apprehension turned to disbelief then, as she raised her head to look for answers she saw Maddie looking perfectly sane and grinning all over her face. At that point, realisation dawned that she had been well and truly duped and red-faced rage become predominant.

'You bitches!' she screamed, her face contorted with anger. 'What have you made me do?'

Maddie laughed aloud. 'You've given us the key of the door, Hilary, and we're truly grateful.'

Hilary's fat body was quivering as she strained to get at them. 'I'll get you both for this,' she shrieked. 'I don't care how long it takes, I'll . . .'

Maddie laid a finger to her lips. 'Ssh! Not so loud! You'll burst a blood vessel. You don't want Miss Ames to find you, do you? After what you've done to her, to say that she is going to be a teensy bit pissed off with you is a bit of an understatement. Remember how handy she is with that cane when she's not upset. Imagine how she'll be when she's hopping mad! You don't really want her to find you, do you?'

Hilary paled at the prospect and fell silent. 'No!' she whispered with feeling.

'That's better,' Maddie said. 'Then we'll help you out by hiding you here until things cool off. But if we do that for you, you'll have to co-operate and not kick up a fuss when we let you down. Is that a deal?'

158

'All right,' Hilary said, sulkily. 'But let me down, will you? These straps are beginning to be uncomfortable.'

'Presently,' Maddie glanced at her watch. 'We've got an hour or so to kill and you've been so good to us that we thought we'd give you a little parting gift.'

Hilary gazed at them suspiciously. 'What sort of gift?'

'Well, since you're hung up there with your legs open and your pussy so readily available, we might tickle you a bit and give you your jollies.'

'What! No! You can't! I don't feel like it. I'm too upset.'

'Oh dear!' said Maddie, soothingly. 'We can't have that, can we? Let's see if we can massage your cares away.' She stepped close to her captive so that her face was only inches away from bright red hairs which adorned her crotch and blew gently on them.

'No, please!' Hilary begged. 'Don't do it. I really don't want it.'

'Your mouth says that, Hilary, but your pussy is saying something quite different. Look at this, Fliss. What do you reckon? Is that a clitoris beginning to bulge, or isn't it?'

Fliss bent close to get a better view. 'Mmm! Difficult to tell.'

Red faced again, this time not with rage but with embarrassment, Hilary strained her head back to avoid seeing them and closed her eyes.

'Come on, Hilary. Don't be coy,' Maddie said. 'We'll even let you choose how we do it. Would you like a straightforward finger-fuck or a dildo? We have lots for you to choose from.'

Hilary bit her lip in chagrin at the effect she could feel these words having on her lower body. Before the interested gaze of her tormentors, the bright pink clitoral hood swelled enormously, until there was no possible doubt as to what was happening beneath it.

'There! Look at that!' said Maddie with satisfaction.

'And she said she wasn't in the mood. I wonder if she's wet, too?'

'Perhaps I should put my finger in and see,' Fliss said.

'No!' Hilary's head was forward again as she craned to watch what they were doing. 'Don't do that! Don't touch me, please! Don't . . . Oh! Ooh!' The intrusion of Fliss' right forefinger into her soaking vagina caused ripples of anticipation to pass over her rounded belly, making it shudder and twitch.

Maddie placed her thumbs on either side of Hilary's outer labia and stretched them apart so that her clitoris emerged, already thrusting beyond it's protective sheath. Maddie stared in genuine surprise. 'Golly, Fliss!' she said. 'Have you ever seen one as big as that?'

Fliss' experience in such matters was severely limited, but she was forced to agree that Hilary's clitoris was extraordinarily large. 'It's as big as my thumb.'

'Just like a little penis,' Maddie said. 'I wonder if it behaves like one?'

She grasped the short shaft of the pink protuberance between finger and thumb and began to masturbate it slowly and with an infinitely delicate touch, eliciting groans from Hilary which were not entirely of humiliation and anguish.

'See! It does!' Maddie said, drawing a little to one side so that Fliss could see better. 'It's already grown some more!'

'Oh God!' Hilary moaned, her plump hips making involuntary circling movements as far as they could within the confines of her bonds. 'What are you doing to me?'

'Why Hilary,' said Maddie, smiling up into her face with mock innocence while she continued her movements. 'I thought you knew. We're subjecting you to forcible masturbation and we're going to keep doing that until you come.'

These words had the stimulating effect on Hilary

which Maddie had known they would. Hilary clenched her teeth and drew in her breath with a sharp hiss, the ripples across her belly becoming more pronounced. She fought madly to control what she was feeling, closing her eyes again and shaking her head vehemently in denial.

'I won't come! I won't give you the satisfaction. You can't make me.'

'No?' Maddie continued her irritating manipulation while Fliss exchanged one finger for two and pumped both slowly up and down. 'Not even if I do this?' Without stopping her right-handed masturbation, she raised her left and tapped a light, rapid, Morse-code message right on the tip of Hilary's very exposed and very erect clitoris.

The effect was instantaneous. Hilary's eyes and mouth shot open and she began a series of hoarse screams and grunts in time with her pronounced pelvic thrusts. 'No! Oh no, please,' she begged. 'Don't do that! Don't touch me there! Oh! Oh! You're making me . . . I'm going to . . . Oh God! Yes! Yes!! Do it! Do it! I'm coming. Ooh! Ooh!'

With a great, gasping shudder, she let down profusely, spending floods of slippery liquid which flowed over Fliss' hand as well as her intrusive fingers. When it was over she hung exhausted in her straps, her head lolling forward and her mouth hanging open.

Maddie and Fliss took her down and allowed her to sit on a chair at the table to recover. She flopped forward, resting her head on her forearms.

'We're going to leave you, now,' Maddie said. 'We've left you food and you'll find a bathroom through there. Be a good girl and behave yourself. You're safer here than anywhere else, right at the moment.'

They went out of the room. Maddie closed the door behind them then knelt with her burglar tool at the lock. Usually so quick at such tasks, she seemed to take a little longer over this one and Fliss said, 'What are you doing?'

'Busting the lock,' Maddie replied over her shoulder. 'Well, not busting it really. Just misplacing one of the tumblers so that the right key won't work. Just in case anyone comes this way.' She rose, dusting her knees. 'I'll do the same to the one at the bottom of the stairs as a double security. Anyone trying it will just think it's not working. By the time they've sent for a locksmith, we'll have done the necessary.'

'OK,' said Fliss. 'What comes next?'

'Well, I think we can say you're finished for the night. Look! It's just getting light. You get back to your room and get some sleep while you can.'

'What are you going to do?' Fliss asked.

'Sneak out now while the coast is clear and wait for Fergus down at the boathouse. I'll parcel up the papers first and write a note to go with them, then I'll be off.'

They parted and Fliss went back to her room as advised. Still dressed, she threw herself down on the bed and tried to sleep but, tired as she was, sleep would not come. She tossed and turned and imagined a host of scenarios, each more dreadful than the last. Maddie had been caught sneaking out by some early-rising tutor. Fergus' boat had broken down and he was drifting out to sea while Maddie and her papers waited and looked for him in vain.

It was quite a relief when the bell rang which signified that it was time to get up and dress. She splashed water on her face and pulled her clothes into some semblance of order, glad of the minor distraction. When she went down to breakfast she was able to appear almost normal.

Nemesis arrived in the shape of Miss Ames during the first class of the day. Fliss' heart sank as she watched the formidable figure enter the Art Appreciation classroom and whisper to Miss Blair, the tutor in charge.

From the way both pairs of eyes turned on her, Fliss knew that she was the subject of the conversation.

Sure enough, when it ended, Miss Blair called to her. 'Felicity. Go with Miss Ames, please!'

With anxious foreboding, Fliss followed her through the maze of corridors and into her office. Miss Ames closed the door behind them, locked it then went across to her desk and seated herself behind it.

She pointed at the strip of carpet in front of the desk. 'Stand there please, Felicity. Now, what is it that you have to tell me?'

Fliss was annoyed to find that her face had begun to burn with a bright red glow. 'I ... I ... Nothing, Miss Ames.'

Agnes Ames stared straight into her eyes and Fliss could feel that gaze rifling through all the compartments of her brain, throwing great shafts of laser light on to many guilty secrets. Her colour heightened. Unable to meet that gaze with boldness, she dropped her head and shuffled her feet.

'This morning, Hilary and Madeleine were nowhere to be found. Tell me what you know about them.'

Fliss was acutely aware that she was no use at all when it came to lying. Maddie would have been able to deal with this situation with ease and probably turn it to her own advantage. Fliss could only squirm and stammer, tears not far away.

'Please Miss Ames ... Please Miss ... I can't!'

'Can't or won't?'

Fliss shook her head, dumbly.

'I see! Very well, then. We've been in this situation before, haven't we, Felicity. You know what is required of you. Raise your skirt, please. Yes, you know how to do that. All the way round, back and front. Now drop your knickers, please, and bend over the desk.'

This was dreadful! Fliss obeyed the instructions, raising her skirt and pulling her knickers down to mid-thigh, baring her bottom for what was to come. She shuffled forward and laid her upper body across the broad desk, reaching forward to grasp the far side. With deliberate cruelty, Miss Ames left her in that ignominious posture while she went to a cupboard and brought out the instruments of chastisement. With a sinking feeling in the pit of her stomach, Fliss saw that this time there were other items besides a cane. There was a well-worn, rubber-soled gym slipper, a leather strap and another, broader strap which was divided into several strands at the end.

Miss Ames laid these things on the desk in front of her face. 'We shall start with a hand spanking, of course. That goes without saying. I can't tell you how many you will get. It's early in the day and it may take some while for my arm to get tired.' She picked up the slipper and flexed it. 'From there, I shall move on to the slipper. When your bottom is nicely sore and glowing, I shall cane you, then use the strap and the tawse. And in case you think that will be the end of the matter, I shall then call my assistant, Miss Moncrieff, who will start all over again and perform the same sequence. By the time she has finished, I shall be refreshed and ready to repeat the dose. Between us, we can keep on all day. Which will give way first, do you think? Your obstinacy, or the skin of your bottom?'

Fliss shuddered and braced herself, biting her lip. She was determined not to reveal anything to this woman but she was uncertain of the extent to which she could bear the pain which was to come. Her last beating had been mild by comparison with what had just been described. She only hoped she could hold out.

Miss Ames came around the desk and stood to Fliss' left, as before. Fliss felt her fingers hook into the ruffled material of her knickers and draw them down to her knees, signalling that not only her buttocks but the backs of her thighs were to be targets. Her skin in those

164

areas twitched and crawled in awful anticipation, yet there was nothing she could do. If she struggled, Miss Ames would simply send for Miss Moncrieff and other tutors and have her held in position for punishment.

Fliss did the only thing open to her which was to hang on to the desk with whitened knuckles, close her eyes and wait for the first stinging blow.

165

Eight

To Fliss, who had been expecting something quite different, the knock at the door was such a shock that she jumped convulsively as if she had been struck and almost lost her grip on the edge of the desk. She remained where she was, not daring to move as Miss Ames went to the door and unlocked it. Unable to see what was taking place behind her, Fliss was acutely aware of the embarrassing exposure of her naked hindquarters to the gaze of whoever was talking in a low voice to Miss Ames.

The first clue she had as to what was happening was when she heard Miss Ames say more clearly, 'Thank you, Miss Moncrieff. I can deal with this now. You may go. Madeleine, you will come over and stand by your accomplice.'

So Maddie had been caught, after all! How long had she been a prisoner? Was she caught on the way out, or on the way back in? The difference was crucial!

Miss Ames resumed her seat behind the desk. 'I will ask you the same question I asked Felicity. Have you anything to tell me about Hilary's disappearance?'

Maddie appeared to think hard. 'You know,' she said slowly, 'I don't think I have.'

'Very well. If that's your attitude, you shall join Felicity over the desk. Skirt up and knickers down, please.'

'Nice invitation, but I'll decline, I think,' Maddie's voice was cool and casual. 'And do get up and pull your knickers up, Fliss. You look ridiculous with your bum stuck up in the air like that.'

'Stay where you are, Felicity,' Miss Ames snapped. 'Madeleine, if you have some idea of overwhelming me by force, you can forget about it. I have only to call out and help will be here in seconds. Do you want me to do that?'

Maddie shrugged. 'Please yourself, Aggie. Before you do, though, I should have a look in your grey filing cabinet.'

'What?' Miss Ames was genuinely bewildered.

'You heard. Take a look. Second drawer down. Red folder at the back.'

Miss Ames face drained of all colour and she stared hard at Madeleine for long seconds before she turned away and crossed hastily to the grey cabinet in the corner of the office. Producing a key from her pocket, she had a little difficulty in fitting it into the lock. Trembling with impatience mingled with apprehension, she tore open the drawer and plunged both hands inside.

Her face even more ashen, she turned to face the two girls. 'What have you done with it?'

'Don't panic, Aggie,' said Maddie. 'It's as safe as if it was in the bank. In fact,' she added, 'that's exactly where it is. In a bank on the mainland with a note to say that if we don't collect it in two weeks' time it's to be sent to the Police.'

'How much do you two know about what's in that folder?'

'Enough!' Maddie said. 'Isn't that right, Fliss?'

Fliss, who had just finished rearranging her clothing, nodded vehemently in agreement.

Maddie continued, 'By "enough" I mean enough to put you and Selina Doyle and probably Hilary, too, behind bars for a very long time.'

'Oh my God!' Agnes Ames came back to her desk and collapsed into her chair. She leaned her elbows on the desk and buried her face in her hands.

'However,' Maddie went on, 'that needn't necessarily happen. It's up to you.'

167

Miss Ames raised her head and a little of her colour returned. 'Of course,' she said. 'If there has been any misunderstanding between us, I'm sure we can talk about it and resolve it.'

'Mm! Exactly what I had in mind,' said Maddie, encouragingly. 'No need to involve the Law.'

Miss Ames was recovering her composure now that a tiny fragment of hope had appeared on the horizon. 'Good!' she said. 'You know, of course, that if there is anything I can do to ...'

'Funny you should say that, Aggie, because there is something you can do right away.'

'Of course, of course.' Miss Ames smile was creamy and ingratiating. 'You have only to say the word.'

'Well, it was more than one word I had in mind,' said Maddie. 'In fact, the words I was thinking of were, "Come round this side of the desk, pull your dress up and get your knickers down." Perhaps you'd like to do that for us now?'

Miss Ames' mouth fell open in astonishment. 'I beg your pardon!'

'We accept your apology,' Maddie said, deliberately misunderstanding. 'But it's not enough. We need some tangible sign of contrition, don't we, Fliss?'

Fliss, who had been just as astonished at what she had heard as Miss Ames, could only nod in agreement again.

Miss Ames prevaricated. 'But surely, you can't mean that I ... That you ... It's preposterous and I won't do it.'

Maddie shrugged again. 'Please yourself. I was only trying to keep you out of trouble. Would you rather deal with us or with the Courts?'

'But it is so inappropriate for a respectable woman of my age to undress herself in front of others.'

'Ooh! Porky pies, Aggie! Your nose will grow. That's not what you were saying last time I saw you. On video, that was. At least, I think it was you. Your voice was a bit indistinct because your mouth was buried in Celia Moncrieff's pussy, so you can get down off your high horse and get 'em off!'

Miss Ames' face had now regained all its colour with an added bonus as her face flamed into redness. 'You've been in my room! Oh my God!' She buried her face in her hands again.

'Cheer up!' Maddie said. 'We can keep that secret and others. As long as you don't annoy me too much,' she added, meaningfully.

Miss Ames pulled herself together with an effort. 'I understand,' she said, slowly. 'Not annoying you means doing what you tell me?'

'There! I knew you'd catch on. Now come round here like the naughty girl you are and stand on the carpet.'

Trembling a little and trying to move with dignity, Agnes rose from her chair and stood in front of the desk.

'Good!' said Maddie. 'Hands to sides, please, and stand to attention. That's it. Now then, up with that dress. You know exactly how it should be done, don't you?'

Agnes nodded. Stooping, she grasped the hem of her dress and raised it to waist level, front and back, bunching it to hold it there. Fliss stared at the lower part of her body thus vulgarly displayed. She had expected to see that Agnes Ames practised what she preached and wore sensible, matronly underclothes. To her surprise, what were now revealed to her interested gaze proved to be lacy, black, French knickers. Not only that, but instead of the expected pantihose, Agnes was wearing black stockings held up by what appeared to be quite an abbreviated black suspender belt.

Maddie, too was impressed. 'Well, what have we here?' she said, bending a little so as to make it obvious to Miss Ames that she was being scrutinised. 'That puts a different complexion on things. Perhaps we ought to see what other outrageous garments you favour, Aggie. What do you think, Fliss? Should she take the dress right off?'

'Oh, I think so.'

'Right! Off with it then, Aggie!'

Miss Ames' discomfiture was apparent. 'Please, no! Surely this is enough?'

'No it's not! Take off the dress and look sharp about it!'

Resignedly, Agnes dropped the part of the green dress she was holding and unbuttoned it. She crossed her arms, grasped the hem and drew the garment off over her head, revealing that her breasts were encased in an equally feminine brassière; black and silky on the underside of the cups, but transparent and lacy on the upper part so that her brown nipples were clearly delineated through the material.

'Fold your dress neatly and put it on the desk!' ordered Maddie. 'You know, of course, that only regulation underwear is to be worn? Of course you do. What am I thinking of? After all, it was you who made the rules, wasn't it?'

Maddie leaned forward and stroked one black bra strap between finger and thumb. 'Off!' she said.

Agnes reached behind her and, after a short struggle, unclipped the offending garment and slid it down her arms.

'Put it on the desk with your dress! No! Don't hide yourself with your arms. Stand up straight! Now let's have a look at you. I expect you'd prefer to keep your knickers on, wouldn't you?'

Agnes looked at her with a mixture of gratitude and hope. 'Yes, please!'

'Tough!' said Maddie. 'Put them on the desk with your other things.'

Utterly defeated, Agnes hung her head as she hooked

her thumbs into the elasticated waistband of her French knickers and pulled them down to mid-thigh, revealing an attractive expanse of white bottom which they had as yet seen only in the form of a video recording. That recording did not, Fliss thought, do Miss Ames full justice. The jiggling movements of her buttocks and breasts as she bent and stood on one foot to take the things off emphasised the fact that she had a voluptuous and sexually attractive body; nothing to be ashamed of.

Fliss watched her remove her lower covering with mixed feelings. Part of her rejoiced in the triumphant sensation of revenge. Another part of her recalled the humiliation of having to go through just such a ritual so that she experienced a pang of sympathy. She hardened her heart. This woman was part of the conspiracy against her; no better than a common thief. Whatever happened to her was justly deserved.

Maddie was speaking again. 'My, my, Agnes! You really are hairy down there. Don't you ever wax? We've all learned from you that such a growth is unhygienic. It'll have to come off, you know. But not right now,' she went on, as Agnes buried her face in her hands again. 'Ours were public, as well as pubic shaves, so I think yours ought to be the same. Now bend over the desk! Legs apart!'

The sight of Agnes Ames bent in the subservient posture of one about to be spanked, her naked breasts flattened against the cold, hard surface of the desk, caused little quivers of excitement in Fliss' lower stomach. She noticed that her vagina was liquefying spontaneously as she gazed at that perfect bottom, so invitingly presented and vulnerable to anything they might care to do to it. The exact centre of the two flawless orbs of her bottom cheeks was marked by a fascinating crease which was filled with a forest of dark curls; verification of Maddie's assessment of the profuse nature of her pubic hair. At the junction with her thighs, which were parted in accordance with Maddie's instruction, a bulging and even more hairy oval delineated the pouch of her vaginal mound. The black strip of her garter belt which encompassed her narrow waist and the blackness of her stockings against the white flesh of her quivering thighs emphasised her semi-nakedness while they marked the upper and lower limits of the target area. Fliss discovered the greatest possible satisfaction in seeing this authority figure translated into a sacrificial object. The spanker stripped and readied for a spanking. How delicious that thought was!

It was, perhaps, a little alarming to discover in herself a growing excitement. She knew that this excitement was entirely sexual because she could feel it in the depths of her belly and in her vagina. Her nipples, too, were erect and tingling. She knew, also, that it had nothing to do with the administration of fair retribution for Miss Ames' part in the conspiracy to rob her of her inheritance. Fliss could be honest with herself and acknowledge that it would not have mattered who was bent over the desk. What mattered, she fully understood, was that there was a naked bottom presented for her to do with as she wished and what she most earnestly wished to do was to exert power over that bottom; to feel it jump and wobble under her hand as she spanked it with all her strength until it blushed into redness; to see evidence of the discomfort she was causing in the form of cries of pain or, better still, tears from the owner of that bare flesh.

Fliss had always known that there was an element of masochism in her make-up. Her fondness for being tied was clear evidence of that. She had not previously guessed that she might also carry a streak of sadism. If asked, she would have described herself as someone who wouldn't hurt a fly. She drew in her breath and gulped a little as she was forced to recognise what was, for her, an ugly fact. She was very much looking forward to inflicting considerable pain! For a moment, her mind withdrew from such an unpalatable truth and she considered relenting; asking Maddie to allow Miss Ames to get up and dress; forgiving and forgetting. At that prospect, the sexual demon within her released a fresh flood of adrenalin which carried her forward on a tide of lust which she could not deny.

Fliss gulped again and emerged from her reverie to find Maddie looking enquiringly at her flushed face and bright eyes. 'You all right, Fliss?' she asked.

'Yes. Oh yes!' Fliss' heart was thudding now and her hand itched to begin. 'May I be first?'

'Be my guest! I'll take over when you get tired.' Maddie stepped back with a courtly gesture which ushered Fliss to Miss Ames' left side.

Fliss took up her position and braced herself. She saw Miss Ames tighten her grip on the opposite edge of the desk and noted with grim satisfaction that the bare white buttocks were quivering and twitching in anticipation, just as her own had quivered and twitched so recently.

She laid the first blow on the left buttock cheek. It was a little tentative; merely a light slap but Miss Ames grunted and winced. Perhaps it would have been better for her if she had been able to show no emotion because that sound and movement, slight though it was, was enough to turn up the wick of Fliss' recently discovered craving. Her next slap was delivered with more force on the right cheek, producing a distinct gasp and an involuntary knee-jerk which was highly satisfactory.

Fliss paused for a moment and inspected her handiwork. On each side of Miss Ames' bare behind, there was now a clearly delineated red patch. That on the right side was already beginning to show the marks of individual fingers. Fliss was panting with excitement, now. She trembled as she waited as long as she could bear before beginning again. When she did, her slaps were delivered with all the force she could muster. One close after the other, they fell indiscriminately on Miss Ames' buttocks and the backs of her thighs so that these areas quickly ceased to be white and became a fiery red lake. The reflex knee-jerks had become a constant, wriggling movement of torment, while the hissing moans of pain were much more pronounced.

Not enough! Not enough to satisfy Fliss' overwhelming desire. In a frenzy now and close to spontaneous orgasm, she beat harder still, panting with her efforts. 'Scream, you bitch!' then, timing to words to coincide with individual slaps, she panted, 'I want . . . to see . . . tears! I want . . . to hear you . . . howl! Come on, bitch! Scream! Scream!'

Miss Ames' head shot back and her whole body arched in agony. Unable longer to keep her grip on the desk, she released it and used her fists to pound on its surface in front of her face. No longer the icy autocrat, she lost all inhibitions in her anxiety to prevent further pain. Tears rained down her face as she began to babble, 'Stop! For God's sake, mercy! No more! Oh God! Make her stop, please!'

The threatened orgasm overwhelmed Fliss at this complete fulfilment of her sadistic pleasure. The sudden dampening of her underclothing did nothing to diminish the rate or force of her slaps until suddenly she felt her wrist grasped, preventing her from striking again. Through the red mist which had blinded her, she slowly became aware of the fact that it was Maddie who was restraining her while looking at her curiously.

'Hey! Come back, Fliss. You OK?'

Fliss stood, white and shaking. As the rage of lust cleared from her brain she saw, for the first time in proper perspective, the reality of that glowing, tortured bottom. Her own palm was smarting considerably.

She collapsed, sobbing, into Maddie's arms. 'Oh God! Oh Maddie! What have I done?'

'You've given Aggie's bum a thrashing it won't forget in a hurry. There, there! Calm down, kid. It was only what she deserved.'

'No, Maddie. It's not that. You don't understand. It's ... I ...' Fliss was quite unable to put her emotions into words. How could she explain the trauma of the self-discovery process through which she had just passed and her guilt at the way in which she had allowed this new passion for sadism to overwhelm her normal psyche?

'I can't explain,' she confessed, defeated.

Maddie embraced her, patting her heaving shoulders. 'Don't worry about it. No explanation necessary. You just got carried away, which isn't surprising after what's been going on. You achieved an object, anyway. Watch this.'

She detached herself, went around the desk and sat in the chair then leant forward to give herself a face-level view of their victim. 'My turn now,' she said, with slow emphasis.

Miss Ames clasped her hands in an attitude of prayer. 'No! No! I beg you, please! You couldn't!'

'You know I could and I would. I can spank harder than she can, too. And I will unless you do what you're told from now on.'

'Yes! Yes! Anything! Can I get up now?'

'No! Stay where you are for a minute while we talk. I don't want to have all the trouble of stripping you off again if things don't work out.'

'But they will! You'll see!'

'OK then, here's the deal. You understand that we'll be leaving here soon?' The tear-stained face before her nodded in acquiescence.

'We shall be going to visit Selina Doyle. She is not to be warned about what's happened. You will show me where the telephone line to the mainland comes in and we'll cut it off. Understand?'

175

Miss Ames nodded again. 'Agreed.'

'Before we go, there are some scores to be settled with some members of your staff. You will see to it that they offer themselves for punishment and give us no trouble.'

'I'm not sure that . . .'

'Let's say a prayer for your powers of persuasion,' Maddie interrupted. 'Because if they don't co-operate, it's your arse and your prison sentence.'

'All right. I'll try.'

'After we've left, you will not continue to run this school in the same way. We'll check from time to time. There will be no more compulsory sex-baths; no more pubic shaves; no more spankings or canings. Look, Aggie,' Maddie continued in a more conciliatory tone, 'you run a fine school apart from those things. The food; the education; the games. They're all fine and just as they should be. You can keep your secret room and still play sex-games, but only with members of staff who are inclined that way. Leave the pupils strictly out of it. And import a few blokes from the mainland from time to time for a dance or a social evening. Run like that, you'll double or treble your numbers.'

'But I must keep order! There must be discipline!'

'So there will be. The worst punishment anyone could get in a school like yours would be to be expelled.'

'I see,' said Miss Ames, slowly. 'I'll think about it.'

'You'll do better than that,' said Maddie. 'You'll do it. Keep your part of the deal and, as far as we are concerned, there is no need for any of the girls to know about what has happened today or will happen soon. You can keep it entirely between you and your staff. The only girl who knows anything is Hilary, and I assume she won't be staying.'

'Why won't she?'

'Because it was Hilary who sold you down the river. She was the one who told us where to find the red folder.'

'I see!' Miss Ames digested this information. 'Just where is Hilary?'

176

'Safe from your spite for the moment, and staying where she is until we leave.' She leaned back. 'You can get up and put your clothes on now.'

Nine

The panelled interview room with its padded bench
upon which Fliss had been strapped down for her first
encounter with the bizarre induction procedures of Draco House was occupied again. The five women there
represented the whole of the tutorial staff, apart from
their Principal, whose arrival they were awaiting with
some curiosity. It was not unusual for individuals to be
summoned from their classes for a conference with their
leader but for all of them to be called for at the same
time and for the meeting place to be this room usually
signalled the arrival of a new pupil. This, they knew,
was not the reason on this occasion, giving rise to much
speculation.

All eyes turned to the door when it opened. Miss
Ames came in, closely followed by Maddie and Fliss.
The women nodded among themselves. The mystery
was solved. Obviously these two young women had
committed some heinous breach of the rules and they
were there to ensure that the appropriate discipline was
successfully administered in order to inhibit such con-
duct in the future.

Miss Ames took up a position in the centre of the
room, flanked by the two girls. She braced herself for an
unpleasant task, adopting an air of quiet dignity.
'Thank you for coming, ladies,' she said. 'The first thing
I have to tell you is that there is a grave danger that this
school will be closed down with the consequent loss of
your employment.' The shocked gasp which came sim-

ultaneously from all five women was evidence enough that she now had their full attention.

'Why that should be so is something I cannot reveal,' she went on. 'All I can tell you is that what takes place in the next few hours, however strange it may appear, is critical to the school's survival. All of you, I know, have enjoyed the work and have been well paid. If that work is to be open to you in the future it is essential that you comply without question with any request made by either Felicity or Madeleine. I ask this of you as a matter of personal loyalty to me. Miss Moncrieff? Miss Kelly?' One by one, she elicited bewildered nods from her staff.

'You will now see that I do not ask of you anything I am not prepared to undergo myself.' Miss Ames turned to Maddie. 'You're quite sure you want to go through with this?'

'Oh, quite sure. Start now.'

As Miss Ames began to unbutton her dress, a sigh of amazement came from the onlookers and a couple of them got to their feet as if to protest. She held up a restraining hand. 'Please! I know you don't understand but this is something which has to be done.'

Puzzled, but obedient, the women who had jumped up resumed their seats on the long bench and watched as their headmistress divested herself of the rest of her clothes. Fliss noted that she had abandoned her sexy black underwear in favour of the regulation issue. When she took down her white knickers, the murmur of consternation which could be heard showed that the tutors had seen her marked buttocks, the redness already turning to bruises to show the severity of the spanking she had undergone. They were only now beginning to have some inkling of what would be the nature of the 'strange' things she had talked about.

When Miss Ames was quite naked, Maddie said, 'You know the procedure?' Miss Ames nodded.

'All right. Hands behind you. Legs apart.'

As Miss Ames adopted the ordered pose and Maddie produced a small torch the watching women realised that what they were about to witness was the same humiliating inspection she herself had given to every new pupil. They watched her raise her arms then bend to touch her toes and all became very aware of the procedure which inevitably followed such an inspection. None of them wanted to believe that the austere Miss Ames was about to submit to having her pubic hair shaved off but it was impossible to doubt the evidence of their own eyes when, inspection completed, she gestured to the padded bench and said, 'On there, I suppose?'

Maddie pointed. 'Yes. On there.'

With the same calm dignity which Fliss was beginning to admire, Miss Ames sat on the edge of the bench, swung her legs up, then lay flat on her back. She raised her knees and parted them wide. 'It won't be necessary to strap me down,' she said.

'Oh, but it will,' said Maddie. 'You don't get the full effect otherwise.' She turned to the seated row of tutors. 'You know how this is done, ladies. Do it!'

With eyes as large as saucers, Celia Moncrieff glanced up and down the row, then said, 'Oh, we couldn't!'

Standing alongside her nude victim, Maddie idly flicked one bare nipple with her finger-nail. 'Oh dear, Aggie,' she said. 'They don't want to play. You know what that means?'

Miss Ames propped herself on her elbows and appealed to her reluctant staff. 'Please! Please do what they say. Come and strap me down.'

Without enthusiasm, they got up and came over to the bench. Watching them go through the same process to which she had been subjected, Fliss felt a twinge of sympathy, then that newly discovered imp inside her took over and she could feel nothing but an erotic crav-

180

ing to exert power; to humiliate and hurt. She watched with satisfaction as the leather bands went about Miss Ames' wrists, securing them to the top corners of the table. When the women doubled her up and passed the straps over her thighs, widely separating them and forcing her knees down beside her body, Fliss experienced an internal quiver like a mini-orgasm which made her shift uneasily and rub her thighs together. Miss Ames was now totally exposed. Last time Fliss had seen her naked, it was apparent that her pubic hair was abundant. In this wide-stretched position, it seemed like a forest. Starting almost as far up her stomach as her navel, it marched on down her body and was still profuse when it reached the area around her anus. In the centre of this dark brown bush, her vagina gaped pinkly and obscenely, opened by the straps which strained her thighs down and apart.

Maddie tested the tension on the thigh-straps. 'I think your girls did a half-hearted job. These seem a little loose to me, Aggie. What do you think?'

Miss Ames, already wincing with the hip-dislocating effect Fliss remembered so well, murmured, 'No!'

Maddie bent closer. 'What was that? I didn't quite catch it. "Tighter!" Is that what you said?'

Miss Ames twisted her head as though seeking some way out of her predicament, even while knowing that there was none. 'Yes!' she hissed, through clenched teeth. 'Tighter!'

'You heard her, girls!' Maddie said. 'Get to it!'

As Miss Kelly and Miss Snaith on either side of the bench took up the last remnants of slack, Miss Ames was provoked into a sharp cry of distress then she was rigorously confined, the clenching of her fists and the feeble waving of her lower legs in the air the only movement she could make to indicate the discomfort she was feeling.

Fliss positioned herself at the foot of the bench and

stooped a little to stare at her former tormentor's embarrassing exposure. She told herself that she was doing so simply in order to make it plain to their captive what she was doing and thereby increase her shame. However, she knew the truth to be that she was completely fascinated by what she saw. Miss Ames' inner labial lips were quite large. Pink and wrinkled, they were stretched even more widely apart by the recent tensioning of the straps so that the warm tunnel of her vagina was clearly visible. Fliss noted that, while it was glistening a little, it was not particularly wet. Above it, the fleshy lump with the distinct division at the bottom which was her clitoral hood showed no sign of swelling. Remembering her own discomfiture at the way her body had let her down when similarly placed, Fliss felt a little aggrieved at Miss Ames' apparent self-control and resolved that she would alter that state of affairs shortly. She allowed her eyes to rove downwards to inspect the upturned anus with its surrounding thatch of brown hair. That, too, would receive due attention.

The glint of light on the pubic curls before her caught her attention and her stomach contracted as she thought about what she knew she was about to do. As in the study, when Miss Ames had been bent over her desk, the element of punishment or retribution had faded into insignificance. She was about to shave someone's pubic hair completely off; leave her totally naked. Bald! That Miss Ames was the victim was irrelevant. Anyone would have done. This was pure, sadistic lust. Fliss knew it very well and didn't care. She also knew that for her own complete sexual satisfaction the recipient of that shave had to acknowledge her subservience; feel the humiliation of involuntary arousal as she had done. On an impulse, she pulled her grey sweater off over her head and unclipped her brassière. Sliding it down her arms, she dropped it on the floor with the sweater, allowing her breasts to fall free, the nipples already erect. Leaning forward between the strained thighs she allowed her left breast, apparently by accident, to brush against the forest of pubic curls while she asked, 'Are you ready for me to begin?'

Miss Ames shuddered a little at the touch. 'Yes!' she said, shortly. 'Get it over with.'

Fliss teased a little. 'We don't want to rush, do we? You might miss out on the full effect. Before we start, you'd better tell your friends what I'm going to do, hadn't you?'

'They know!'

'I'm sure they do, but I want you to tell them, just the same.'

Miss Ames shut her eyes tightly. 'Damn you!' she hissed.

This evidence that her captive realised the ignominy of her position gave Fliss a jolt of sensual pleasure which she sought to intensify. 'Come along, Aggie,' she said encouragingly. 'Tell them exactly what I'm going to do. You know you've got to. And look at them when you tell them.'

Miss Ames grimaced then, realising the hopelessness of her position, complied. Raising her head, she stared down between her breasts at the wide-eyed group she could see behind Fliss. 'She's going to shave me!' she gritted, her head falling back.

'No, Aggie, not good enough. Lift up your head again; look at them and tell them what I'm going to shave.'

There was a pause so long that Fliss thought the order would not be obeyed, but then the head was raised again. 'I'm going to have my pubic hair shaved!'

Fliss uttered a patient sigh. 'Oh dear! Still not good enough. I'd better tell you what to say. You have to say, "I've been such a naughty girl that I have to have my pussy shaved." Can you say that?'

Miss Ames rolled her eyes in desperation. 'I can't!' she muttered. 'I can't! Please don't make me!'

Fliss said nothing, but just stared. Miss Ames read no compassion in those eyes. Finally she gave up. With face aflame, she raised her head again. 'I've been such a . . .' she faltered.

'Such a naughty girl!' Fliss encouraged.

' . . . such a naughty girl that I have to have . . . I have to have . . .'

'My pussy shaved!' prompted Fliss.

' . . . my . . . my pussy shaved!' The last two words were almost a shout and, when they were uttered, she dropped her head back again, murmuring, 'Oh God! Oh God!'

Fliss thrilled at this certainty that Miss Ames was shamed and disconcerted. She felt her knickers dampening at the crotch and knew that she was ready to begin.

The clippers were in their rightful place under the table. She brought them out and, holding them ostentatiously in sight, switched them on. The noise they made brought memories flooding back. Her palms began to sweat a little and it was only with difficulty that she restrained herself from going too fast and cutting a great swathe of hair straight away. She laid the cold metal of the clippers on Miss Ames stomach, delighting to see the flesh instinctively recoil.

'Put a pillow under her head, Maddie!' Fliss said. 'I want her to watch!'

With great self-discipline, Fliss contented herself with little, nibbling bites at the upper part of that brown thatch where it blended with the flat, hairless belly, dividing her gaze between two almost equally enjoyable sights. The little curls she stooped to blow away were a joy, but so was the expression on Miss Ames' face. Total subjection and shame were apparent, but was there, too, just the tiniest trace of excitement? For a moment, she moved the clippers down and, not cutting, held the vibrating heel just above that clitoral hood. Yes! There was that tell-tale jerk and now Miss Ames' eyes told of her imminent arousal.

184

Fliss clipped on more rapidly now, though still at a pace which maximised her enjoyment. The pubic mound, deprived of most of its covering, was more clearly delineated, as were the outer labia. She took particular care over the inner thighs, then moved down to her final target. Pressing the humming clippers in closely all around that puckered anus, she noted that Miss Ames' hands and toes were clenching and unclenching; a sure sign that she was susceptible to stimulation in that area.

Then the first stage was done. Fliss put down the clippers with some reluctance but consoled herself with the thought that what was to come would be just as pleasurable; maybe to tormentor and victim as well, she thought. The shaving foam was icy on her palm and she deliberately held it up to be looked at before applying it liberally around the whole area she proposed to denude, provoking a gasp and a spasmodic jerk from Miss Ames.

Perhaps it was that jerk which put the idea into Fliss' head. For whatever reason, she experienced a wild and unstoppable urge. The rubbery inner labia were considerably engorged now, acting as guiding markers in a thick sea of foam. Fliss inserted all four fingers of her foamy right hand into the space between the lips and pushed hard. Miss Ames grunted. Her back arched and her legs below the knees, the only other part of her free to move, kicked wildly. Fliss pushed again, feeling the warm flesh around her fingers resisting, then giving a little. A final shove and the whole of her fingers disappeared so that her thumb pressed against the clitoral bump. There was now no doubt that an erection was in progress. The hump was pushing up from the foam in a demanding fashion and Fliss wiggled her thumb against it for only a moment.

The effect was highly satisfactory. Fliss could feel her fingers being sucked at. Miss Ames' head rolled from side to side. 'No, no!' she gasped. 'No! Agh! Not that! Oh!'

Fliss withdrew the intruding fingers and allowed her forefinger to stray downwards, feeling through the foam until it was centred over the dent of her anus.

Miss Ames threw her a pleading look. 'No! Oh no! Not there! You mustn't . . . Ooh! Uh!'

As Fliss thrust the questing finger forward she felt the sphincter muscles tense, at first resisting ingress. She maintained the pressure and waited, knowing from her own experience what would happen. Sure enough, the hard muscle slackened a little then pushed out with little kissing motions, welcoming the intrusion as the finger slid in up to the foamy knuckle. She withdrew that finger, added another to it and pushed with both.

'Oh God, no!' Miss Ames screamed. 'Not that! Too big! It won't . . . ! Oh! Ooh!'

Just as Fliss' body had done, Miss Ames' was overcoming its owner's will and opening like a flower, unable to resist the torment because of its accompanying promise of sexual gratification. Satisfied that Miss Ames was well aware of that fact and mortified by it, Fliss withdrew her fingers. Neither she nor her victim could be sure whether the sigh which that movement elicited was of discomfort or disappointment.

When Fliss picked up the razor, she found that she was trembling with suppressed excitement and she had to steady her wrist with the other hand. The bite of the blade into the clipped hairs on the foamy belly was just as satisfying as she had thought it would be, as was the band of white, hairless skin which followed each stroke. She did not linger over this part of the process, yet performed it with precision and completeness. When she was done, she wiped away the foam's residue with a damp cloth and revelled in what she saw. Miss Ames was completely smooth and hairless. Every detail of her sex and anus was clear to see. There could be no concealment now of her state of arousal. Her labia, inner and outer, were swollen and pink and, most satisfactory of all, from the division at the base of her hood, the tip of an engorged clitoris could just be seen. The watching tutors would be able to see these things. More importantly, Agnes Ames would know that they could see them. Fliss felt that her triumph was complete except for one detail. She had experienced an involuntary orgasm during her own shave and she was determined that Miss Ames should do the same. With both thumbs, she pressed upwards and outwards just above the fleshy hood so that it retracted, leaving the full length of erect clitoris exposed and vulnerable. Leaning forward again, she centred her right nipple exactly on it and by rotary movements of her upper body contrived to masturbate it very gently in slow circles, staring into Miss Ames' face at the same time.

The fleeting expressions she read there pleased her very much. Lust! Lust denied! Lust recurring! Lust resolutely thrust aside! Lust returning with reinforcements! Resolution faltering! Annoyance! Shame! Humiliation! Lust not to be denied! Lust unbearable! Lust! Lust! Lust! Miss Ames threw back her head and gave a great shriek. 'God! Oh God! What are you doing . . . ? It's coming . . . ! No, please don't . . . Not in front of everyone! Not here . . .' With a huge, sighing groan, she climaxed, her stomach ripples clear for everyone to see, her legs kicking.

Fliss stepped back and to one side so that everyone should have a clear view of her bald pubes and vagina. No trace of dryness now. Love juice trickled down her cleft and over her anus, dripping off on to the leather padding underneath her. She lay with her eyes closed and head turned to one side, biting her lower lip and very aware of what she had been made to do.

She was aroused by Maddie leaning over to whisper in her ear, 'My turn now!'

Miss Ames' eyes jerked open and she turned her head to stare at her persecutor. 'What? No! You can't!'

'I don't see how you're going to stop me.'

'No ... You don't understand. I don't mean you can't ...' She lowered her voice. ' ... I mean, I can't,' she hissed. 'I can't come twice. I never have been able to.' There was, perhaps, a trace of satisfaction in her tone as though she thought that in this respect at least she would be able to thwart their intentions.

'Well, we'll just have to do our best,' said Maddie, matter-of-factly. 'I'm glad you told me straight away. I can adjust accordingly. I was just going to masturbate you again but it seems that you might need a bit more than that. Hold on, don't go away!'

Maddie passed out of sight behind her head for a moment, then came back. Miss Ames eyes opened wide in horror. Maddie was holding up an enormous, pink, rubber dildo. It resembled none that Miss Ames had seen before. The head of it, which would have been the swollen glans in a real penis, was completely circular and covered in tiny rubber bumps like the grips on a finger-stall. The shaft was heavily veined and from near the base two rubber protrusions sprouted at an angle, one at the front and one at the back. These protrusions were shaped like birds with long, flexible rubber beaks. The beak of the rearmost bird was much thicker; about the size of a little finger. Maddie twisted the base and Miss Ames eyes, already wide, opened still further. The whole of the bumpy head revolved slowly like a lighthouse. She twisted again and the front projection vibrated fiercely, the bird's rubber bill pecking furiously at thin air. She twisted a third time and the bird with the fatter bill pushed it vigorously up and down.

'Still think I can't do it?' asked Maddie, switching off this fearsome tool.

'Please don't!' Miss Ames begged. 'I implore you! Please don't try.'

Seeing her torturer implacable, she temporised, 'Then at least not here. Not in front of everyone! Have mercy!'

'Sorry, Aggie,' Maddie said. 'Not only must they be here but, because of what you've said, they have to help.' She turned to the group of tutors.

'Celia! Come over here. I don't want her making a lot of noise and fuss. Get at the top of the table; lean over and put your tongue in her mouth. Go on! Do it now! And don't take it out until I tell you. Maggie Snaith, come here! You'll be on her left side, sucking that nipple. Mary Kelly, you're on her right side doing the same thing there. Well? Don't stand gawping! Get on with it! And nothing half-hearted, either. I want to see lots of sucking, tonguing and nibbling, understand?'

Maddie watched until she was certain that the tutors she had chosen had well and truly begun their appointed work. She could tell the effect they were having by the movements Miss Ames' body was making, closely strapped as it was. When she was satisfied, she moved to a position between those agonised thighs. With great care, she separated the labia and inserted the very tip of the huge mechanical dildo into the still-wet space between them. With gentle, pumping strokes she pushed it further and further in until most of its length had disappeared and the rubber birds were poised to strike at clitoris and anus. In spite of Celia's flickering tongue in her mouth, Miss Ames was still able to make grunting noises which showed that she was very well aware of what was going on, even though she couldn't see. When Maddie switched on the revolving head it evoked a particularly loud groan of protest and Miss Ames legs waved even more frantically. Maddie looked up for a moment to check that her nipple-suckers were performing at their peak. They were. The movements of their heads and jaws made it apparent that they were devoting more attention to their jobs than if they had been merely obeying orders and it seemed as though there was some pleasure for them in what they were doing.

Maddie switched on one pecking bird and advanced the giant penis a fraction so that its bill beat rapidly on Miss Ames exposed and swollen clitoris. Her grunts became a series of frantic, muffled, mewing noises and her stomach contractions were unmistakable. A sudden flow of clear liquid emerged from the tight-stretched labial lips, almost squirting from the tiny gap where the dildo met the entrance to her vagina. Maddie smiled to herself and pushed the tool a little further so that it's revolving rubber head must have been right up into the neck of her womb. With care, she centred the other bird's beak on her puckered anus and pushed until it went in to the hilt. She turned on the third mechanical stage.

The convulsive leap Miss Ames gave threatened to break the thick straps which bound her. In spite of Celia's restraining grip on her head, she tore her mouth free. Face purple, head back, neck muscles and tendons straining, she screamed loud and long. 'Grr! Oh! Oh! It's happening! It's happening! I'm coming again! Oh! Aaah!' Spasms of an extremely intense climax made her naked belly jump and dance as even more fluid spurted from her. The bursting of the one-climax barrier seemed to release some long-dormant capacity within the deepest recesses of her libido. That orgasm was hardly over when she jerked straight into another. Now she was hardly coherent as climax followed climax in swift succession. Again and again, she jerked to her peak. 'Yes! Y . . . Y . . . Ooh! Ooh!' A few panting breaths, then, 'Yes! Y . . . Y . . . Do it! Do it to me! Yes! Ooh!'

At last, she could do no more and lay still, completely exhausted. Maddie had her released and she rolled over on to her face resting her head on her forearms. 'Thank you! Oh, thank you!' she murmured, though whether that was for her release from the straps or her release from the thrall of one-peak inhibition, no one could be sure.

'One down and two to go,' Maddie declared, smiling brightly at the awed tutors.

With her headmistress temporarily disabled, Celia Moncrieff assumed the mantle of command. 'What do you mean?' she asked.

'We have to give June Blair and Patsy Colforth a bath.' As the two named tutors recoiled, she went on, 'Surely you'd enjoy that. You seemed to enjoy bathing us when we arrived.'

'You can't be serious.' June Blair sounded incredulous.

'Deadly serious, June. We're going to bath you and Patsy, so you'd better get your clothes off.'

'Absolutely not!' Patsy Colforth said. 'It's out of the question.'

Miss Ames raised herself weakly on her elbows. 'Please ladies! Please! Do what they say! It's important for all of us.' Suddenly wearied with the effort of speaking, she collapsed on to her face again.

'Well? You heard Aggie. What's it to be?'

The two women looked at one another, then June spoke for both. 'It's no! We won't do it and you can't make us!'

Maddie shrugged. 'OK, if that's your decision. It means that the school will close and all these other nice ladies will be out of a job but, as you say, we can't make you and we won't try. We'll just leave you to talk about it amongst yourselves for a while.' She glanced at her watch. 'Fliss and I will be in the shower room in twenty minutes time. If you're both there by then, voluntarily or not, naked and with your hands tied, then these ladies keep their jobs. If you're not there, we will leave and there'll be no second chance. Perhaps that's something you others would like to consider.'

June and Patsy looked at their fellow tutors confidently, certain of their support. Maddie paused momentarily on the pretext of gathering her equipment into a bag. It was long enough to see that confidence turn to doubt then apprehension as the others weighed

191

a bit of discomfort for two of their colleagues against a worrying search for any jobs as good as the ones they were in danger of losing. Half smiling to herself, she gestured to Fliss to follow her and stalked out of the room.

It took a little while for Maddie and Fliss to complete the preparations they had already begun in the shower room and the stipulated twenty minutes had almost elapsed when the double doors flew open and a small group erupted into the room. June Blair was between Celia Moncrieff and Agnes Ames, the latter having apparently recovered all her strength. June wore a white towelling bathrobe, the sleeves of which were empty and flapping. That her presence was involuntary was clear from the way she was throwing herself about and trying to break away. Maddie was sure she would have been screaming and yelling, too, but for the fact that her mouth was stuffed full of what appeared to be cotton wool which was secured in place by several layers of bandage tied around her lower face. The doors hardly had time to stop swinging when they burst open again and a second group entered. This time, it was Patsy Colforth, identically dressed and gagged, who was being propelled by Mary Kelly and Maggie Snaith.

Both women were pushed to their knees in front of Maddie and Fliss and held there, their captors panting a little from their exertions.

'I thought I said naked and tied,' Maddie said.

'They are!' Agnes Ames reached for the tie of June Blair's robe and, in spite of her frantic wriggling, unfastened it. It slipped back from her shoulders to reveal that she was indeed quite nude. Maddie could also see why she had not been able to put up a better struggle. Her wrists were crossed in front of her and tied together with more bandage, the ends of which had been taken around behind her back and secured there.

'And Patsy?' asked Maddie, nodding towards the second prisoner.

'The same,' Agnes said. At a gesture from her, Patsy's robe was removed to show that she, too, was naked and trussed.

Maddie smiled. 'I see you managed to convince them.' She pointed to two of the stout shower heads above them which protruded about four feet from the white, tiled wall, supported by brackets attached to the ceiling. 'Tie their wrists to those. One shower for each. Use these skipping ropes.'

When the bandages which secured their bound wrists to their bodies were removed, both women made another determined bid for freedom, but were severely outnumbered. There was a brief flurry of naked arms and legs, then they were both secured with arms stretched above their heads, a pose which lifted their breasts and thrust them forward, emphasising their nudity. They stopped struggling then and stood quietly, eyeing Maddie and Fliss apprehensively from above their cotton wool gags.

Maddie turned to Agnes Ames. 'Where are all the girls?'

'All on the playing field. Organised games supervised by prefects. I thought it best.'

Maddie nodded approvingly. 'No one will hear if they scream a bit, then?'

'No.'

'Good! Take those things out of their mouths. If they get wet they might have a bit of trouble breathing. Anyway, we want to hear them, don't we Fliss?' Fliss nodded in complete agreement. The urge was upon her again. She not only wanted to hear them. She was itching to get on with what they had planned.

The gags were removed and, as soon as she was able, Patsy said, 'What are you going to do?'

'What do you think we ought to do?' Maddie asked. 'Shave you as well?'

Both women instinctively crossed their legs. 'No!'

193

'Cane your bottoms?'

'No, please!'

Maddie smiled at their horrified expressions. 'Don't worry. You're getting off lightly. We're just going to wash you, like you wash all new arrivals. Lather you up, then hose you down. That won't be too bad, will it?'

Compared with the alternatives which had just been proposed, that didn't sound so awful and both June and Patsy relaxed a little.

'But you see,' Maddie went on, 'You're not really dirty and that would be a waste of a wash. So I think we ought to make you really filthy first.'

'What do you mean?' Patsy asked, apprehension returning.

Maddie removed a towel which had been concealing two plastic buckets. She picked up one of the buckets and the thick, black, sludgy liquid in it sloshed to and fro. Maddie dipped a wide brush into the liquid, stirred it briefly and brought it out dripping. 'We're going to make you black all over. When we've done that, we're going to soap and hose you clean. Don't worry,' she continued, seeing their horrified expressions, 'it's only water-based colour from the Art Room. It'll wash off easily enough.'

'But you can't mean to . . .' Patsy Colforth spluttered. 'You can't . . . I mean, you just can't!'

'Oh I can, Patsy, and you know it. Just watch and you'll see. Anyway, I was in your Art Class just the other day and you said we should paint a nude if we got the chance. We'll just be doing what you told us. Grab a brush and a bucket, Fliss.'

As the two girls advanced upon them, June and Patsy backed away as far as their strung-up position would allow until they were standing on tiptoe, bending forward to keep their balance, their stomachs tense and pulled in while their breasts swung free in dangling vulnerability.

'You can wriggle and kick about if you like,' said Maddie. 'The only difference that will make is that it will take longer and you'll probably finish up with more on you. I should stand still if you can but it's up to you.'

With tantalising slowness, she advanced the dripping brush towards Patsy's bare belly, staring intently into her face all the time. Patsy watched it come in mesmerised horror, unable to shrink further away. When the cold blackness touched her skin and striped a broad band of black across her navel a grimace of distaste crossed her face and she gasped. 'Ugh! Oh, yurgh! It's all slimy!'

Maddie refilled the brush and slapped it upwards twice, blackening the nipple area of each hanging breast. The paint splattered up across Patsy's upper chest and neck. Some of it went on her face and she gasped in distaste again.

Maddie glanced across to see that Fliss was subjecting June to the same indignity before she went around the back of Patsy's suspended nakedness. Patsy craned anxiously over her shoulder and saw Maddie load the brush again. The coldness on her buttocks told her that her bottom was being coated with the stuff, then she felt a liberal dose being rapidly applied to her bare back. She was methodically painted all over, from her hands to her feet. Only her face was ignored, together with her genital area which she protected by keeping her thighs pressed together. Presently, even this solace was taken from her.

Maddie paused in her labours to beckon to the watching tutors. 'Come and hold one leg out for me,' she said. 'I need to get at everything.'

'No!' Patsy screamed. 'Not there! Don't put it there! Keep away! Oh God!' She lashed out feebly with her feet but they grasped her left ankle and pulled her leg out horizontally to the side, exposing her completely. She thought her misery was complete when she felt the gooey stuff being sloshed around her vagina and worked into her anal crease. There was worse to come.

As Maddie advanced the dripping brush slowly towards her face, she twisted her head about in a fruitless attempt to avoid the inevitable. 'Please, no! Not on my face. I beg you not to do that.'

'Shut your eyes tight!' Maddie ordered. 'I don't want to get paint in them. I should shut your mouth, too!'

Realising the hopelessness of resistance, Patsy took a deep breath and screwed up her face to be painted. The cold slime of it on her face and in her ears was almost more than she could bear. Maddie emptied the remains of the bucket over her head and plastered her brown, curly hair into a flat, shiny cap close against her skull then stepped back and stood with Fliss to admire their work.

Their victims were a sorry sight. Completely blackened from head to foot, only the whites of their eyes and the pink orifices of their mouths broke the sheen of darkness all over their bodies as they hung by their wrists, trickling and dripping. Shiny, slimy, black skin twitched and rippled involuntarily in reaction to the itch of the little runs of paint.

'Great job, eh Fliss?' Maddie said, with deep satisfaction. 'Shower time now!' They turned on the shower heads above their respective captives and a stream of warm water descended. What Maddie had said about the paint was proved true. It washed off with the greatest of ease. Within seconds of the first blast of water, pink and shiny flesh replaced the black coating while the white tiled floor ran grey into the gutter. With soapy sponges, Fliss and Maddie lathered up the women and scrubbed them with a will, not neglecting their most intimate parts. When they had finished, both were very clean and pink.

'Is that it?' asked Patsy. 'Can we be let down, now?'

'Not quite yet,' Maddie replied. 'You haven't been hosed down yet.'

'I don't understand,' June said. 'We've showered already. We're clean.'

'Ah! These are very special hoses we've rigged up just for you.' Maddie dragged two black, rubber hoses across the tiled floor, then returned to their point of origin to turn them on. They were not connected to taps, but to a pair of shower outlets. Maddie had removed the perforated heads and attached the hoses in their place. She tested the water for warmth, then adjusted the spray until it got finer and finer. Maddie had also tampered with the spray control so that finally the jet from each hose was no thicker than a needle, yet carried all the force of a full shower. She handed one to Fliss, who tested it against her hand and winced at the tickling sting.

Each girl turned her hose upon her chosen victim, at first directing the tiny jets at their feet and toes. A frantic dance at once ensued as the naked women attempted to remove themselves from the over-stimulating irritant. They were reasonably successful until the jets moved higher, when it proved impossible to prevent some part of their body being under attack, however much they jigged and threw themselves about. Inevitably, their nipples came in for severe abuse and were soon red, erect and straining.

At an order from Maddie, the other tutors came forward. Two went to Patsy and stooped to grasp an ankle each. They marched backwards and apart, dragging her to the near-horizontal and widely separating her legs. While they held her firmly, Maddie directed the needle jet at close range on to her clitoris and held it there until she jumped and bucked into orgasm. Not content with that, she had the tutors walk forward until Patsy was near the horizontal in a face-down position. While they held her bottom cheeks open, Maddie subjected her anus to needle-spray torture until she climaxed again. Meanwhile, June was receiving the same treatment from Fliss.

Leaving the women to tend their maltreated colleagues, Maddie and Fliss went to the turret room. Hilary jumped up as they came in. She had twisted the remnants of her nightdress into a sort of loose sarong. 'Did you bring more food?' she asked.

'No,' said Maddie. 'You'll be able to get your own, now. We're letting you go.'

'What about Miss Ames?' Hilary asked, anxiously.

'We're going to fix that for you. All you have to do is what we tell you.'

'Oh! Well, if you're sure . . . What do I do?'

'First,' said Maddie, 'you take off that garment and come over to the bench, here.'

'I don't understand.'

'Look,' said Maddie, impatiently. 'Do you want us to help you or not?'

'Yes, of course, but I don't see . . .'

'There's no reason why you should. Just do what I tell you.'

Hilary shrugged. 'OK.' She removed the sarong and, quite naked, followed Maddie to the low bench. When told, she knelt at one end of it and leaned forward so that her breasts were pressed against the cold, leather padding. They cuffed her wrists and pulled them forward so that they could be roped to the legs at the front end of the bench. They got her on to her feet, awkwardly stooped forward and tied her knees to the tops of the back legs, spreading her thighs wide. They attached her ankles to the bottom of the bench's back legs. Passing a broad strap across the small of her back and under the bench, they strained it as tight as they could so that she was doubled in two, her upper body crushed against the leather, but her lower part arcing up in a curve which left her fat bottom sticking up in the air, well clear of the padded surface, her thighs severely parted by the width of the bench and her vagina and anus completely exposed.

198

They left her there, completely puzzled, and went down to Miss Ames' office. She was there again, fully dressed and utterly composed, as though the bizarre events of the past couple of hours had never happened.

'We've sent for the boat. We're leaving now. We've packed some of the things from your turret room. We'll take them with us in your motor caravan when we get to the mainland. We'll bring them back when we've finished with them. The telephone is on again but don't forget what I said about not warning Selina. We can always come back, you know.'

'It's all right,' said Miss Ames wearily. 'As far as I'm concerned, it's over. I shouldn't have got involved in the first place. I was a fool,' she added, simply, 'and I am lucky to get off as lightly as I did. Thank you both for that.' She paused for a moment. 'And for other things,' she said. 'I promise you that I will run the school as you suggest. You're welcome to check.'

'I'm sure you will, Aggie,' Maddie said. 'Now we've a parting gift for you.'

'Oh? What's that?'

'Hilary!'

Miss Ames' face lit up. 'Ah!' she said. 'I was wondering what you were going to do with her.'

'Wonder no longer,' Maddie said. 'She's waiting for you in the turret room. Might be one of your leather suit jobs. What do you think?'

Miss Ames licked her lips. 'Yes! I think so. Definitely.'

'Good,' Maddie said. 'We'll be off then.' She held out her hand. 'Good luck with your new system.'

Miss Ames took the proffered hand and shook it. 'Thank you,' she said, 'and goodbye.'

Shortly afterwards, Hilary looked up from her helpless and cramped position on the bench to see Miss Ames staring at her with glittering eyes. Hilary's lower lip quivered and her eyes filled with tears. 'It wasn't my

199

fault, Miss,' she whimpered. 'They made me tell them. You don't know what they did. They . . .'

Miss Ames wasn't listening. She had crossed to the closet and taken out her leather discipline suit and whip. As she pulled it on with slow, caressing movements, she stared intently at the naked posterior so conveniently presented.

'Oh dear, Hilary!' she murmured. 'What have you done, you silly girl? You've been so naughty and so weak! I am very seriously annoyed with you. Fortunately, you will find that I am very skilled in the matter of character building. When I have finished with you, you will never, ever, want to do such a thing again. I must say that I am pleased with the way you have been presented to me. Such a splendid bottom. Such succulent thighs. I will take my time over those. Tell me, though, Hilary, have you ever been whipped between the legs? Ever had your inner thighs and pussy striped with thin, whippy leather again and again? No? It stings, Hilary! It burns! It hurts almost as much as what you did to hurt me. Soon, Hilary! Very soon! Think about it!'

Hilary sniffled quietly in self-pity. She watched her own image in the full-length mirror and now fully understood why she had been pinioned in that fashion. Her reflection told her that the large moon of her bare behind was sticking up as though inviting painful punishment, yet there was nothing she could do to protect it. Beyond that obstruction, she could see Miss Ames completing her preparations. The sinister leather suit did nothing to calm Hilary's fears. When Miss Ames got up and came towards her, swishing her leather whip through the air and smacking it into her gloved palm she threw herself about, tugging at her bonds in a frenzy. They did not budge an inch. As her fate drew nearer still, Hilary stopped struggling, mesmerised by the icy intent in those eyes set in the black leather cat mask. She could do nothing but stare and wait.

Ten

Selina Doyle was sitting at the desk in the study which had belonged to Fliss' father. She was intent on her accounts and paused to mark her place with her finger before looking up to see who had knocked and entered. Mrs Carstairs, her normally reserved and severe housekeeper, was looking unusually flustered. 'Miss Doyle,' she said. 'There's someone to see you. I told them . . .'

'It's all right, Mrs Danvers,' Fliss said, pushing past her into the room. 'Selina will want to see us.'

Selina looked as if she could not believe the evidence of her eyes. 'You! What are you doing here? How did you . . . ?'

'Explanations later, Selina. Sufficient that I'm here, for the moment.' She turned and gestured to Maddie, who had followed her into the room. 'This is my bosom pal, Madeleine Doran. "Maddie" to her friends, so you may call her Madeleine. She'll be staying for a few days. I invited her.'

Selina pursed her lips and reached for the telephone. 'I wouldn't do that, if I were you,' Fliss said. 'Who would you call, anyway? Your friend Agnes? No help there. She wants nothing more to do with you. She's only thankful I didn't have her arrested. Of course, if you were thinking of calling the Police that's a different matter. It'd save me a job. I expect I shall be doing that myself, presently. There are lots of lovely, incriminating letters with your name on them they'd just love to see.'

Her face white and set, Selina withdrew her hand

from the telephone. Her lip curled. 'That Agnes,' she said, bitterly. 'I should have known she couldn't be trusted.'

'Oh, Agnes wasn't your undoing, Selina. It was Hilary. You remember Hilary. You couldn't be satisfied with just locking me away. You had to go one better and pay someone to make my life more miserable. It was that spitefulness that laid you low. And you are brought down; you realise that, don't you?'

Selina nodded slowly then stared at Fliss with calculating eyes. 'Why are you here?' she said, slowly. 'If your evidence is so good, why didn't you just call the Police?'

Fliss hitched her bottom on to the corner of the desk and swung her leg, completely at ease. 'Well, I'll tell you, Selina. I think it's a personal thing between you and Alice and me. I'm prepared to settle it on a personal basis, just between the three of us – well, the four of us, counting Maddie. I've got a proposition for you. If you agree, you can avoid all the messy complications of Courts and the Law, prison uniform, bars, locks and slopping out.'

Selina narrowed her eyes. 'What's your proposition?'

'Well, of course, you turn over all your accounts to me; sign over the estate now and also sign anything else that's necessary to undo the transfer of my assets to you.'

Selina saw that she had no option. 'Agreed.'

'Get rid of Mrs Carstairs. Tell her to go today. I'll stand for a month's wages in lieu of notice. You can keep Alex on for a while.'

'All right,' Selina said. 'What else?'

'For a period of time – maybe a few days, maybe a week or longer, depending on how you behave, you and Alice do all the work around the place. You wear the uniforms we provide and you obey all orders . . .' she leant forward and laid stress on the word, ' . . . *all* orders, without question, however strange they may be.'

'What sort of orders,' Selina asked, suspiciously.

'Ah well! That will be a surprise. I'll give you a clue, though. Think about what you and Alice did to me in the stable and rack your brains. I'm sure you'll get the idea.'

'What you're proposing is slavery!'

'Ooh! That's a harsh word, Selina. Let's call it getting a bit of my own back for a while. Anyway, slaves aren't free to leave and you will be. Just walk out any time. Of course, you'll be a fugitive from justice. That sounds rather fun, doesn't it? Your picture on the Wanted posters; living life with your chin on your shoulder all the time; changing addresses every week to keep one step ahead of the posse . . .'

'All right! All right! You've made your point. I agree!'

'Can you speak for Alice, too?'

Selina's pause was only momentary. 'Yes!'

'Mm! Interesting! You got a little thing going with her, perhaps? She wears the dress and you wear the trousers? Is that it?'

Fliss was gratified to see Selina flush slightly. 'None of your damn business!' she said.

'I'm in a good mood today so I'll let you off that one,' Fliss said. 'Don't try my patience too far, though. Now get out and do as I've told you. Give me the key of the safe before you go. And the key of the door. This is my office now and you won't come in here again unless I give you permission. When you've sent Mrs Carstairs away, run me a bath and put out some fresh towels. I'll see you and Alice in the library in . . .' she checked her watch, ' . . . in one hour's time. Don't be late!'

Promptly at the set hour, Selina and Alice kept their appointment. Maddie and Fliss, sitting side by side on the great sofa, watched them enter with some satisfaction. Selina wore an air of bravado but Alice was definitely uneasy. Her colour was high and she fidgeted nervously with her hands.

Fliss looked at her watch. 'Good! Not late. Alice, has Selina explained what this is all about?'

'Yes, Felicity . . . I mean Miss Marchant. She told me but I . . . I mean . . . Look!' she burst out, impetuously. 'This wasn't my idea, you know. I thought you might let me off. She made me! I hope you realise that . . .'

Selina interrupted her. 'Oh, shut up, Alice, do! I'm sick of your whining. You didn't say "no" to the money, did you? Well then, don't beg and plead now. Just take what's coming to you like I've got to.'

'Well said, Selina!' Fliss grinned at Alice. 'She took the words right out of my mouth. You're in this right up to your titties.' She had guessed aright. Her deliberately coarse expression had a definite effect on Alice, whose colour deepened as a slow blush spread into her face. 'And speaking of titties,' Fliss continued. 'It's time we saw yours. Your uniforms are in these boxes.' She patted two large cardboard boxes on the sofa beside her. 'This is what you will wear while you are working here, so get undressed now.'

'Here?' exclaimed Alice. 'While you watch?'

'Certainly! Where else?'

Maddie and Fliss watched as the two women took off their outer clothes. Their styles were distinctly different. Selina stripped stoically and seemingly without emotion. Alice undressed much more slowly with nervous, fluttering movements, her embarrassment apparent.

In brassière and panties, Alice implored, 'Can't we keep our underthings on?'

Selina, already naked, became impatient again. 'I shall slap you in a minute, Alice. Don't give them the satisfaction. If I can do it, you can do it!' She planted her legs astride, put her hands on her hips and faced the two girls, daring them to embarrass her.

Alice removed her last two garments and stood crouched, one arm shielding her breasts and one hand over her pubic area.

Fliss held out the boxes and Alice and Selina took one each. There was a pregnant silence after they opened them. 'Why, they're empty!' Alice said, wonderingly. 'There's nothing in them!'

'Exactly!' said Fliss. 'That is your uniform. That is what you will wear at all times from now on while working around the house. Nothing!' She was pleased to see that even Selina was a little taken aback at this prospect and had lost some of her air of nonchalance. Alice, of course, was in a positive tizzy, as Fliss had known she would be, and that was very satisfactory, too. 'And now,' she continued. 'Maddie wants a word with you.'

Maddie got up and faced the two women. 'Stand up straight! Don't slouch! Alice, take your hands away from yourself. Put them on your head if you can't think what to do with them. Good! You've remembered that you are to obey all orders. Fliss has made me responsible for discipline while you are here and it's my job to see that you work conscientiously at any task you are given.' She indicated the short, flat, plastic ruler in her hand, flexing it for greater emphasis. 'I will use this on you if I find you slacking or disobedient, so we'll make a start on the drill you have to learn. When I say, "bend over," you will immediately turn away from me, put your legs apart, bend down and hold your ankles. We'll try that now. Bend over! No, no! That won't do at all. You have to move much more quickly than that. Get up again. Face me! Now, bend over! That's better. Let me see it like that every time. Legs a little further apart, Alice. I can't see your pussy properly.'

Maddie patrolled up and down behind the stooped figures, allowing Fliss time to admire the ignominy of their position. For their ages, both had remarkably good figures. Selina had a lean and cat-like build with relatively small breasts and stout, protruding nipples. Alice was a little plumper but by no means fat. Her nipples were small pink buttons but, in compensation, her breasts were rounder; fuller; milky-white except for traces of tiny blue veins. They swung free now, wobbling slightly with the small movements she made. Her bottom, too, was very white and plumper than Selina's, though both made gorgeous targets.

Maddie stopped beside Alice, who craned anxiously to see what was going on. 'When I am displeased with you,' Maddie said, 'I shall slap your bottom with my ruler, like this.' She administered six stinging strokes with the ruler which made Alice's unmarked buttock flesh dance and jiggle.

'Ow! Ow!' Alice screamed, her knees bobbing in her efforts to avoid the blows. Six distinct red bands sprang up to mark where the plastic ruler had fallen. 'Ow! Why me? What did I do?'

'You didn't do anything, Alice. This is just a demonstration. And I chose you because your pussy is much hairier than Selina's. Maybe I'll have to shave it for you. I'll see how you get on.' Maddie moved on and stood behind Selina. 'Now Selina's pussy, as I'm sure you know, Alice, has hardly any hairs at all around it down below, which is why I've saved her for my next demonstration. If I am more than a little displeased, I shall spank your pussies with my ruler, like this.' She brought the ruler up from below, between Selina's spread legs, so that the flat of it smacked against the divided bulge of her outer labia. Selina grunted, but made no movement or sound throughout the six strokes. Nevertheless, the reddening in that area showed that the smacking must have smarted.

'Right! Get up and face me!' Maddie ordered. Both women did so, Alice rubbing her stinging backside. Selina did not deign to touch her sore place. 'If I am particularly displeased, I shall order you to hold out your tits for a spanking. Hold out your tits, Selina!'

'Damn you!' Selina spat, venomously.

'Now, now! None of that! Hold out your tits. Put

your hands underneath and lift them up.' With murder in her eyes and in her heart, Selina did as she was bidden and Maddie smacked the soft, upper surface of each breast, once, with her ruler. This time, she was pleased to notice, Selina winced in discomfort.

Maddie moved on to stand in front of Alice who stared at her as does a rabbit at a snake. 'Hold out your tits, Alice,' Maddie said, gently.

Alice cowered, shielding her large white breasts with her hands. 'No, not me! Please! Do her again! Don't do it to me!' she gibbered.

'Come on, Alice, pull yourself together,' Maddie commanded, 'or I'll have to demonstrate all over again, using just you. Bum, pussy and all. You don't want that, do you?'

Alice shook her head. 'No!' she whispered.

'All right, then, hold out your tits!'

Slowly, and with the greatest reluctance, Alice cupped her twin orbs and lifted them, offering them for sacrifice.

'Good!' Maddie said. 'Now, when I am really pissed off with you, I shall spank you across the nipples, like . . .'

With a great shriek, Alice dropped her breasts and clutched them protectively, crouched and cowering again.

Maddie shrugged and moved back to Selina. 'Hold out your tits, Selina!'

'Wait a minute! It's her turn!'

'Yes, I know, but she won't hold her tits out,' Maddie explained, patiently.

'Oh yes she bloody will!' exclaimed Selina. She marched across to Alice and got behind her. She hooked her arms inside Alice's and pulled them back cruelly, locking her elbows into hers and forcing her chest forward. 'If you think I'm taking it for you, you've got another think coming, you whining little bitch!' she snarled. 'Come on!' she invited Maddie. 'Do it and get it over with. I've got her!'

Maddie took up her position in front of the weakly struggling Alice. 'No, no!' Alice pleaded. 'Don't smack my nipples. I couldn't stand it! Really! I . . . Ow!' As the flat of the ruler landed with a distinct thwack across one pink button, Alice danced impotently and raised one knee in a futile attempt to cover herself. Maddie smacked it down with the ruler and struck again at the other nipple, eliciting the same howl of surprise and pain. Selina released her captive and Alice doubled over, rubbing her breasts in an attempt to assuage the sting which was, even now, bringing a pink blush to her tender flesh.

'Very well,' Maddie said. 'Now you've learned the drill, you may go. Your first job is in the kitchen. There are lots of dirty pots and pans and the floor's all greasy. No gloves; no aprons; no clothing at all. You'll just have to be careful where you splash the hot water. When you've done the washing-up, you'll scrub the floor. On hands and knees, mind! No mops! I shall come and inspect it shortly and it had better be good.'

Maddie and Fliss watched the two naked, dejected figures trail away to begin their drudgery. 'Oh, Maddie,' Fliss said. 'Do you think we're going a bit too far? Maybe that's enough and we should let them off?'

'It's your game,' Maddie said. 'You can blow the whistle any time. Is that what you want to do?'

Fliss thought about it for a while. The sight of those two bare bodies and what Maddie had done to them had been most stimulating and she felt the dragon of sadism breathing its fiery breath into her loins. The truth might be unpleasant but at least she had the courage to face it squarely. She knew that she wanted to see more humiliation and discomfort. The need was like a thirst which had to be assuaged. 'No!' she said, decisively. 'That's not what I want. Let's keep on for a while longer.'

'OK by me,' Maddie said.

* * *

The sight and smell of the stables were like a friendly home-coming to Fliss. King was safe and sound, apparently well and happy which was a great relief to her. She petted him and fed him pieces of carrot she had taken from the kitchen. The sight of her two thwarted enemies on their hands and knees, scrubbing, while Maddie supervised, occasionally encouraging one or the other with a swipe at their bare bottoms had been most pleasant. She savoured the recollection of their subservience; their nudity; their dangling breasts moving rhythmically with their scrubbing motions; the perspiration which beaded their bodies as evidence of the fact that they were being forced to work hard. At the memory, she felt her own breasts tingle and her nipples harden, pushing against the light silk blouse she wore, while her vagina echoed the message of power and lust created in her mind's eye.

A movement in the other part of the stable interrupted this train of thought and she came out of King's stall. 'Hallo, Alex,' she said.

He turned at the sound of her voice. 'Why, hallo Miss Marchant. They told me you had been sent away.'

'I was, Alex, but I'm back now.'

'To stay?'

'Yes.'

'I'm glad.' Fliss found herself being quite unreasonably pleased about that. 'I was afraid in case it was my fault you got sent away,' Alex said.

'Because we got caught doing naughty things together?'

He nodded.

'Don't worry. It wasn't your fault. It would have happened, anyway. I was afraid you would have got the sack over it.'

He shook his head. 'No, I didn't.'

Suddenly curious, she asked, 'Would it have been worth it?'

He looked away, unwilling to meet her eye. 'If I had got the sack, you mean.' He paused and for some reason Fliss found herself holding her breath. 'Yes,' he said at last, 'it would have been well worth it.'

'Ah!' Fliss found that this came out almost as a soft sigh. 'Remind me exactly what it was we were doing. I've forgotten.'

'You have?' He stared hard at her and Fliss found that this time it was she who was obliged to look away.

'No, not really,' she admitted, 'but remind me anyway.'

He smiled down at her with his head slightly tilted; something which she suddenly found most attractive. 'Well, Miss Marchant, as far as I remember . . .'

'Not "Miss Marchant", please. Fliss.'

'Well, Fliss. I was hot and had taken my shirt off . . .'

'You look hot now. Why don't you take it off again?'

He smiled again. 'All right.' He pulled his shirt off over his head and stood looking at her. His body looked every bit as good to her as it had on that first occasion and her love juices began to gather in a way which made her want to rub her thighs together, though she refrained, for fear that he would notice the movement and interpret it correctly.

'What happened then?' Fliss was annoyed to notice that her voice had a little tremble in it and hoped it was apparent only to her.

'Well, you sat down on that bale and took your blouse off.'

'Like this?' She went over to the bale and sat down. She stared hard at him as she slowly unbuttoned her blouse. She wore no brassière and when she cast off the silk garment her breasts pushed up and out, free and uncovered, the nipples hard brown stalks against her pale skin. She rubbed her palms gently across them, partly to excite herself and partly to observe the effect on him. She was pleased to see the bulge in the front of his tight, blue jeans grow noticeably.

'You're not going to make me stand on a bale again, are you?'

'No,' she said. 'No, I'm not. Come over and sit by me.'

She shifted along a bit and he joined her on her bale, sitting on her left and putting his right arm around her waist. She rejoiced in the touch of his warm hand on her cool, bare skin. His left hand was lying in his lap. She picked it up and placed it underneath her left breast so that her firm young flesh was cupped in his palm. His hand moved upwards, brushing at her nipple and she sighed deeply, pushing her breast towards the source of that pleasure. She felt him shudder and turned her face towards him. 'Kiss me, please, Alex,' she said.

He was a good kisser. His hot, urgent tongue thrusting into her mouth, turned her mind to thoughts of other things thrusting into other places and her vagina liquefied and flowed as she sucked with equal urgency at the sweet intruder.

She broke away, panting a little. 'Let me see you, Alex. Take all your clothes off. I want to see.'

He got up and unfastened his leather belt. He kicked off his shoes and pulled off his socks. He unzipped his jeans and climbed out of them. She pointed at his undershorts. 'Those too. I want to see everything.' When he had taken them off, she stared at his naked body in complete fascination. His penis was long and hard and thick, rising from a knot of curly brown pubic hair at the junction of his body and his thighs. The large testicles which swung beneath this mighty instrument were equally interesting to her and she tried to imagine what they would feel like in her hand. Or in her mouth, she thought, with a sudden quickening of arousal.

'Would you like me to undress for you?'

'Please.'

'Sit down, then.'

He resumed his seat on the bale and she stood in front

of him to strip. She did so in a daze of dreamy pleasure and when she was done she stood quietly before him, her hands at her sides, hiding nothing, but enjoying the admiration she could read in his eyes. Naked, she dropped to her knees on the dusty floor in front of him. She put her elbows on his knees and cupped her chin in her hands as she gazed up into his face.

'May I touch it?'

He gulped, unable to speak, then nodded. She leant into his lap and inspected her prize with care. She had seen only one erect penis before and that had been in the half-light and at some distance. This thing, in close-up, she thought quite beautiful. She felt her clitoris expanding and the pink lips which lined her slit swelling as never before. She imagined the head of this beautiful object probing between those soft lips; pushing up inside her love canal where no penis had ever come. Would it be warm or cold? Experimentally, she encircled the thick trunk of his organ with her finger and thumb, masturbating instinctively but gently. He drew in his breath sharply and a small pearl of fluid emerged from the tiny slot in the tip. She bent forward and licked it off, moving her tongue inside her mouth afterwards to experience the flavour. It was a very distinctive taste and smell, like nothing she had tasted before. Perhaps a tiny bit salty. A trickle of love-juice ran down her thigh unheeded.

'Sorry,' he said. 'I'm leaking.'

'So am I,' she confessed, smiling up into his face conspiratorially and was immediately amazed. She would never have imagined herself capable of such boldness. Her whole body was throbbing from want of him. She glanced down and saw that the aureola behind each straining nipple was a solidly inflated lump. She knew exactly what she wanted; how she wanted it and in what order.

'I'm being very naughty, aren't I, Alex?'

He smiled into her shining eyes. 'Yes, a bit.'

'Do you think I deserve a spanking?'

His smile broadened. 'Probably.'

'Why don't you do it, then, Alex? Why don't you put me across your knee and smack my bottom.'

'But I love your bottom. Why would I want to spank it?'

'Because I want you to. Because having my bottom smacked does things to me. Won't you do it for me, please?'

He stared at her. 'You're serious! You really want to be spanked?'

She jumped to her feet in pretended pique, careful to stand a little to his right with parted thighs and upper body thrusting so that he could obtain the most impressive view of the aroused state of her pink labia and erect nipples. She tossed her head. 'Of course, if you're afraid to . . .'

He reached out and grabbed her left wrist, pulling her forward so that she stumbled and fell across his knees. His left arm encircled her waist, pressing her close against his nakedness and she rejoiced as she felt the heat of his hard penis pressing against her left side.

She was carried away on the rising thermal of her lust. 'Yes! Oh yes, Alex! Do it now. Smack my bare bottom. Make it sting!' The delicious smacking noise as the flat of his right palm rose and fell, connecting with her yearning bottom-flesh, drove her to fresh heights of ecstasy. She struggled to get her right hand underneath her body, feeling for her bloated clitoris. 'Put your left hand under me, Alex! Pinch my nipple! Yes! That's right! Do it! Harder! Hurt me! Make me feel it! Oh God! I'm coming! Don't stop! Don't stop! Smack me harder! Harder! Yes! Yes! Ohoo!' She shuddered into glorious climax, her whole body jerking, tensing and relaxing in regular pulses across his knees, then her straining head fell forward and her tight muscles turned to water and flowed. 'You can stop, now!' she panted. 'Ooh, how marvellous! Glorious! Thank you, Alex.'

He smiled down at her naked back, admiring the bright red patch which had so recently been tender white skin. 'My pleasure,' he said, quizzically.

She had recovered enough to twist her head and return his grin. She scrambled off his lap and knelt in front of him again, holding both his hands in hers.

'Is that it?' he asked.

'Oh no, Alex! Most decidedly not. That was only the start. Now I want you to take me over to that pile of straw and fuck me. You'll be my first and I'm awfully glad it's you. I'm not a virgin, though, so there's no need to be gentle with me. Fuck me hard, Alex, until I scream for mercy and come again. Only, I want everything all at once. As well as being fucked, I want to work you off with my hands and my mouth afterwards, so if you can manage to hold out and not come, I'd like to see you spurt when it happens. That's something that really interests me.'

She pulled him eagerly by the hand across the stable and arranged herself on her back in the pile of straw. The individual stalks tickled and scratched her naked skin in a delightful way as she spread her legs as wide as they would go and drew him down on top of her. She reached underneath his straining body to grasp his penis and lead it to the entrance which awaited it with such enthusiasm. His penetration of her was every bit as delicious as her imagination had led her to believe it would be. This was no courgette; no cold, hard dildo; no tiny finger. This was hot, pulsing man-flesh. She remembered her own chagrin at not being able to feel what Maddie was doing to an artificial penis and concentrated on making her vagina vibrantly active for him. Not that this required much concentration. Without her conscious volition, it was twitching and sucking at his organ as it pounded into her. His balls slapped against the cheeks of her bottom and her breasts joggled mightily with each colossal thrust. This was her very first real fuck and she was enjoying every second of it. In her aroused state, she could not long tolerate this treatment and, too soon, felt the familiar signs of imminent orgasm. She gasped and moaned her way through it, her strong young thighs clamped around his waist and her ankles crossed behind his back drawing him further in, if that were possible. When it was over she lay under him, content to stroke his body and his face, murmuring sweet endearments.

Presently she stirred. His penis was still hard inside her. 'You didn't come?'

'No,' he said. 'As instructed.'

'There's a good boy,' she said, shoving at his shoulders. 'Get off me then and I'll see to you.'

He rolled off her willingly enough and lay on his back beside her, his penis standing up at an angle. She knelt in the straw beside him and once again took this object of her affection in her hand. She saw again in her mind's eye what she had seen Maddie do to Fergus. Leaning forward, she encompassed the tip of it with her lips and sucked, her hair falling down on to his bare stomach. She had never tasted her own juices and had to guess that this was what she now experienced in her mouth. It was, she found, exciting and drove her to take more of his organ into her mouth, sucking hard and encircling it with her tongue. She felt pulsings beneath her fingers. 'Is it coming?'

He was breathing heavily, his eyes closed and his head straining back as if in pain. 'Yes! Yes! Don't stop! Rub me! Rub me hard! Make me come!'

Fliss removed her mouth and substituted a very hard, fast, masturbating action, her encompassing fingers near the head just underneath the glans. Her left hand sought his testicles, fondling and rolling them gently. His body bucked as though to escape and the pulsings grew stronger. She leaned forward again, her gaping mouth just above the reddened tip of the flesh she was pumping so vigorously. 'In my mouth, Alex! Squirt it in my mouth! I want to drink you!'

The suddenness and violence of his ejaculation took her by surprise so that she instinctively jerked away as the fountain of creamy white liquid shot from his reddened knob, so that some of that first flow missed her mouth and splashed her face. She quickly repositioned herself so that the rest spurted into her open mouth. It seemed to go on for a long time and she licked and gulped in her effort to swallow as much as possible and not spill too much. She was only partially successful so that some was deposited on his belly. As he sighed and relaxed, she licked at these little pools with a busy tongue, rejoicing in the strange musky smell and the salty taste of it.

At last she flopped down on her back beside him and they linked hands, lying in companionable silence for a while until he said, 'Phew! That's what I call a work bonus!'

She giggled. 'Want to do it again?'

'What? Gosh! Not for a couple of hours, at any rate.'

'Tomorrow!' Fliss said, decisively. 'We'll do it again tomorrow! Keep your strength up. You'll be amazed at the number of places I can find for you to put it.' She was pleased to see that even in his recently-drained state that provocative statement raised a responsive twitch in his flaccid organ. Still smiling, she got to her feet and searched for her cast-off clothing. She'd have to get the straws out of her hair before she saw Maddie again.

Eleven

Alice's naked buttocks were quivering in a most tantalising way as she moved around the bedroom, polishing
and dusting. Maddie, stretched at full length on the
large double bed, watched her for a while, remarking the
red ruler marks still clearly visible on that white bottom.
There was something enticingly vulnerable about Alice
which was quite absent in Selina who was even now
performing a similar clean-up job in the library. The
way she kept flicking nervous glances in the direction of
her new Mistress, of whom she clearly stood in great
awe. Maddie felt the first stirrings of sexual arousal.
Perhaps this train of thought was worth following up?
There might be some sport to be had.

'Alice!'

Alice started as violently as if Maddie's voice had
been a gunshot in the silent room and almost dropped
the ornament she was holding.

'Put that down and come over here.' Obediently,
Alice replaced the ornament on the dressing table and
padded across to stand beside the bed, her fingers twin-
ing nervously in front of her.

'Yes, Miss Doran?'

'Don't fidget, Alice. Anyway, you're blocking my
view of your pussy. Put your hands on your head.' This
pose, when immediately adopted, lifted her breasts and
displayed them to best advantage and Maddie felt a
surge in her own bosom. The two ruler marks across
each nipple were fading, but could still be seen. The

217

knowledge that Maddie was staring at her pubic hair made Alice blush prettily and Maddie did nothing to ease her embarrassment.

'You're very hairy down there, Alice,' she said. 'Ever been shaved?'

Alice's blush deepened and she looked away. Her voice was the merest whisper. 'No.'

'Selina never did it for you?' Alice shook her head, not trusting her voice. 'So you do have sex with her? Come on, answer up. I've got my ruler about here, somewhere.'

'Yes, we have sex.'

'Tell me about it. What's it like?'

Alice's eyes darted around the room, seeking any distraction from this unwelcome inquisition. 'I . . . I can't, Miss. It's embarrassing.'

'No need to be embarrassed, Alice. I won't tell anyone. Look, take your hands off your head and sit down by me.' She patted the side of the bed and Alice perched there like a wild bird, poised as though ready for flight. Maddie laid a comforting hand on her bare thigh. 'That's better. Now tell me all about it.'

Alice gulped, uncomfortably aware that Maddie's fingers were only inches away from her pubic hair. 'What do you want me to tell you?'

'Well now, let's start with something easy. She masturbates you?'

'Yes.'

'With her finger inside your pussy?' Alice nodded.

'Do you like it when she makes you come?' Alice nodded again.

'Come along, now. You're making me do all the work. I shall become seriously displeased in a moment and you know what that means.'

'I'm sorry.' Alice was desperately anxious to please the person who could and would inflict physical punishment on her body. 'I don't know what you want to

218

know. She kisses me . . . down there and I do the same to her. Sometimes we use things on each other.'

'Things? What things?'

'You know. Artificial things . . .'

'Dildos?'

'Yes. Dildos. Please Miss Doran . . . Please! Your hand's moving!'

'It's all right, Alice. I'm just checking to see if talking about it is making you wet. No, don't clamp your thighs together. Open your legs. Wider! Wider than that! Now, hold still while I check you out.' Maddie's left forefinger sought and rubbed at Alice's pink slit where it nestled amid its protective shield of curly brown hair. 'Why, you are getting moist, aren't you, you sexy little thing?'

Alice endured in silence, but Maddie noticed that her little pink button nipples had stiffened into erectness and were becoming almost respectable in size while the squirming of her body was not entirely predicated by distaste.

'Selina seems like the bossy one. Is she bossy in bed?'

'Yes. She makes me do . . . things.'

'What sort of things?'

'I can't say . . . Really I can't!'

'All right. You don't have to. I just wanted to find out which one of you was the dominant one. Do you like being made to do things?'

Alice gazed at the floor. 'Yes,' she whispered.

'Just by Selina? Suppose I make you do . . . things now?' Alice blushed again and hung her head again, but a sudden gush of warm, slippery fluid against Maddie's finger told a tale of its own.

'All right, Alice. Stand up and put your hands on your head again. Stay there!' Maddie got off the bed and went to a chest of drawers. When she came back, she was carrying her plastic ruler and a long, pink, flexible dildo. The dildo was unusual in that it was attached to a broad, flat base and was obviously designed to stand up on its own.

'Kneel down. Legs wide apart, please.' Maddie knelt with her and positioned the dildo with care directly under Alice's quivering bottom. 'Keep your hands on your head. Now sink back on your heels. Slowly, now!' As Alice's body came lower and lower, Maddie adjusted the position of the dildo until the head of it was well centred between her parted sex-lips. 'All the way, now,' she ordered. 'Right down as far as you can go.' With a sigh, Alice sank back on to her heels and almost the whole length of the tool disappeared into her vagina.

Maddie got up and sat on the bed close to and facing the kneeling figure. She flexed her plastic ruler in her hands. 'Here's the deal, Alice,' she said. 'You are not to take your hands off your head or to touch yourself in any way. Most particularly, you will not; I repeat NOT move up and down on that thing inside you. If you do any of those things I will beat your bottom and your nipples very hard and for a very long time. Do you understand?'

Alice nodded. 'Yes. I understand. How long must I stay like this?'

'Until I tell you to move. Do you think you can do that?'

Alice nodded again. 'I think so.'

'Good! Remember, I shall be watching closely.' Maddie stretched out both hands and caressed the naked breasts so conveniently presented.

Alice jumped in surprise and Maddie said, accusingly, 'Did you move?'

'No! No! I swear I didn't! It's just that it's difficult to keep still when you touch me.'

'Of course it is! You didn't think I was going to make it easy for you, did you?' Maddie took one of the straining pink nipples between each finger and thumb and manipulated them. Alternately pulling, rolling, squeezing, then pinching, she used every ounce of her skill to tease and torment Alice. She knew exactly what effect such treatment ought to be having on a body which was already semi-randy and she watched carefully for signs that it was working. Presently, such signs came in abundance. Alice began to breath heavily. She screwed up her face in concentration and tried to keep herself resolutely still but little nervous tics kept jerking beneath the smooth skin of her stomach. Maddie pretended not to notice this trivial disregard of her strict orders and maintained her torture, well aware of the overwhelming urge Alice must be feeling to move on her impaling dildo to extract pleasure from it.

'Please! No more! I can't stand it!' Alice begged.

'Yes you can!' Maddie was remorseless. 'You'll stay still like that until I tell you to move!'

Alice was becoming hysterical with pent-up longing. 'I can't! I can't!' she shrieked. 'I've just got to move!'

'Even if it means having your bottom and your nipples beaten?'

Alice paused and Maddie watched her most closely. This was the point towards which she had been working. She knew how badly Alice feared a beating. Maddie would be certain of her mastery when Alice became so eager for sexual release that her desire overcame that fear. Even as she watched, that moment arrived. Alice reached her crisis point and plunged headlong into the abyss.

'I don't care,' she shouted, beginning to jig frantically up and down. 'You can beat me black and blue. I must have it! I must!'

Maddie leaned nearer to the agonised face which was working and contorting ferociously so close to her own. 'Yes!' she hissed. 'Go for it, Alice! Do it! Put your hand down and work yourself off! Let me see you come!' She pinched and twisted almost viciously at the burning nipples she still gripped.

Alice's hands flew to her crotch and she masturbated her clitoris frantically, redoubling her bobbing movements.

'Yes! Oh yes!' she panted, in an ecstasy of relief. 'Oh! Ooh! Here I come! Here I . . . come!' For a moment, she detached her hands from her groin and held them out towards Maddie, fingers wide-stretched and quivering with tension as she hung on the edge, prolonging the magnificence of the moment while her belly visibly churned. Then, quite suddenly, her whole body relaxed and she fell forward on to her elbows, her forehead resting on the floor while she struggled for breath.

When at last she looked up, her eyes had a peculiarly soft and sated look while her mouth hung open, still urgently seeking air. She stared at Maddie as though she were a stranger until full comprehension returned. 'God! Oh God! What have you made me do? Are you going to beat me?'

'Maybe not,' said Maddie comfortably, beginning to unbutton her blouse. 'It all depends how I feel after you've finished sucking my nipples and kissing my pussy.' Observing a fractional hesitation on Alice's part, she stopped what she was doing and picked up her ruler. 'Of course,' she said, 'you may prefer to have your nipples smacked. I hadn't considered that.'

'No! Oh no!'

'Or maybe,' Maddie continued, driving the message home, 'Maybe I should just tell Selina what you've been telling me and what we've been up to while she's been slaving away downstairs?'

That was a telling point which confirmed her estimate of the relationship between the two women. Maddie could see from the flicker of fear which passed across Alice's face that the threat of Selina's displeasure carried more weight that any ruler smacking she could administer. Satisfied, she continued to undress while Alice knelt, meek and irresolute, beside the bed. When she was wearing only panties, she stopped again. 'Well?'

Alice made her decision. She got up and crawled on to the bed alongside Maddie who humped her bottom upwards in invitation and said, 'You can pull my knickers down for me.' Alice hooked her fingers into the waistband of the flimsy garment and drew them down to mid-thigh. The touch of her fingers was pleasant and it was gratifying to notice that Alice was definitely displaying an interest in the area she had uncovered.

'Are you looking at my pussy, Alice?'

Alice coloured and averted her eyes with a guilty start. 'No!' she said, hastily and in some confusion. 'I wasn't really . . .'

'It's all right. I want you to. Take my knickers right off.' When Alice had obeyed, Maddie raised her knees and spread her thighs wide. 'Kneel between my legs and have a good look.' She placed her forefingers on either side of her slit, pressed and moved them apart so that her labia gaped, revealing the shiny inner surfaces and the button of her erect clitoris, 'Come closer! No, closer than that! Closer! Put out your tongue! You know what to do? Good! Agh! Aha!' The flicker of Alice's warm, wet tongue on those surfaces already sensitised by desire sent Maddie into a trauma of pleasure and her hips began a slow undulation. 'Yes! That's it!' she breathed. 'Stick your tongue right inside! Mm! Now higher. Tickle my button. Gently! Oh, so gently, Alice. Keep it gentle, even if I tell you to be rougher. Keep me on the edge.'

Maddie closed her eyes and abandoned herself to the pure pleasure of what was being done to her. Alice was no novice in this department, she could tell. In a little while she murmured, 'Now my nipples. Move your hands up and feel for them. There! Aren't they nice and big and hard? Don't you love them? Show me you love them, Alice. Squeeze them and stroke them, but gently. Everything gentle, Alice. Good!' Now Maddie knew that her pleasure was at a point where it could not be increased without climax and she wanted to stretch it out; to delay the moment when the bliss of orgasm would also signal the end of the joys of anticipation.

Her breath was hissing between her clenched teeth in short sighs of pure pleasure and she could feel her wetness bathing Alice's lower face and her eager mouth as it burrowed into her groin, sucking, tickling and licking.

'Always slow and gentle, Alice, no matter what. It's near, now. You'll like that. Nearer! Here I come! Now! Hard and fast! Bite me! Pinch me! Finish me!' The fact that Alice had remembered her orders and did not alter her soft, tantalising stimulation was highly satisfactory to Maddie. She squirmed in ecstatic frustration and her clenched fists beat on the covers beside her body. To be at such a high point and to be held there for long, long seconds was the goal she had been striving to achieve. She was being driven mad with longing. Her mouth opened wide in a soundless scream but her breathing was suspended so that all that emerged was a long, rasping gurgle. When the dam finally succumbed to the pressure and climax flooded through every part of her body, the sensation was every bit as intense as she had hoped. She clasped her thighs against Alice's ears and pressed on the back of her head, holding her mouth tightly in position while she humped and writhed through the throes of her peak. For some time afterwards her vagina, driven by violent stomach contractions, continued to suck at Alice's tongue still embedded inside her. Finally, she relaxed and released her grip, her head falling back.

Alice raised her head and regarded Maddie from between her still-gaping thighs. She wiped shiny liquid from her mouth with the back of her hand and smiled shyly so that Maddie could tell that the experience had not been entirely unpleasant for her.

Maddie smiled back. 'Phew! One-all, I think, Alice. Come up here and lie down by me for a minute while I rest.'

They lay side by side for a while, neither speaking, until Maddie raised herself on one elbow and leaned over the naked, white figure on her right. With her left forefinger, she traced a light circle around one of Alice's pink nipples, then allowed that finger to trail down across her belly until it scratched gently at the brown patch of pubic hair which bloomed at her groin. 'You're quite a sexy little thing in your own way, aren't you? Ready to do it again? This time, I'll give you one at the same time.'

Alice neither nodded, nor spoke, but Maddie could read the eager light of acquiescence in her eyes. Maddie's estimate had been proved right again. This one was a little goer. 'Right!' she said, kneeling up. 'This time I'm going to sit on your face, OK?' Alice nodded, blushing slightly.

'Put your arms up above your head!' Maddie straddled her, facing her feet and shuffled backwards. With her arms now trapped where they were, Alice's reach was not great enough to touch her own body or to interfere with anything Maddie might care to do to it. Indeed, she could not even see it, her view being blocked by Maddie's magnificent, tanned buttocks and back. Maddie lowered herself until she felt Alice's tongue begin its task, then she put her hands down on to the plump white breasts between her own thighs and began to play with the nipples, tweaking and pinching a little. Muffled little noises indicated that this manipulation was felt and appreciated, so she allowed her hands to stroke downwards away from her, caressing the smooth white stomach skin and tickling in circles around the pretty dimple of Alice's navel. Unbidden, Alice's knees came up and her plump thighs parted until her knees almost touched the bed on either side, inviting investigation. Leaning still further forward, Maddie opened her sex and began a gentle masturbation of Alice's clitoris, occasionally delving further to trail her finger up and down the wet aperture below. Propelled by spasmodic jerks from the gluteal muscles in her backside,

Alice's lower body began to hump upwards towards this source of excitement.

Encouraged, Maddie slid her wet finger further down still, feeling for the puckered eye of Alice's anus. She found it and pressed gently, demanding entrance. Alice immediately clapped her thighs tightly together and beat on Maddie's back. Unable to articulate, she shook her head violently, making noises of protest. Maddie stopped what she was doing and got off her, turning to kneel beside her. 'What's the matter, Alice? Don't you like that?'

'No!'

'You mean Selina's never used that hole? You've never had anything in there?'

Acutely embarrassed, Alice whispered, 'No.'

'You don't know what you've been missing. We must remedy that at once.'

'No, please! I don't like it! Really!'

'How do you know you don't like it if you've never done it?' asked Maddie with irrefutable logic. 'Now let me see. What shall we use?' She rummaged in a bedside drawer and brought out a different pink penis. 'See!' she said, holding it up for Alice to inspect. 'That's not so big, is it? What else shall we need? Oh yes!' She brought out a very large tube of cream and laid it on the bed beside the dildo.

Alice eyed these preparations with considerable trepidation. 'You're not ... You're not really going to, are you?'

'Of course I am,' Maddie said, then suddenly stern, she added, 'Look here, Alice. Either you let me fuck your bum or I'll smack it with my ruler. After that, I'll smack your pussy and your nipples and after that I'll tell Selina all about our little session. It's up to you.'

It was Hobson's choice and Alice knew it. She lay there, gnawing her lower lip for a while. 'Will it hurt?' she ventured, at last.

'Probably, to start with,' Maddie said. 'I'll do my best to see that it's no more uncomfortable than it has to be. After a while, I promise you that you won't care if it does hurt.'

'All right,' Alice said, timidly. 'What do I have to do?'

'Not very much. I'll be doing all the work. All you have to do is to kneel on the side of the bed here where I can get at you. That's right. Bum outwards facing me. Now go down on to your elbows and stick it out. Right down! Legs wide! Put your forehead on the bed!'

As Alice adopted the required pose, her buttock cheeks widely separated and her anal area completely available, Maddie reached into the drawer again and brought out a long, white, tapered nozzle. She removed the cap from the tube of cream and replaced it with the nozzle.

Alice, straining around, saw her do it. 'What are you doing with that?'

'I'm going to squirt it up your bum.'

'Oh!' Alice digested this information. 'Must you do that?'

'Believe me, you wouldn't like it one bit if I didn't. Now hold still.' She expressed a small amount of the cream from the nozzle on to her finger and smeared it on the tight brown nut of Alice's sphincter. She squirmed and jumped.

'Still!' Maddie commanded. She placed the tip of the nozzle in the exact centre of the puckered target and pressed. Alice bucked forward. Maddie slapped her bottom with the flat of her spare hand. 'Keep still, I said! This is just a thin little thing. How are you going to manage if you can't even take that. Now, when I press again, you push out. Strain a bit, as if you were trying to go.'

'I'm sorry. I'll try.' Quivering with fear of the unknown, Alice managed to control herself sufficiently to do what she had been told. This time, when Maddie

227

attempted to insert the tip of the nozzle, her sphincter relaxed. It was only for a second, but that was sufficient for the required entrance to be gained.

'Ooh!' Alice wiggled experimentally. 'Is it in?'

'Just the tip. How does it feel?'

'Funny.'

'Nasty?'

'No . . .' Alice explored the sensations she was experiencing. 'No, not nasty. Just funny.'

Maddie squeezed the tube so that a small drop of cream would lubricate the nozzle's further ingress, then she pushed steadily until the whole length of it had disappeared. Alice felt the stretching effect as the wider part of the nozzle stretched her anus and she panted, her thighs trembling.

Maddie held the tube in place with one hand while she placed the other reassuringly in the small of Alice's back, holding her still.

'All right?' she enquired.

'Yes. Is that all of it?'

'Yes. Now hold still again.' Maddie used both hands to squeeze the tube, rolling it up from the bottom so that a gush of the contents exuded from the tip where it was embedded high up inside Alice.

'Oh! Oh! It's cold! What are you doing?'

'It's all right. Nearly done now.'

A third of the tube still remained when Alice suddenly cried out. 'Ow! Ouch! Stop!'

'What's the matter?'

'I can't take any more. I think I must be full. It aches when I move.'

'That's OK. You've just cramped up a bit.' Maddie reached underneath Alice, kneading and massaging her lower stomach where she could feel a knot of hardened muscle. 'Relax. Breathe deeply. That's it. Better now?'

'Mm. Is there much more?'

'Just a bit.' Maddie completed the emptying of the

tube without further interruption then withdrew it with great care. Knowing what Alice's natural reaction would be, she took care to plug her anus with her fingertip as the end of the nozzle came free.

'Oh! Ooh! I can't hold it. I have to go to the bathroom!'

'No you don't!' Maddie slapped the bare bottom again. 'Just hang on for a moment. It will pass!'

'But I feel so full!'

'That's the whole idea. You're going to feel even fuller in a moment.' She picked up the flexible dildo and pushed the tip of the head against Alice's sphincter. 'Push out!' she ordered.

A tiny spurt of cream bathed the head of the dildo, lubricating it. Maddie shoved abruptly, so that the head of it disappeared inside. Alice bucked violently forward, wriggling madly. 'Ow! Oh no! I can't . . . It's too big! Take it out, please!'

Maddie held Alice firmly with her left arm in front of her thighs, preventing further forward motion while she continued to push until almost the whole length of the imitation penis was firmly embedded. 'There!' she said. 'That's just about all of it. Just relax and get used to it for a while.'

'I'll try. Just don't move it, please.'

'I won't. Not until you're ready. Calm down.'

Alice rested for several minutes with her head on her forearms, sighing deeply, then, 'I think it's better, now,' she said. 'I really need to go to the toilet, though.'

'Good! That's all part of it. Let me show you.' She slid her left hand under Alice and felt with her forefinger for her clitoris. As she had known it would be, it was a very solid lump in a high state of excitation. She massaged it and Alice reacted immediately. The end of the dildo which was held lightly between Maddie's finger and thumb jerked frenziedly.

'Oh! Ooh!'

'Feel good?'

'Oh yes!' said Alice, wonderingly. 'It's sort of different. Is it that thing in me that's doing it?'

'You bet! Want me to move it now?'

'Maybe just a little bit.'

Maddie resumed her masturbation of Alice's clitoris and, at the same time, began a slow, gentle, pumping motion with the dildo, moving it only a little way in and out so that its surrounding web of tight-stretched skin alternately pouted and indented. Little gobs of cream exuded at the junction of plastic with flesh, forming a slippery white film which prevented friction and soreness.

'Oh!' Alice cried. 'Oh fantastic! Why didn't you tell me?' Her whole body was jerking with pleasure.

Maddie smiled. 'I did, but you wouldn't listen. Want me to do it some more?'

'Oh, yes please!'

'Ask me nicely, then.'

'What do you mean?'

Maddie stopped her movements altogether. 'Talk dirty. Ask me to fuck your bum.'

'I can't . . . I can't use those words.'

'Then I don't do it.'

There was a lengthy pause then, from Alice's lowered head came the faintest of voices. 'Fuck my bum, please! Do it! Oh yes! Yes! Ooh! Oh God! I'm coming already! I can't wait! Do it to me! Fuck my bum! Oh fuck . . . Oh . . . bum . . . Oh! Aah!' She peaked quite suddenly, hot juices almost squirting from her love-cavern in her excitement. She rested then, her head still lowered, only gasping a little now and then as Maddie, with enormous care, extracted the dildo from her anus. With that obstruction removed, her need became abruptly urgent and her sphincter twitched spasmodically in tune with her instinct for expulsion.

She scrambled off the bed. 'I must . . . I've got to . . .' She looked wildly about her.

'I should hurry, if I were you,' Maddie said. Smiling indulgently, she watched the naked Alice hurry towards the bathroom in a crouched, anxious run.

Maddie was sitting in the library reading a magazine when Fliss came back from the stables. She looked up as her friend entered. 'Hallo,' she said. 'You look pleased with yourself. What have you been up to?'

'Oh, nothing much,' Fliss said. 'Just this, that and the other, but it was nice. What have you been doing?'

'Funnily enough,' Maddie said, 'I've been doing this, that and the other as well. That was nice, too,' she added, with a dreamy look in her eyes.

Twelve

Mr Silsby, as short, bald and fussy as ever, was in his place at the small reading table in the library. Could it really be so short a time since he had been there before, Fliss wondered? So much had happened in the interim that it seemed to be more like years than months. She leaned over his shoulder to sign the deed of transfer and he blotted her signature with care and precision.

He peered over his glasses to where Selina, elegant in a smart cream linen trouser suit sat on the large sofa. 'And now your goodself, Miss Doyle.' She got up and came over to stand beside Fliss but Mr Silsby did not immediately hand her the pen. Instead, he put his fingertips together and pontificated for a while.

'I must say that I am most gratified that you have so quickly discovered that Felicity is quite capable of running her own affairs. You must have built up quite a relationship in this short space of time.' He beamed from one to the other while Selina said nothing, then he went on, 'And I must congratulate you on the excellent care you have taken of the money and properties entrusted to you. I must confess that when I went through your accounts I was astonished at the size of the dividends you obtained from some of the companies in which you chose to invest. In some cases as much as one hundred per cent. Quite extraordinary!'

Fliss did not permit her smile to show on the outside. She and Selina both knew that these companies were ones created by Selina and were merely pieces of paper designed for only one purpose; to leak away the estate's assets. They were supported only by Selina's personal wealth so that the dividends on which Fliss had insisted were coming directly out of Selina's pocket.

'Yes,' Mr Silsby babbled on. 'Felicity must have been impressively convincing. I remember one client . . .'

'Just give me the pen,' said Selina, shortly.

She signed her name and he blotted it with the same care then folded up all his paperwork and put it in his briefcase. 'Well, ladies, I must be getting along. So nice to have met you all again. Yes, indeed.' He beamed again. 'Ah yes. Such a happy outcome!'

Fliss showed him out and closed the great door behind him. She heard his car start and move away as she went to the kitchen, expecting to find Maddie and Alice there. The large room appeared to be empty and she was about to close the door again when there was a shuffling noise and Maddie's head appeared above the far edge of the large, scrubbed table which occupied the centre of the kitchen.

'Oh Maddie. There you are. What are you doing?'

Maddie stood up. 'I was just showing Alice how to scrub the table legs properly.' At that, Alice's head appeared alongside Maddie and she also climbed to her feet. She had, thought Fliss, been scrubbing hard, because her face was red from the exertion and there was a faint sheen of perspiration on her bare body.

'Can you both come into the library for a moment?'

'Oh sure,' Maddie said. 'Come along Alice.'

Fliss stared at her. 'Are you all right? You look flushed. You're not catching a cold?'

'No, I'm fine. It was just the stooping down. You know.'

'Oh, I see.' Fliss led the way back to the library and the pair followed along behind. Selina had resumed her seat on the sofa and Fliss made Alice sit alongside her. Maddie perched herself on the corner of the reading table.

'You'll be glad to know that this is your last day here,' Fliss said. 'The paperwork is all complete and there is nothing left for you to do. My old staff will be back tomorrow, all except Mr Lupton. I'm retiring him on a pension and keeping Alex on.'

'Thank God it's over and good riddance,' Selina said, rising. 'Come on Alice. Let's pack.'

'Oh, but it's not quite over yet, Selina.'

'It's not? You said we could go.'

'No, I said you would go today. But not right now. There's a little matter to settle first.'

'What little matter?'

'Well, I seem to remember someone being hung up in the stable and spanked. Nothing I've done to you yet has been quite as bad as that.'

Selina stared. 'Good God! You can't mean that you . . . that we . . . Oh God! You do mean it, don't you?'

''Fraid so,' Fliss said. 'Time to strip off again, Selina. We're going to the stable.'

'Me too?' asked Alice in a small voice. Fliss thought it a little strange that Alice's appealing gaze was fixed not on her, but on Maddie.

'Surely you too. You enjoyed spanking me. Now I'm going to enjoy spanking you.'

Selina objected. 'But we can't go out of the house with no clothes on.'

'Yes you can. There's no one to see you. I've given Alex the day off. Besides, the fresh air will do you good. Brace you up. You've been cooped up in the house too long. Now get your clothes off before I have them taken off by force.'

With a look that would have paralysed an adder at twenty paces, Selina disrobed and soon stood as naked as Alice.

'Right!' Fliss ordered. 'Off we go to the stables.'

She and Maddie followed the nude women across the yard and Fliss was pleased to note that being unclothed outdoors was the source of some embarrassment to both. Although they knew there was no one to see, they crouched a little and hurried, protecting their breasts and genitalia with their hands.

Once in the scented dimness of the stables, Fliss set down the small bag she was carrying and said, 'Sit down!'

'Sit down?' asked Selina, looking around. 'Where?'

'On the floor. No, not there. Here!' Fliss pointed to the spot. 'Sit facing each other, put your legs apart and put your feet against each other's.' Puzzled, but obedient, they did so. Fliss took leather ankle and wrist cuffs from the bag and attached them to Selina's limbs, while Maddie did the same to Alice. From where it was leaning against a stall, she brought one of the trapeze bars she had gleaned from Miss Ames' turret room and laid it across Selina's ankles. She pulled Selina's legs a little further apart and attached clips on her ankle cuffs to rings in the ends of the bars then did the same thing to Alice clipping her ankles to the same rings.

'Lean forward!' Selina leant and Fliss clipped her wrist cuffs to the same rings so that she was obliged to remain leaning forward, her wrists now attached to her spread ankles. Meantime, Maddie was attaching Alice in a similar fashion.

'What are you doing?' Selina demanded. 'I don't see . . .'

'Shut up! I'm busy!' Fliss reached up above them to where a twin cable ran through a pulley attached to a beam. She pulled down on the ends of the cable and clipped them to the rings in the end of the trapeze. She stepped back and surveyed her handiwork, hands on hips, checking that all was secure before she nodded to Maddie. Maddie went to the wall at one side where she and Fliss had spent some time and effort in installing one of the winches from the turret room. She turned the handle and the pawl clicked over the ratchet as the cable tightened.

235

Alice uttered a little scream as she felt her feet being drawn upwards, then overbalanced backwards, her legs and arms sticking up, for all the world like a dead spider. Selina remained as near to upright as she could manage for as long as she could but eventually she, too, succumbed to the inevitable and toppled on to her back. After that, further retraction of the cable caused their bodies to be dragged towards one another along the dusty floor. When their bottoms were only a few inches apart, Maddie stopped turning the handle. With considerable agitation, both women's eyes turned to follow Fliss as she again delved into her bag. This time, she produced a double-ended dildo and proceeded to lubricate both ends from a small bottle of oil. The dildo was further unusual in that each end was divided from the other by a flattened rubber disc in the centre which meant that neither participant in its use could get more than her fair share of the thing.

When Fliss crouched beside their upturned bottoms with this instrument in her hand, Selina divined her intent. 'No!' she cried, struggling as best she could. 'Not that! Spank us, but surely there's no need to . . . Ooh!' She grunted as Fliss inserted one end of the pink dildo into her vagina and pushed it in until the disc nestled against her pubic hair.

Fliss nodded to Maddie again and, as the turning of the handle was resumed and the two vaginas drew ever nearer, she centred the other end of the dildo on Alice's, holding it in place until each of their bare bottoms finally swung clear of the floor and were pressed so closely against the other's that there was no possibility of the tool slipping out.

Alice wriggled uneasily. 'Keep still!' Selina snapped at her. 'You're doing things to me. Stop it!' Alice stopped wriggling and bore her ordeal with more fortitude as the pair were slowly winched higher and higher until their buttocks were a good three feet from the floor and they hung there nude and vulnerable, suspended by wide-spread wrists and ankles. Joined like Siamese twins at the vagina, any slight movement by one was immediately felt as sexual stimulation by the other, so they remained as still as possible, swaying gently to and fro.

Their discomfort was still not complete. Fliss dragged over a bale and stood on it so that she could conveniently reach Selina's breasts. She held two little brass objects in her hand.

'What are those?' Selina asked.

'Nipple clamps. See! I tighten them like this and they grip on to your nipples.'

'Oh dear God! Oh, no!'

'If you make a fuss, I'll tighten them really hard and hurt you. If you're good, I'll just screw them up far enough so they can't slip off. Come on, now, let's tease them out a bit and get them nice and long and hard.' She suited her actions to her words while Selina, mindful of her threat, bit her lip and said nothing, even when the clamps were firmly applied.

Alice, being simultaneously clamped by Maddie, did not react with such stoicism. 'Ow! Ouch! Ow!' she yipped as her small nipples were also gripped in tiny brass vices. With two short lengths of light chain with clips at each end, Fliss fastened their clamps together, Selina's right nipple to Alice's left and vice versa, adjusting the tension with precision so that there was a slight pull which elongated their breast flesh just a trifle.

The final item she brought from her bag was a short, light, very broad leather strap, guaranteed to sting but to cause no great injury. 'Alice first, I think,' she said, handing the strap to Maddie.

Maddie stood back and measured her length. Striking upwards from below with such a puny instrument, it was certain that the smacks carried no great force but from the fuss Alice created one would have thought that she was being flogged unmercifully with barbed wire.

She shrieked and yipped endlessly, struggling and bucking at each slap, her arms and legs flexing frantically in an effort to haul herself higher and so escape the bottom strapping she was receiving. These movements were inevitably transmitted directly to Selina's body in the form of vaginal stimulation and nipple pulling.

'Keep still!' Selina yelled. 'Stop wriggling, you silly little bitch! You're making me come. I don't want to let them see me ... I don't ... Oh no! Oh no! Oh shit! Ooh!' Although she did her best to conceal her orgasm, it was obvious to Maddie and to Fliss. Maddie stopped spanking and handed the strap to Fliss.

Fliss had half-thought that Selina would bear her smacking in silent immobility, but she had reckoned without the recent humiliation of being brought to orgasm by Alice's lack of self-control. For whatever reason, Selina didn't yell but she did use the excuse of a smacking to wriggle mightily, heaving her body backwards to tug at Alice's nipples. In this, she was inhibited by the fact that an equal and opposite strain was placed on her own nipples. There was nothing inhibited, however, about the fashion in which she bounced her buttocks repeatedly against Alice's, jiggling the double dildo in her vagina each time.

Even so, Alice might not so easily have come to climax had not Maddie, standing beside her, discreetly felt under her and found her anus with her forefinger. This triple stimulus was too much for Alice and she, too, came mightily, with little gasps and cries of mingled discomfort and pleasure.

When Maddie lowered them to the floor and Fliss released them, both women's arms and legs were sore and strained from their recent ordeal and they spent some time stretching and rubbing before they were able to rise.

'Is that it? Do we go now?' Selina asked, craning over her shoulder to see how badly her bottom had been marked. It was hardly marred at all, so light had the strap been; just a little pinker than the rest of her.

'Just one more thing,' Fliss said. 'This!' From her bag, she produced a large, heavy, glass paperweight.

Selina stared at it. 'That? I don't understand.'

'You will,' Fliss led the way out of the stable and across to the far corner of the yard. This was the location of the slurry tank which dated from the time when cows had been regularly confined and milked in that place. It resembled a concrete swimming pool, being about forty feet long, twenty feet wide and four feet deep. There the resemblance ended. Here was no crystal clear, blue, filtered water. This was filled with a foul and stinking mixture of cow muck and water, product of many swillings of the concrete yard over many months. Selina and Alice stared at it uncomprehendingly.

Fliss tossed the paperweight into the centre of the tank. So thick was the mixture there that after the paperweight plopped on to the surface it actually remained there for a fraction of a second before sinking from sight, releasing a stream of bubbles which popped oozily in the yellowish slime.

'Oh dear!' said Fliss. 'I've dropped my paperweight. Go and fetch it for me, would you?'

Selina turned pale. 'Who, me?'

'No, both of you. It'll be quicker if there are two looking.'

'You want us to get in there?'

'Well, I don't see how you're going to get it otherwise. Very fond of that paperweight, I am. I shall be quite cross if I don't get it back. Cross enough, maybe, to cancel the arrangements for you to leave today.'

Selina locked eyes with Fliss and the two women stared hard at each other for long moments. This was the final battle of wills; Selina filled with hatred, refusal very close to the front of her mind and Fliss resolute and implacable. Selina was the first to break eye contact; to flinch and look down. The refusal died stillborn. She shrugged. 'And this is the last thing? There'll be nothing else?'

'The very last, I promise you.'

'All right. How deep is it?'

'About four feet. You'll be able to wade and feel for it with your toes.'

'I'm not going in there!' Alice wailed. 'I won't!'

Selina rounded on her fiercely. 'If I'm going in, you're going in. I'm nearly through this thing and I'm not going to let you screw it up for me. Now, are you getting in, you silly cow, or am I going to push you?'

Whimpering, Alice knelt down with her back to the tank and extended a cautious foot into the slime behind her. It crept glutinously up her ankle and she felt it squelch between her toes. 'Ooer! Yuk! I can't!' she sobbed.

Selina stooped in front of her, put both hands squarely on her shoulders and shoved. Alice squeaked. 'No! No! Don't push me! I'm going!' Grimacing with distaste, she moved her other knee back over the edge and slowly lowered herself into the tank. The gooey mixture climbed further and further up her body, coating first her calves, then her knees and thighs. The feel of it intruding between her bottom cheeks and soaking into her pubic hair was almost a sticking point and she stopped, her face working in disgust, before she continued her downward progress, allowing the mire to rise up and submerge the flinching white skin of her rounded belly. Then her feet were on the bottom and it lapped gently just underneath her breasts. She rested her elbows on the concrete side, panting. 'Pooh! It stinks!' she said, wrinkling her nose.

'Of course it does!' Selina muttered, impatiently. 'Move over. I'm coming in now!'

Copying Alice's technique, but with much less ado, she lowered herself into the filthy effluent. 'Come on!

Let's get it over with!' With arms held high out of the clinging ooze, she led the way towards the spot where the paperweight had disappeared and, after a brief hesitation, Alice followed her. Their movements were slow, as in some nightmare. The texture of the mixture through which they were obliged to wade was such that it took time and a lot of effort to move it aside to allow progress.

Eventually, they reached the spot and moved around, feeling with their feet until Selina exclaimed, 'I've got it. It's under my foot.'

'Can you pick it up with your toes?' Alice asked.

'Of course I can't. You'll have to duck under and get it. You can feel down my leg.'

'Duck under! Duck under! I'm not ducking under this stuff! Why don't you . . .'

Selina's patience ran out. Maddened by the ignominy of what she was being forced to do, she vented all her pent-up exasperation on the hapless Alice. Pushing herself as high out of the ooze as she could, she put both hands on the top of Alice's head and forced her under the surface so that there was nothing to be seen of her except a pair of sticky hands which clawed frantically at Selina's breasts. The head which emerged when Selina let her up bore no resemblance to that which had disappeared. Coated thickly in sludge and featureless except for the open, pink mouth from which issued wail after wail of distress, Alice appeared more like some primeval slime monster. 'Oh! Ugh! Pooh!' she spluttered. 'Why did you do that?'

'Because you are so stupid! Now, are you going to get it or do I duck you again?' Suddenly, Selina changed her tone and tried reasoning. 'Look,' she said. 'You're all mucky already and you can hold your nose this time.'

Alice caved in. She took several deep breaths, grasped her nose and ducked again. She seemed to be under for a long time, but when she came up, she was waving the paperweight. She wiped most of the goo from her face with her spare hand, blinked and beamed like a child who has won a prize at the bran-tub. 'Look! I've got it! I was brave wasn't I, Selina? I did it all by myself!'

'Well done!' Fliss called. 'Bring it over here and come out, Alice.'

Alice waded to the side of the tank, her disgusting trophy borne triumphantly aloft. Fliss took the weight from her. 'Give us your wrists!' She and Maddie took hold of a wrist each and, with a heave, dragged her from the tank and allowed her to plop down on the concrete like a giant seal, all shiny, slippery and stinking from her immersion.

Selina, close behind, held up her arms to them. 'Pull me out!'

Fliss stared at her, then deliberately dropped the paperweight back into the tank. Selina made a despairing grab at it, but missed and it sank as before. She pounded with her fists on the smooth concrete at Fliss' feet. 'Bitch! Bitch! Bitch!' she screamed at the top of her lungs.

'Yes, I know,' Fliss said. 'Just get it, will you?'

With a severe effort, Selina controlled her rage. She grasped her nose, took a deep breath and ducked out of sight. When she came up, she was already holding up her arms to be rescued. They grabbed her wrists and dragged her, too, from the sucking embrace of the tank. Maddie had already laid out the fat yard-hose and now she turned it on both women. Ordinarily, the shock of the cold water would have been unpleasant, but on this occasion, they rejoiced in it, revolving and dancing about; pulling apart the creases and crevices of their bodies so as to ensure that the blessed, cleansing stream would wash the last traces of foul muck from them.

Epilogue

Mrs Bedwell closed the library door behind her and left Maddie and Fliss eyeing the tray of home-made scones and pot of tea she had left. Maddie stretched her long legs luxuriously towards the glowing fire. 'You know,' she said, 'I could get to like this life-style.'

'You'll stay, then. I hoped you would.'

'For a while, anyway.' Maddie buttered a scone. 'I shall quite miss not having Alice about the place,' she said, reflectively.

'Mm! I thought you might!' Fliss took a scone of her own. 'Never mind, I'll make it up to you. I'll even let you share Alex.'

'Ooh! A threesome! How jolly!' Trying to eat and giggle at the same time, she choked a little and melted butter ran down her chin. Instead of trying to wipe it off, she extended her tongue as far as it would go and waggled it suggestively in search of the errant butter.

Fliss watched her. 'How coarse!' she said. 'I know what you need. A good Finishing School!'

NEW BOOKS

Coming up from Nexus and Black Lace

Dark Desires by Maria del Rey
May 1996   Price £4.99   ISBN: 0 352 32971 8
A subtle taste of the bizarre renders each of Maria del Rey's kinkiest stories strikingly original. Fetishists, submissives and errant tax inspectors mingle with bitch goddesses, bad girls and French maids, in settings as diverse as an austere Victorian punishment room and a modern-day SM dungeon, in this eclectic anthology of forbidden games.

The Finishing School by Stephen Ferris
May 1996   Price £4.99   ISBN: 0 352 33071 6
Young heiress Felicity Marchant is sent, by Selina, the corrupt trustee of her estate, to be disciplined at a sinister finishing school on a remote island. There, she is subjected to all manner of indignities and humiliations, and must outwit a spy planted by Selina if she is to give her tormentors a taste of their own perverse methods of control.

Dear Fanny by Michelle Clare
June 1996   Price £4.99   ISBN: 0 352 33077 5
Inspired by Fanny's Hill's *Memoirs*, Lady Charlotte Spicer recounts her own life of pleasure. Captured by pirates and sold to an Arabian sultan, the wholesome Charlotte soon adjusts to her debauched new life in his harem and, as she discovers her capacity for perverse pleasures, her personality becomes increasingly depraved and wanton.

Candy In Captivity by Arabella Knight
June 1996   Price £4.99   ISBN: 0352 33078 3
When work takes the ambitious Candy Brompton to a remote Hebridean island, she stumbles upon a dark and enigmatic all-female community. Spirited and defiant, Candy lets curiosity get the better of her, and soon discovers the exquisite pleasures which can be derived from the judicious use of the cane and other instruments of correction.

Pandora's Box Anthology, Ed. Kerri Sharp
May 1996   Price £4.99   ISBN: 0 352 33074 0

This unique collection brings together new material and extracts from the best-selling and most popular titles in the Black Lace series. *Pandora's Box* is a celebration of the revolutionary imprint which puts women's erotic fiction in the media spotlight. The diversity of the material is a testament to the many facets of the female erotic imagination.

The Ninety Days of Genevieve by Lucinda Carrington
May 1996   Price £4.99   ISBN: 0 352 33070 8

Genevieve Loften discovers that a 90-day sex contract is part of a business deal she makes with the arrogant and attractive James Sinclair. Thrown into a world of sexual challenges, Genevieve is forced to balance her high-flying career with the twilight world of fetishism and debauchery.

The Black Orchid Hotel by Roxanne Carr
June 1996   Price £4.99   ISBN: 0 352 33076 7

As joint owner of the Black Orchid Hotel, Maggie can enjoy the services of its obliging male and female staff at any time. But she soon becomes jaded and seeks new lovers, whose raw, unpredictable sexuality more than compensates for their lack of sophistication. Maggie may not, however, be the only one playing with fire . . .

The Big Class by Angel Strand
June 1996   Price £4.99   ISBN: 0 352 33076 7

1930s Europe. As Hitler and Mussolini prepare for war, Cia, a young, Anglo-Italian woman, returns to England, leaving behind a complex web of sexual adventures. Her English friends appear to be leading a carefree and hedonistic lifestyle, but Cia is soon embroiled in its underlying tensions and rivalries – and enjoying its darker pleasures.

NEXUS BACKLIST

All books are priced £4.99 unless another price is given. If a date is supplied, the book in question will not be available until that month in 1996.

CONTEMPORARY EROTICA

THE ACADEMY	Arabella Knight	
BOUND TO OBEY	Amananda Ware	Feb
BOUND TO SERVE	Amanda Ware	Sep
CANDY IN CAPTIVITY	Arabella Knight	Jun
CHALICE OF DELIGHTS	Katrina Young	Mar
THE CHASTE LEGACY	Susanna Hughes	Aug
CHRISTINA WISHED	Gene Craven	Apr
CONDUCT UNBECOMING	Arabella Knight	
CONTOURS OF DARKNESS	Marco Vassi	
DARK DESIRES	Maria del Rey	May
DIFFERENT STROKES	Sarah Veitch	
THE DOMINO TATTOO	Cyrian Amberlake	
THE DOMINO ENIGMA	Cyrian Amberlake	
THE DOMINO QUEEN	Cyrian Amberlake	
ELIANE	Stephen Ferris	
EMMA'S SECRET WORLD	Hilary James	
EMMA ENSLAVED	Hilary James	
EMMA'S SECRET DIARIES	Hilary James	
EMMA'S SUBMISSION	Hilary James	Oct
FALLEN ANGELS	Kendal Grahame	
THE FANTASIES OF JOSEPHINE SCOTT	Josephine Scott	
THE FINISHING SCHOOL	Stephen Ferris	May
THE GENTLE DEGENERATES	Marco Vassi	
HEART OF DESIRE	Maria del Rey	

STEPHANIE'S REVENGE	Susanna Hughes	
STEPHANIE'S DOMAIN	Susanna Hughes	
STEPHANIE'S TRIAL	Susanna Hughes	
STEPHANIE'S PLEASURE	Susanna Hughes	
THE TEACHING OF FAITH	Elizabeth Bruce	
FAITH IN THE STABLES	Elizabeth Bruce	Mar
THE TRAINING GROUNDS	Sarah Veitch	
UNDERWORLD	Maria del Rey	

EROTIC SCIENCE FICTION

ADVENTURES IN THE PLEASUREZONE	Delaney Silver	
RETURN TO THE PLEASUREZONE	Delaney Silver	
FANTASYWORLD	Larry Stern	

ANCIENT & FANTASY SETTINGS

THE CLOAK OF APHRODITE	Kendal Grahame	
DEMONIA	Kendal Grahame	
THE HANDMAIDENS	Aran Ashe	
THE SLAVE OF LIDIR	Aran Ashe	
THE DUNGEONS OF LIDIR	Aran Ashe	
THE FOREST OF BONDAGE	Aran Ashe	
PLEASURE ISLAND	Aran Ashe	
WITCH QUEEN OF VIXANIA	Morgana Baron	
SLAVE-MISTRESS OF VIXANIA	Morgana Baron	

EDWARDIAN, VICTORIAN & OLDER EROTICA

ANNIE	Evelyn Culber	
ANNIE AND THE SOCIETY	Evelyn Culber	
ANNIE'S FURTHER EDUCATION	Evelyn Culber	Aug
THE AWAKENING OF LYDIA	Philippa Masters	
LYDIA IN THE HAREM	Philippa Masters	
LYDIA IN THE BORDELLO	Philippa Masters	Jul
BEATRICE	Anonymous	
CHOOSING LOVERS FOR JUSTINE	Aran Ashe	
DEAR FANNY	Aran Ashe	

Please send me the books I have ticked above.

Name   ....

Address   ....

                ....

                ....

                .... Post code ....

Send to: **Cash Sales, Nexus Books, 332 Ladbroke Grove, London W10 5AH.**

Please enclose a cheque or postal order, made payable to **Nexus Books**, to the value of the books you have ordered plus postage and packing costs as follows:

UK and BFPO – £1.00 for the first book, 50p for each subsequent book.

Overseas (including Republic of Ireland) – £2.00 for the first book, £1.00 for the second book, and 50p for each subsequent book.

If you would prefer to pay by VISA or ACCESS/MASTER-CARD, please write your card number and expiry date here:

....

Please allow up to 28 days for delivery.

Signature ....